"It's going to happen, Lash.

"If not now, then later. You know it as well as I do. I want you, and I'm not ashamed to admit it. You want me, too, though you're having a little more trouble accepting it. We're both adults, and you don't have one thing to be afraid of. Not me, and not my brothers. I think what you're really scared of is yourself. But this thing between us isn't gonna go away, no matter how much you try to ignore it."

He couldn't breathe. "When you're ready for me, Lash, you let me know. But don't wait too long, 'cause I'm not going to."

Then she slipped away, and he managed to breathe again. Damn, he was in trouble. Deep trouble. It would take a saint to resist that woman.

And Lash Monroe was no saint.

Dear Reader,

Welcome back to another month of great reading here at Silhouette Intimate Moments. Favorite author Marie Ferrarella gets things off to a rousing start with *The Amnesiac Bride*. Imagine waking up in a beautiful bridal suite, a ring on your finger and a gorgeous guy by your side—and no memory at all of who he is or how you got there! That's Whitney Bradshaw's dilemma in a nutshell, and wait 'til you see where things go from there.

Maggie Shayne brings you the next installment in her exciting miniseries, THE TEXAS BRAND, with *The Baddest Virgin in Texas*. If ever a title said it all, that's the one. I guarantee you're going to love this book. Nikki Benjamin's *Daddy by Default* is a lesson in what can happen when you hang on to a secret from your past. Luckily, what happens in this case ends up being very, very good. Beverly Bird begins a new miniseries, THE WEDDING RING, with *Loving Mariah*. It takes a missing child to bring Adam Wallace and Mariah Fisher together, but nothing will tear them apart. Kate Hathaway's back with *Bad For Each Other*, a secret-baby story that's chock-full of emotion. And finally, welcome new author Stephanie Doyle, whose *Undiscovered Hero* will have you eagerly turning the pages.

This month and every month, if you're looking for romantic reading at its best, come to Silhouette Intimate Moments.

Enjoy!

Leslie Wainger

Leslie Wainger
Senior Editor and Editorial Coordinator

Please address questions and book requests to:
Silhouette Reader Service
U.S.: 3010 Walden Ave., P.O. Box 1325, Buffalo, NY 14269
Canadian: P.O. Box 609, Fort Erie, Ont. L2A 5X3

THE BADDEST
VIRGIN IN TEXAS

MAGGIE
SHAYNE

Silhouette®

INTIMATE™MOMENTS®

Published by Silhouette Books

America's Publisher of Contemporary Romance

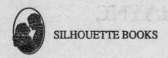

SILHOUETTE BOOKS

ISBN 0-373-07788-2

THE BADDEST VIRGIN IN TEXAS

Copyright © 1997 by Margaret Benson

MAGGIE SHAYNE,

a national bestselling author whom *Romantic Times* magazine calls "brilliantly inventive," has written thirteen novels and one novella for Silhouette. Her last novel, *Born in Twilight* (3/97), a Silhouette single-title release, was based on her popular vampire series for Shadows, Wings in the Night.

Maggie has won numerous awards, including a *Romantic Times* magazine Career Achievement Award. A three-time finalist for the Romance Writers of America's prestigious RITA Award, Maggie also writes mainstream contemporary fantasy.

In her spare time, Maggie enjoys collecting gemstones, reading tarot cards, hanging out on the Genie computer network and spending time outdoors. She lives in a rural town in central New York with her husband, Rick, five beautiful daughters and a bulldog named Wrinkles.

Prologue

Little Lash Monroe sat in the hard wooden pew in the front row and listened to his foster father, the Reverend Ezekiel Stanton, pontificate in a loud, booming voice about the wages of sin and the wrath of the Almighty. Hellfire and damnation tended to be at the heart of most of the preacher's sermons. And Lash, being only nine, supposed one day he'd understand why the bumper sticker on the back of the Reverend Mr. Stanton's battered pickup truck read God Is Love when he talked about God as if He were a fire-breathing dragon from a horrific fairy tale. His words sent chills down Lash's spine.

And the light in the preacher's eyes gleamed like... like that new gray-blue cat's-eye marble Lash had won this morning from Gulliver Scuttle. Lash smiled and tucked his hand into his pocket to feel the cool, smooth marble he'd been gunning for all these weeks. His at last. Then the smile leaped from his face when the

preacher struck his fist hard on the podium in front of
him to punctuate the word *Vengeance* in the quote Lash
figured must be his favorite, "Vengeance is mine, say-
eth the Lord."

Lash met the preacher's piercing gaze, and forced
himself to stop thinking about the marble, and the
shooting match this morning, and to pay attention. After all, the preacher wasn't so bad. Strict, yes, but not
mean. It wasn't his fault Lash was miserable living
with him and Missus Olive, who would have blown
away in a strong wind or fainted at the sound of a cuss
word. Yeah, they were wearing on him some. Especially her, being so helpless and delicate and requiring
a houseful of men and boys just to take care of her
every little need. Lash had never known a whinier,
more dependent woman in his life. But still and all, she
was better than his own mom, who'd been drunk most
of the time, and even more helpless. So helpless she'd
said she couldn't take care of two boys all alone, and
dumped Lash and Jimmy off at a shelter one night.

Jimmy had been sent to live with a family in Texas.
And Lash had been brought here, to the preacher, who
wanted plenty of sons, and his wife, who was unable
to give him any. And really, despite their shortcomings,
they'd treated him just swell.

It was the boys he couldn't stand. They were the
ones who made his life pure misery in every way they
could think of. All older than him, all bigger, and every
one of them way meaner. Especially Zane, the oldest,
biggest, meanest, of them all. Zane was twelve, Jack
eleven, and Peter—who claimed his name was really
Pedro and that he had a rich uncle in Mexico who
would come for him one day—was ten. Peter made
them all call him Pedro when the Stantons weren't

within earshot. And if they forgot, they were liable to get clubbed for it. Lash tended to call him Petey, despite the repercussions, just because it bugged the other boy so much. Rich relatives, indeed. The king of beef, Peter said they called his uncle. Sure. The kid was full of blue mud.

In comparison to Lash's measly nine years of age, they were practically grown-ups. They didn't act that way, though. Lash still had sore ribs from the minor beating they'd given him last week, when Zane ordered Lash to do his share of the chores, and Lash was foolish enough to refuse. He'd ended up doing Zane's chores anyway, only doing them while hurting like crazy. Next time he'd just agree right off the bat.

But he had a feeling that wouldn't be enough to satisfy Zane. He thought Zane *liked* tormenting him.

It was as this thought entered Lash's mind that he first felt the itching, creeping sensation around his ankles and calves...and then higher. He dropped one hand to scratch his leg, all the while keeping his eyes respectfully focused on the preacher. But the itch didn't go away. In fact, it spread higher. And then, all of a sudden, it became a pinching feeling. Lash slapped hard at his legs, jerking his gaze floorward at the same moment. Oddly, he noticed several other members of the congregation itching and slapping themselves, too.

And then he saw them. Ants. There must have been a million of 'em. It looked as if someone had scattered handfuls of them across the floor near the front pew. A hundred of the shiny black buggers—some the size of guinea pigs, Lash noted with alarm—were swarming over his shoes and disappearing beneath the hem of his pant legs. He jumped to his feet, howling out loud and hopping up and down like a Mexican jumping bean,

slapping his legs as if they were on fire. And he barely
noticed at least six other people doing a similar jig.
They looked like Indians from a John Wayne movie
doing a war dance before the big shoot-'em-up scene.
Mrs. Potter threw her walker so high and so hard that
it formed a perfect arch in the air before coming down
hard on the three people in the pew behind her. Sally
Kenyon was standing in her seat, screaming at the top
of her lungs and tugging on her blond ringlets. Girls.
Sheesh, did she really think all that fussin' was going
to help anything? Old Leroy LaRue just stood there,
stooped as always, nailing ants one by one with his
walking stick, just lifting it up and jamming it down,
again and again. With his snow-white hair sticking up
and his beak of a nose crinkling, he grinned toothlessly.
"Gotcha, ya sneaky little buggers!" *Bam, bam, bam.*
"There! Ha! Gotcha!" *Bam-bam!* "An' you, too! I see
ya sneaking away!" *Bam-bam-bam-bam.*

Lash would've laughed at Leroy's counterattack if
he hadn't been so busy trying to shake the entire ant
army out of his pant legs. He managed to kick off his
shoes in a frenzied effort to rid himself of the biting
little demons. The shoes flew forward, and one hit the
Reverend Mr. Stanton square dead center of his forehead. The second one landed on the podium, no doubt
leaving a dirty mark all over the fire-and-brimstone ser-
mon the preacher had spent all week composing. Lash
barely noticed that the fire and brimstone from the ser-
mon was becoming apparent in the Reverend Stanton's
face. He was too busy hopping on one foot to peel off
the other sock and then reversing the procedure.

It was only as Lash accomplished this and danced
his bare feet away from the platoon of ants trooping
over the church floor, that he noticed Zane, sitting

safely two rows back. He was doubled over, clutching his spare-tire belly and laughing so hard his face was beet red and tears squeezed from the corners of his eyes.

And then Lash's view was blocked by the members of the congregation, all rising and making their way toward the exits, to avoid being attacked by Zane's killer ants.

Safe for the moment, Lash stood there shaking his head. And then a heavy hand clapped down on his shoulder from behind, and he knew full well whose hand it was. And he also knew he was in major trouble. Because of all the boys in the preacher's household, Lash was the only one with an ant farm. And even if he denied responsibility for this, it wouldn't hold water when Zane and Jack and Peter gave their version of things. They'd make sure their stories matched, and they'd make sure Lash was implicated. They always did.

"I think," said the Reverend Mr. Stanton, "that you are going to have some new Bible verses to memorize."

Lash glanced up at the preacher, and he could have sworn that behind that weathered, stern face, the preacher was battling against the urge to grin. But he couldn't be, Lash reasoned. The preacher was too upstanding to find any of this funny. Still, Lash found himself awfully glad that memorizing Bible verses was the most severe punishment in the man's collection. It wouldn't be so bad.

"How many this time, sir?" Lash asked.

The preacher's bushy brows rose. "For this? Oh, I'd say…a hundred might be sufficient."

"A hundred!"

The preacher nodded. "You may recite them before the entire congregation next Sunday—after you've delivered your apology to them, of course."

With a heavy sigh, Lash nodded. "Yes, sir."

"I swear, Lash, I've never come upon a boy with such a love of mischief-making as you. But I'm bound to reform you, son. Or die trying." His hand, leathery and firm, gave Lash's shoulder a squeeze.

He'd die trying, Lash thought. Lord, but *he* wasn't the one who was supposed to learn a hundred Bible verses in one week's time. *He* wasn't the one who'd be embarrassed right to the roots of his teeth getting up in front of all these people, who'd probably still be itching from their ant bites, to apologize and recite all those verses. Lash was. But Lash *wasn't* the one who'd orchestrated this whole fiasco in the first place.

He met Zane's triumphant beady little eyes across the room. An ant bit hard, and Lash jumped and slapped at his leg, and when he did, that pretty gray-blue cat's eye marble he'd been trying to win for a month popped right out of his pocket, rolled under the pew behind him and kept on rolling. And before he could get hold of it again, pudgy Zane with his ugly mug was knocking people out of the way to wedge himself under a pew two rows back. When he got up again, he held that marble between his thumb and forefinger and admired it, just to be sure Lash would see. Then he dropped it into his own pocket, and turned to saunter out of the church, acting like he wasn't even aware of all the hopping and slapping and shouting going on around him.

Silently Lash vowed that he would never, never for the rest of his life, want to be plunked down into the middle of a huge family. Especially one with so many older, bigger, meaner brothers! Never!

He made his way out of the church, and on the way, he caught the pale gaze of Olive Stanton, his foster mom, and he knew just by looking at her that she'd seen what Zane had just done. She knew that Lash wasn't the one responsible for all of this. Heck, as far as brains went, she had twice as many as her husband, even if he *was* a preacher and all.

But all Missus Stanton did was shake her head sadly and send a reproachful look toward Zane's retreating back. She wouldn't say anything. The woman didn't have any backbone at all when it came to telling her husband—or anyone else, for that matter—that they were wrong. She'd sooner be hung by her toes than disagree with anyone, and she never raised her voice above a whisper. Lash wasn't sure if that was because she appreciated all their coddling so much she didn't want to seem ungrateful, or if she just didn't have a lick of courage. But he did know he didn't want to be around females who got themselves used to being waited on. It made them soft and yellow, as far as he was concerned. Nope. Once Lash grew up and moved away from the Stantons of Maplewood, Illinois, he was going to keep himself clear of coddled girls, big families and older brothers for the rest of his life...and maybe even longer than that!

He didn't like having chores to do, Bible verses to memorize. He didn't like having to answer to the Reverend Mr. Stanton. He detested having to wait on Missus Olive. He just plain hated having to watch his every step in case he crossed those bullies he was forced to live with.

When he grew up, Lash was never going to have to

answer to anybody. He'd be free as a bird. Why, when he got tired of living in one place, he'd just throw his stuff in a bag and head off to someplace new and different. Every trip would be a brand-new adventure. Life was going to be fun and carefree, not an endless cycle of rules to be followed and orders to be obeyed. Not for Lash.

He was kinda hoping he could look up his real brother, Jimmy, who was in Texas now, and talk him into going along with this plan. They'd be drifters. Free and happy. No women or families allowed.

Meanwhile…Lash picked up his Bible, riffled the pages to be sure no ants were waiting in ambush inside, and then opened it to see if he could find a hundred verses the preacher hadn't already made him memorize. As often as he got himself into trouble—with plenty of help from Zane and Petey the beef prince—he kinda doubted he'd find that many.

Chapter 1

Jessica Brand caught hold of the calf's slippery, translucent front hooves and pulled as the cow strained. The animal was a first-calf heifer. She'd never been through this ordeal before, and she might not make it through this time. The cow was small, dammit. Jessi's brothers never should have kept her as breeding stock.

Jessi tightened her grip on the calf's tiny forefeet and tugged, but her hands slipped. She flew backward, landing butt first on the barn's concrete floor and cussing as those tiny feet vanished back into the haven of its mother. The cow bellowed loud enough to wake the dead.

"Hush, cow! The last thing I need is my brothers out here worrying I might break a nail. I'm a veterinarian now. And I could've handled this even without my brand-new license. Now be quiet and *push*."

She shoved herself to her feet, using her elbows instead of her hands. She didn't want germs all over the latex gloves. Bracing one forearm across the cow's rump, she delved into the birth canal with her free hand, found those tiny cloven hooves and began pulling again.

"That's the most disgusting thing I've ever seen in my life." The deep voice came from the open front doors, and Jessi turned quickly, sighing in relief when she saw Lash lounging there grimacing at her. Better him than one of her oversize, overprotective brothers.

Of course, it couldn't have been one of her brothers. Any of *them* would have rushed her by now, shouting at her for standing close enough to be kicked, scolding that she wasn't strong enough to pull a stubborn calf into the world, yelling at her for even being out in the barn all alone in the middle of the night. She rolled her eyes at the thought of it. Thank God it wasn't them.

It was almost irritating, though, that Lash did none of those things. He just stood there, not so much as offering to lift a finger.

"Get in here and close the door," she told him. "If my brothers see the barn lights on, they'll be swarming all over this place."

"So what? If they swarm, then you get to hand this mess over to them. Seems like an appealing prospect, from where I'm standing."

"If I wanted to hand it all over to them, Lash, I would have just yelled for 'em in the first place. Now close the door."

With a slight frown and a glance over his shoulder, toward the house, Lash complied. Then he moved closer, but the look of distaste on his face only grew more and more pronounced.

"You're just a big fraud, aren't you, Lash?" Jessi said as she pulled, tugged and turned the calf slightly, trying to work him free before he suffocated. "You're no ranch hand."

"Never claimed to be," he said. "I told you before, I'm a firefighter. Or I was, till I came down here." He pursed his lips and narrowed his eyes. "I hate like hell to ask, but is there…something I can do to help?"

"Yeah," she said, glancing sideways at him, seeing the alarm flash in his pale blue eyes. Those eyes of his reminded her of an arctic wolf's. Alarmingly at odds with his silky sable hair. Hair she'd fantasized about running her fingers through…

"Jessi?"

She dragged her gaze from his hair and blinked. "Hmm?"

"You were gonna tell me how I could help?" he said, then glanced at where her hands were and made a face.

She laughed at him. "Don't worry. I want you on the other end. Stroke this big girl's head, or talk to her, or something. Scratch her ears. She's so damn tensed up she's gonna crush the calf instead of birthing him."

Nodding hard, Lash hurried around to the front of the cow and proceeded to stroke her head and whisper sweet nothings in her ear. The cow relaxed slightly. Jessi didn't blame her. That man could melt butter. Well, he could melt *her*, anyway. Jessi smiled when the cow relaxed still more. She could see the calf's wet pink nose now. "You're good at that," she said.

"I'm fair with animals. That's why I offered to stay on and help out while Garrett and Chelsea took their honeymoon." He glanced over the top of the cow to meet her gaze. "Never volunteered for that end of things, though."

Jessi smiled at him. "Well, now that I'm a full-fledged vet, I suppose I'll have to get used to this end of things.''

He shook his head. "Makes me feel ancient. A kid like you is barely old enough to know what that end of things is for," he quipped, and went back to stroking the cow's face, calming her. Too bad he had the opposite effect on Jessi. She felt her face heating, and battled the urge to peel off her latex gloves and slap his face with them. Kid, indeed.

Then she was distracted by the animal actually pushing for once. The calf's head cleared so far she could see the closed eyes and pale lashes. "That's good," she called. "Whatever you're doing, keep doing it."

She got a better grip on the newborn's forelegs, and waited. This time, when the cow pushed, Jessi was ready, and she pulled in sync. The calf's entire head emerged, and Jessi immediately cleared its airways, relieved when the tiny animal made wheezing sounds. But the calf was now hung up at the shoulders. This was the toughest part for the mother, she knew, and she used her hands again, wincing at the viselike pressure on her fingers as she probed. But she had to be sure the calf could emerge.

"So tell me," she said as she explored the poor, long-suffering animal, "Why did you really come here in the first place? I know, you said you had an old score to settle with that maniac who almost killed *my* brother. But you never said what."

Speaking softly, as if still soothing the pain-racked cow, Lash said, "That maniac...killed *my* brother."

Jessi was so startled that she paused in her examination of the animal and looked at him. He only nodded, his hand scratching the cow behind the ear. "Jimmy was with the DEA, investigating Vincent de

Lorean's drug trade. De Lorean found out and had him killed.''

"And you quit your job at the Chicago Fire Department to come to Texas and make him pay?'' She shook her head. "And my brothers call me impulsive and reckless!''

"It wasn't reckless. Hell, it worked. We got him, didn't we?''

Jessi nodded and resumed probing, not wanting to dwell on recent events that had nearly cost her oldest brother his life. "So what now?'' she asked, trying not to sound overly interested in his answer, although she was.

He only frowned at her.

"You got de Lorean,'' she clarified. "You stayed on here to help out while Garrett took his honeymoon. But he and Chelsea will be back tomorrow. So what are you going to do next?''

He shrugged. "No idea.''

Jessi dipped her head quickly to hide her sudden smile from him. The birth canal was clear, so she gripped the calf's legs again, preparing to pull when the cow pushed. Soft baby-brown eyes blinked open and stared at her, unfocused and shining.

"You could stay here,'' she said. Then she peered around the cow to see his reaction. "We were short-handed even before Garrett left.''

"Your brother Ben is home now,'' Lash said. "You have plenty of hands.''

"Adam isn't. He insisted he had to get back to that city-slickin' job of his in New York. Though we all know it's really just that he's scared to death of running into Kirstin Armstrong and finally having to ask her why she left him at the altar and married old...'' The cow pushed, and Jessi pulled. The calf's shoulders passed through. "That's it, girl. Once more. Just once more."

"Come on, girl," Lash said to the cow. "You're doing great."

"Anyway," Jessi continued, as she awaited what would, she hoped, be the final push. "We could use you here. I know *I* could." He glanced at her sharply, eyes narrowed. "You're a natural with the animals," she said quickly. "Why, we could even put you in the extra bedroom up at—"

"Not on your life," Lash said. And again, Jessi popped up to meet his eyes.

"You think there's something *wrong* with my house, Lash Monroe?"

"Just a bit crowded, is all," he told her. "Been there. Done that. Didn't like it."

She scowled at him, but he went on.

"No, ma'am, Lash Monroe doesn't like crowds. And he doesn't like ties, either. Family or otherwise. I may stick around for a while, but then again, I might just pull up stakes and flit off as soon as your brother comes back. I pride myself, you see, on being just as free as a bird. That's all I want out of life, and so far, it's exactly what I got. I aim to keep it that way."

The cow pushed. Jessi pulled. The calf slid into the world with a *whoosh*, and Jessi hefted the hundred-pound baby bull in her arms, not letting him hit the floor. She eased him gently into the fresh hay she had waiting. "Untie her, Lash, so she can meet her newborn."

Lash loosened the halter ropes, and the cow turned around fast, bending her long neck and licking at her infant calf with so much vigor the newborn was knocked over sideways with every swipe of his mother's tongue.

Jessi turned and peeled off the gloves, then headed into the room at the far end of the barn to deposit them in the wastebasket, and scrub her hands thoroughly at the sink there. She hadn't liked Lash's response to her question. Then again, there wasn't much he said or did that she did like. He insisted on seeing her as a kid, just the way her brothers did. It was damned infuriating. Especially when it was coming from him—the one man she'd ever met who made her want to come across as one hundred percent pure Texas woman. Not that she'd shown it. Not yet, anyway. She had to figure out how to proceed first.

"So you're ready to move on, eh?" she asked, pretending it was only small talk. "Well, I can't say as I blame you. The work here is tough."

"I didn't say I minded hard work."

"Right," she said as she cranked off the faucets and reached for a paper towel. "Must be the dirt. You're from the city, after all. Can't blame you for going wishy-washy when it comes to the good fresh smell of cattle, can we?"

"Dirt doesn't bother me in the least," he said. "I was a firefighter, for crying—"

"Yes, but how long ago was that? I mean, you couldn't go back to it now, could you? Feeling as *ancient* as you do, and all."

"Now hold on a—"

"And it stands to reason that if you're getting too old and decrepit to fight fires, then ranching can't be much more to your liking." She sighed as he narrowed his eyes on her. "Probably you'll look for a nice easy job you can do from behind a desk, your butt cushioned by a soft chair as it slowly turns to flab.'' She deliberately craned her neck and focused on the part of his anatomy in question, shaking her head and clicking her tongue. ''Cryin' shame, too.'' She tossed her head and moved past him into the barn. The cow had licked the calf until his curly red-and-white coat stuck up in all directions. The little one had even managed to get to his feet.

''Did I do something to make you mad, Jessi?'' Lash asked, coming up behind her.

She glanced over her shoulder. '''Course not.'' Then she lifted the calf in her arms and carried it around its mother. ''Talk to her again, Lash. Let's see if this little fella is hungry.'' It was always a trial showing a newborn calf where to find nourishment for the first time, but even more of a trial getting a first-calf heifer to let her newborn suck.

Of course, Jessi suspected Lash had no clue about any of that. She listened to him crooning at the cow as she guided the little one's head to its mother's udder.

At the first taste, the calf began sucking madly, then suddenly jammed his head upward, in an action known as ''bunting'' that seemed to be an instinctive one among calves. Unfortunately, his mother did not appreciate her swollen, sore udder being so rudely treated. The cow jumped and kicked. Her hoof caught Jessi along her right temple and felt something like a sledgehammer. Jessi sailed backward from the force of the blow, and hit the floor with an impact that knocked the wind out of her, but good.

''Jessi!'' Lash lunged forward, falling on his knees beside her, and though his face swam before her eyes, she could see the alarm in his expression. She supposed it was directly related to the warm trickle she felt on the side of her head.

He tugged the bandanna from around his Stetson and pressed it to the wound, sliding his other arm beneath her shoulders and lifting her from the floor, searching her face. "Damn, you split your head. Are you okay? Can you see me? How many fingers am I holding up?"

She blinked her vision clear, and stared up into his eyes. Oh, man, she did like this. It was almost worth getting kicked. Lash holding her this way, bending over her—she could easily imagine that he was about to kiss her senseless, instead of just looking after a nasty wound. And she liked the fantasy so much that she moistened her lips, and lifted one hand to fan her fingers into the hair just above his nape. It felt every bit as good as she'd imagined it would. She liked the feel of it on her fingers.

"Jessi?" he asked, and he blinked in confusion. She smiled very slightly, and his eyes showed utter shock. They widened, then narrowed again. His brows drew together, and his gaze shifted downward to her lips. And then he couldn't seem to look anywhere else.

"Just what in the *hell* is all this?"

Lash dropped her so suddenly she nearly cracked her head again. Jessi suppressed a growl of utter frustration, and glanced over to see the calf now feeding happily on his own, the cow twitching and dancing a bit, but no longer fighting so hard. And beyond that, in the once again open doorway of the barn, she saw three big shapes silhouetted by moonlight and angry as all get-out.

"Just what in the *hell* does it look like?" she snapped. "I got kicked. But I'm fine." She got to her feet, ignoring the throbbing pain and the still slightly floaty sensation buzzing around in her head. She didn't forget to send a disgusted glare at Lash as she brushed the hay from her jeans, and then from her hair.

Wes didn't look as if he believed her. His dark Comanche eyes narrowed on her, then on Lash. Elliot just leaned against the barn door, grinning. Ben stood there without a hint of how he felt showing in his blue eyes. His shaggy blond mane moved with the breeze. Gosh, he was so quiet these days. She never knew what he was thinking.

To ease their minds, she lifted Lash's neckerchief away from her head, felt the bleeding start up again, saw her three brothers instantly pale and surge forward. They were so predictable, and all shouting at once.

"Jeez, Lash, how could you let this happen?"

"Damn cow is headed for auction first chance I have!"

"What the hell you doin' under a damned first-calf heifer anyway, Jess? You should have asked one of us for help."

Ben scooped her off her feet and started toward the house. Elliot rushed on ahead to call Doc. Wes headed into the barn to install the mother and newborn in the holding pen in the back for the night.

"Put me down," Jessi ordered. "Dammit, Benjamin, I mean it!" But Ben just shook his head and smiled gently at her, carrying her the rest of the way inside.

"Relax and enjoy it, honey. You're bleeding, and that's no little cut. So tell me, what was our hired hand doing out there, just now?"

Jessi rolled her eyes. "Trying to stop the blood from oozing outta my skull, you big nosy lug. What did it look like?"

Ben shrugged. "Looked like he was fixin' to kiss

you, baby sister. And I can tell you, the day he does will be the day he's hitting the road. *Comprende?*''

"Don't sweat it, Ben. He's already planning to hit the road. Any day now, as a matter of fact. You got nothing to worry about.'' She stared into his blue eyes—dark blue, like the Gulf at midnight, instead of pale silvery blue like Lash's—then she poked him in the chest. "But I'll tell you one thing, big guy. I'm gonna kiss who I want, when I want, and how I want, and if you try to butt in, it's gonna be your rear end hitting the road. And I'll be behind you, kicking it from here to El Paso.''

He smiled at her, or came as close to smiling as he ever did since his wife died, then reached down to ruffle her hair.

Jessi let her head fall backward and rolled her eyes. She was going to go stark raving *mad* if she didn't find a way to change the attitudes of the males on the Texas Brand. One male in particular.

She glanced back toward the barn, saw Lash standing in the doorway, staring after her and looking a little confused. Damn. What would it take to make him—to make all of them—see her as a grown woman with a mind of her own?

What?

Chapter 2

Lash stood there watching Ben carry his kid sister into the house, and he wondered what the hell had come over him just now. For a second there, when he was leaning over Jessi, with her head cradled in the crook of his arm, he'd felt something...something really unexpected. Her shining brown eyes—as big and innocent as the newborn calf's—had met his and held them. Her tongue had darted out to moisten those full lips of hers. And...if he wasn't mistaken...her fingers had threaded into his hair in a purely sensual way. For the barest instant, the thought of pressing his mouth to hers had crept into his mind with an undeniable insistence.

He swept his hat from his head with one hand and pushed the other one through his hair. She was trouble, that Jessi Brand. Trouble with a capital *T*. Good thing her oldest brother would be back tomorrow and Lash's services here would no longer be needed. The sooner he got away from her...and her brothers...the better.

They were bad news. Arrogant and macho, every last one of them, and they tended to remind him of the boys he'd been raised with a bit more than was comfortable.

Well, all except for Garrett, of course. Lash and that big lug had sort of become friends. And friends didn't go around having impure thoughts about a friend's baby sister, now did they?

"Hey, Lash, you wanna give me a hand in here?"

Lash turned, sighing. Wes had installed the cow and calf in the pen. Now he was carrying a pail of warm water toward the pen, the hay having already been there waiting.

Wes didn't need any help. So he must want to talk, and that was the last thing Lash felt like doing just now. Hell, Wes was the hottest-tempered of them all. They all joked it was the Comanche blood in him that made him so, but Lash suspected it was nothing more than pure meanness. And while he was only Jessi's half brother, he took the role as seriously as any of her full brothers did.

Lash replaced the Stetson he'd taken to wearing since coming to Texas, sauntered into the barn and scooped molasses-scented grain from a bin to take back to the cow, since it seemed the only chore left to be done. As Lash lowered the grain into the pen, Wes said, "How old are you, Lash?"

He felt the hairs on his nape prickle. Mean or not, he'd like to grab hold of Wes Brand and shake him, and he didn't give a damn about the bowie knife the guy carried in his boot, or his skill at throwing it, either. This really wasn't any of Wes's business, though he supposed the bastard would disagree.

"Thirty-four," he said, and he faced his accuser

squarely, leaning against the pen as if he hadn't a care in the world.

"Thirty-four," Wes repeated, black eyes piercing. "Jessi's twenty-three. You know that, right?"

"I know it."

Wes nodded. "Just checking. Wouldn't want you to forget it."

"I'm not likely to forget it," Lash replied. And he was telling the truth. He wasn't going to forget it. Jessi was far too young for him. And besides all that, she was exactly the kind of woman he *didn't* want. She was so used to being treated like a fragile princess, to being coddled and spoiled and protected by her big brothers, that she probably couldn't live without it. Why would he be attracted to her, even for that brief, insane instant? It was nuts!

"Garrett will be back tomorrow," Wes went on. He checked the gate on the pen to be sure it was fastened and started across the barn toward the door.

"I didn't forget that, either," Lash said. So Wes intended to give Lash his walking papers, did he?

"You planning to move on once he's back here?"

Lash nodded, heading for the door, as well. "That's the plan." And it was looking like a better plan with every second that ticked by. He was getting tired of the smell of cattle and fresh hay and horseflesh.

And that fresh sunshine-and-green-grass scent Jessi always seemed to exude. He was tired of that, as well.

Wes glanced over his shoulder. "Good," he said. "That's real good, Lash. For the best, I figure." He flicked off the barn lights and stepped outside.

Jessi had three stitches in her temple, a pounding headache and a bad attitude. The stitches hadn't been necessary. She could've slapped a handful of gummy pine tar on the cut and covered it with a bandage and been just fine. But no, her bossy brothers had insisted. And then they'd hustled her up to her bedroom and into her bed as if she were a six-year-old with the sniffles. They'd fussed over her until Doc arrived to throw them all out. And while Doc disappeared into her bathroom to scrub his hands, she'd slipped out of bed, tossing the ruffly pink comforter aside with a grimace and made her way to the window, with its matching ruffly pink curtains, to peer below.

Lash's decrepit-looking black car—the convertible from hell, she liked to call it—had still been parked outside. So he'd stayed. To make sure she was all right?

She scanned the darkness, and then she spotted him. He was perched on a bale of hay near the pasture gate, and every few minutes he glanced up toward her bedroom window.

She smiled broadly. He cared a little bit, then. Maybe. Or maybe he was thinking about that almost-kiss back in the barn. It had been an almost-kiss. She was sure of it.

Then Doc had returned and ordered her back to bed, and she'd suffered through a long night of being fussed over in the room her big brothers had decorated for her. If it wouldn't break their big, dumb hearts, she'd probably burn the furniture and paint the walls olive drab, just for a break from all the frills. But that would hurt them, and she wouldn't do that for the world.

It had been a long night.

This morning had been worse yet. They'd brought her breakfast in bed and informed her she'd be confined to her room. Doc, the old pain in the backside, had said she might have a mild concussion and advised twenty-four hours of bed rest. So Ben had gone off to the airport to pick up Chelsea and Garrett without her. And, dammit, she'd wanted to go along!

Despite Doc's silly orders, she wasn't in bed. She'd risen, showered and dressed and was now sitting in front of the prissy vanity her brothers had bought her, brushing her short rust-colored hair so that it covered the ugly white patch on the side of her head. Barely. With a sigh of disgust, she put the brush down and got up, went to the window and parted the stupid lacy curtains to look outside. She wondered what Lash was doing right now. Had he arrived yet this morning, or was he still at that apartment he insisted on keeping in town? And then she wondered what would have happened if her brothers hadn't burst into the barn when they did.

She'd seen something change in Lash's eyes as he stared down into hers. Something subtle, but real, she was sure of that. And she thought maybe he *had* been thinking about kissing her.

She wanted that man, dammit. Had wanted him since the first day he'd shown up on their doorstep. And what Jessi Brand wanted, Jessi Brand got.

Most of the time.

She wasn't going to give up on Lash. Of course, if he packed up and left town today, she would be doomed to failure.

She was just letting the curtains fall back into place when she saw the dust rising in the distance. Her heartbeat quickened, and she squinted at the road that stretched out beyond the arch over the driveway. And sure enough, Garrett's big old pickup truck bounced into view. Hot damn, Garrett was back!

She whirled around and raced into the hall and down the stairs. Elliot rose from his chair at her arrival. Little Ethan looked up from where he sat on the floor in his diaper and drool-spotted T-shirt and smiled at her, showing off his first two baby teeth. Ol' Blue lifted his head tiredly, but didn't leave his station, right beside the baby, as always. The hound dog acted as if he were Ethan's parent.

"They're back," Jessi said, pausing only long enough to scoop the baby up as she passed. She was on the front porch, baby on her hip, before the pickup came to a dusty stop out front. Then Ben emerged, followed by Chelsea and Garrett.

God, but those two looked happy. That woman was surely the best thing that had ever happened to her big brother. "Look, honey," she cooed to little Ethan. "Your aunt Chelsea and uncle Garrett are back!"

Garrett headed up the porch steps and wrapped Jessi in a bear hug that included the baby. Then he swept the little one from her arms. "Hey, Bubba! You've grown like a weed, haven't you?"

"Bububububu!"

Chelsea came right on his heels, and she hugged Jessi, as well. "How is everything?" she asked. "Did he give you any trouble?"

"Depends on which *he* you're referring to, hon. The baby was a perfect angel. Can't say the same for the rest of these lugheads."

Wes was heading across the driveway from the nearby barn, Lash at his side. They looked up, spotted Garrett and Chelsea and both smiled. Wes's white grin was bright from within his tanned face, and Jessi wished he'd get over his hotheaded attitude and smile more often. Sure he'd done time for a crime he didn't commit, but it was over and it was time he let it go.

Then she met Lash's gaze. His smile faltered a little, but his gaze held hers tight. There was a little hint of alarm that drifted in and out of his eyes, and then he looked away.

There was noise and laughter and plenty of hugging as everyone talked at once. They wound up in the living room, drinking iced tea and hearing the full report on the honeymoon cruise to the Bahamas while Chelsea doled out the gifts she'd brought back for everyone. And that was when the subject finally turned to the big white bandage on the side of Jessi's head, and the entire incident in the barn last night, with Wes making it sound as if she'd taken her life in her hands just by birthing a calf. Lash didn't say much. Just sat in the far corner of the room. But his gaze strayed to Jessi's more than once, though he looked away quickly each time she met it.

Jessi sat quietly, pursed her lips and refused to scream at her brother. Not for the world would she have spoiled this homecoming by starting a brawl. Every time the urge to club Wes upside the head hit her, she took a big gulp of icy-cold tea to distract herself. She'd gone through half the glass already.

"It was pure foolishness," Wes was saying. "Besides risking herself, it was risky for the animals. Jess should've called a vet—"

"Wes," Chelsea said, frowning, "your sister *is* a vet."

"Come on, Chelsea, I meant a *real*..." Wes had the good sense not to finish the sentence. He met Jessi's gaze. "I mean—"

"I know what you mean," she said. She got to her

feet, her hand closing around her glass, crossed the room and poured the tea, ice cubes and all, into Wes's lap. She slammed the empty glass down on the table beside him, turned and left the room to go back upstairs to her own. Her head hurt, and she just wasn't up to dealing with her brothers right now.

Chelsea's voice followed her up the stairs. "Weston Brand, that had to be the most insensitive hogwash I've ever—" And then she heard the tap of Chelsea's feet crossing the floor and heading upstairs after her.

She barely had time to brush the hurt, angry tears away before she heard the gentle tap on her bedroom door. "Who is it?" she asked, just in case she was wrong and it was one of her brothers. If it was, she had every intention of telling them to go to hell.

"It's Chelsea."

Jessi opened the door, and met her sister-in-law's eyes.

"You wanna talk about it?" Chelsea asked.

The tears came fresh and fast, and the next thing Jessi knew she was wrapped up tight in the smaller woman's arms. "I hate this," she said, straightening away and swiping angrily at her eyes. "I never cry."

"I know you don't," Chelsea said. "But those brothers of yours bring it out in the best of us."

"You got that right."

"At least Lash set them straight," Chelsea said.

Jessi blinked and stared at her. "He did?"

Chelsea nodded. "Told them you pulled that calf like a pro. Said he knew he couldn't have done it, and doubted any other vet could've done better."

Jessi averted her eyes, hoping Chelsea wouldn't see how much pleasure that gave her. "Doubt it made any difference to them," she said.

"Probably not. In fact, Wes was sort of glaring at him when I left the room." She paced farther into the bedroom and sat down on the edge of the bed. "It's just because they love you, you know. You'll always be their baby sister."

"But, Chelsea, I'm an adult. When are they going to see that?"

Chelsea shrugged. "They aren't...unless you force them to."

"Yeah, that's pretty much the way I figure it, too." She sighed and went to the vanity, pulled open its drawer and extracted a letter. "Something happened while you were gone," she said, and she turned to face Chelsea again. "Marisella Cordoba...she passed away."

"Oh, no." Chelsea looked stricken. "That sweet lady? Oh, Jessi, I'm sorry. I know how close she was to you."

"Closer than I realized, I guess." She handed Chelsea the letter, and Chelsea, frowning, pulled it from its envelope and unfolded it.

Her eyes scanned the page, then met Jessi's again. "She named you as her sole heiress?"

Jessi nodded. "Her lawyer said she had no family. And I guess she was grateful to me for always taking care of that old cat of hers. She wanted me to turn the house into a veterinary clinic, Chelsea. And the money she had in the bank will be enough to do it, too." Jessi shook her head slowly. "She believed in me that much."

"Of course she did. Anyone with half a brain would."

Jessi smiled. "She left me the cat, too."

"There's always a catch, isn't there?" Chelsea

grinned and Jessi smiled, feeling a bit better. "So where's that old beast now?"

"At the lawyer's house, in town. I'm supposed to pick him up today, when I go in to sign some papers making all this official." She lowered her head and sighed. "Chels, I haven't told anyone about this yet."

Chelsea nodded. "Because you think they'll try to talk you out of it?"

"Yeah. They'll say I'm too young, too inexperienced, too...too everything. But I'm going to do it. And if they give me too much grief...then..." She bit her lip, lowered her head. "Then I'm going to leave. The house Marisella left me is big enough for me to live in, as well as run a clinic from. And I will, Chelsea, if they force me."

"But if you do, you won't be running into Lash Monroe around the ranch every day, will you Jess?"

Jessi's head came up fast. "How did you—?"

"Oh, come on, sweetie. It's written all over your face every time you're in the same room with him."

Jessi felt her face heat. But in a moment she was shaking her head. "Doesn't matter," she said. "Lash is probably going to be leaving, anyway, now that Garrett's home."

"Don't be too sure of that. Garrett's planning to ask Lash to stay on."

Jessi felt her brows arch. "He is?"

"We had a message while we were away. There's been some rustling going on in the area, and Garrett's duties as sheriff are going to keep him busy until he puts a stop to it. He isn't going to have as much time as he'd hoped to help out here on the ranch. And besides all that, he wants Lash to help him with the investigation. I guess he was pretty impressed with

Lash's performance in tracking down Vincent de Lorean."

Jessi licked her lips. "You think Lash will agree?"

Chelsea shrugged. "You know him better than I do. What do you think?"

Jessi smiled slowly. "He'll agree. If I have anything to say about it...and believe me, I will."

"That's more like the Jessi I know and love."

"It's the Brand in me coming out," she said. "Now, if I could just get my brothers to see it."

Chelsea looked Jessi over, head to toe. "Well, we can start right now. You say you're going into town today, to see that lawyer? Well, this is a business trip. You can't go in jeans."

"Gee, Chelsea, I don't own much else."

"I do. You need a power suit today, Jessica. And you might as well be wearing it when you face those bundles of testosterone downstairs to tell them about all this. You're a career woman now. So dress the part." She pursed her lips. "I think my skirts will be quite a bit shorter on you than me." Then she smiled. "All the better." And with a wink, she took Jessi's hand in hers and pulled her down the hall and into the master bedroom, which had once belonged to Jessi's parents, but now had been passed on to Chelsea and Garrett. Several new drawings and paintings hung on the walls. Chelsea's handiwork. She'd made a living as an artist before she came here. Now she divided her time between the ranch and volunteering over at the Women's Crisis Center in El Paso. Fighting domestic violence was one of Chelsea's passions.

Jessi surrendered herself to her sister-in-law's ministrations. A short time later, Jessi looked at herself in the full-length mirror and shook her head. She wore a pencil-slim emerald-green silk skirt that made her legs look endlessly long and slender. The matching jacket was cropped short, showing off her narrow waist. The cream-colored blouse underneath was nothing less than classy. Sheer nylons covered her legs, and she wore a pair of shiny black pumps on her feet. Chelsea had helped her with a light coat of makeup, barely visible, but somehow enhancing her cheekbones and wide-set eyes.

"What about my hair?" she said, giving her head a shake. "It's so tomboyish."

"You've gotta be kidding. Most women would kill for that shade of auburn, Jess. And the cut is what's known as 'short and sassy.' Very chic." She picked up a pair of earrings with green stones set in an intricate gold design and handed them to her. "You look fabulous. All you need is a briefcase."

"A veterinary bag," Jessi corrected. "And I already have one."

"Good. Now for the grand entrance."

"Yeah," Jessi said. "The one where I have to ask my brother for permission to use his pickup."

"Hey, I married him. It's my pickup too." Chelsea fished in her purse for the keys.

Jessi took the keys from her hand, bit her lip and blinked her eyes dry. "You don't know how much..."

"Sure I do."

"I was so young when our parents were killed. I can't even remember having another woman around to...to talk to, you know?"

"I know. Don't forget, I lost my mom, too. And then my sister."

Jessi nodded. "But you have another sister now."

Chelsea met her eyes, and Jessi saw them moistening. "That means a lot to me, Jess."

"Hey, don't get too happy. Remember, you got a houseful of brothers as part of the deal."

"Five brothers and little Ethan. So the Brand women are outnumbered by the men, six to two." Chelsea smiled and gave Jessi a wink. "They don't stand a chance."

Lash had battled the urge to grab Wes Brand by the front of his shirt and shake him after seeing the tears spring to Jessi's eyes—tears caused by her brother's thoughtless remark. Heck, the kid didn't deserve that. And she had done a hell of a job with that calf last night. She might be young, but there was no question she was very good at what she did. Lash had seen her in action too often this past month to doubt that. What he couldn't figure out was why her brothers did. They'd been around her a heck of a lot longer than Lash had.

But he satisfied himself with a few words in her defense, and managed to keep his temper in check. Odd, the way the sight of her tears had roused it to such an unusual level. He was normally slow to anger. He shook his head, and thought it was a damned good thing he'd decided to move on.

The brothers had adjourned to the kitchen and now sat around the table with filled coffee mugs and a heap of doughnuts that seemed to be shrinking at an alarming rate. Lash didn't sit. Instead, he cleared his throat and, when Garrett looked at him, spoke. "Now that you're back, Garrett, I'm thinking it's time for me to be heading out."

It was Wes who replied. "Been nice havin' you here, Lash. You have a nice trip, now."

Elliot shook his head and took a quick sip of his coffee. Looked to Lash as if he did so to hide the grin he was battling. Ben said nothing. The guy never did say much. Seemed locked in a perpetual state of mourning over the death of his young wife, Penny. Jessi had filled Lash in on that sad event, but she'd also told him it had happened over a year ago, and that she was pretty worried about Ben's seeming inability to get past it. Or even to crack an occasional smile.

Garrett sat thoughtfully for a moment. Then he drew a breath. "Lash, is there something pressing you need to see to? Someplace you have to be?"

The question took Lash by surprise. "Well, no, not really. I just thought it was time."

"And you thought right," Wes said.

Garrett shot his brother a quelling glance before returning his attention to Lash. "Then I have a proposition for you." Garrett got to his feet, yanked another mug from the tree and filled it, then set it in front of an empty chair.

Taking his cue, Lash took the seat, and the mug.

"Lash, I could still use you here," Garrett began. Wes rolled his eyes and heaved a sigh, but as a deterrent it was ineffective. "There's been some rustling going on, and it's going to take more than one small-town sheriff to get to the bottom of it."

Lash choked on his coffee, lowered the mug with a bang and swiped at his mouth with his shirtsleeve. "You gotta be kidding me."

Garrett smiled at him. "You did a hell of a job with the whole de Lorean thing. No fed could've done better."

"I'm no lawman, Garrett."

"Neither was I, till they pinned this badge on me. I need a deputy, Lash. Not only that, but I'm still gonna need your help here on the ranch. Especially with rustlers prowling the pastures."

"Damnation," Wes muttered. Garrett glanced toward him, and Wes shook his head. "I don't suppose it ever occurred to you to ask one of us," he snapped.

"It occurred to me. Wes, you have a record, justified or not. You've also got a temper hot enough to melt glaciers, and the whole town knows it. Sorry, but with your reputation, they'd never sit still for me pinning a badge on your chest and handing you a loaded gun." Wes's face reddened a little, but he couldn't very well argue his brother's points. "Elliot's young yet. Maybe not too young, but we all know he can't hit the broad side of a barn with a pistol. 'Course, if he could rope the bad guys, we'd be in good shape, but it's safe to figure they'll be carrying weapons more lethal than lassos. And Ben..." Garrett glanced at the blond man sitting quietly with his head slightly lowered. "Ben's mind wouldn't be on the job. Lash has proven he's damn good at this kind of work, and I want him with me in this."

Finally he met Lash's eyes again. "So what do you say?"

Lash drew a breath and sighed hard. What could he say? Garrett had treated him like family...well, except for that one misunderstanding when he'd damn near broken Lash's nose and Jessi had just about screamed the house down over it.

Jessi. She was his reason for leaving. He wanted to get away from her, because he was sorely afraid she might be developing some silly crush on him. And she was too pretty, too able to make him feel a twinge of temptation every now and then, though he hadn't fully realized the danger she posed until last night.

On the other hand, he owed Garrett Brand. Owed him big. If not for the big guy, Jimmy's murderer might still be walking around a free man.

So which was more important? Risking a little temptation or doing right by a friend?

And, as it often did, the voice of the Reverend Stanton rang through Lash's mind like some kind of born-again Jiminy Cricket, acting as his conscience. "'...*Is this thy kindness to thy friend? Why wentest thou not with thy friend?' Second Samuel sixteen–seventeen, Lash, my boy. Memorize it.*"

Lash sighed and wondered if he'd ever find an occasion in life that didn't call some applicable verse to mind. Heck, probably not. He'd memorized most of the good book before he grew old enough to move out of the Stanton house. It came in handy at times. At others, it just gave him twinges of guilt.

Like now. A twinge just big enough to make him do the right thing.

He sighed once more, and finally nodded. "All right, Garrett. I'll stick around. But understand that this is temporary, okay? Once this rustling thing is over, I'll be leaving."

Garrett's face split in a broad smile. "Understood."

Lash reached his hand across the table to shake Garrett's. Then he caught Wes's eye and knew the man still didn't approve.

"Well, Lash, since you're staying on," Wes said, "maybe you can take the pickup into town for that load of feed that's waiting to be collected. It'll give me a chance to have a talk with my brothers."

"Be glad to," Lash said, but he knew his smile didn't reach his eyes. He and Wes were going to have to come to an understanding, and Lash suspected it wasn't going to be pretty. Fact was, he was eager to get out of here and think about what he'd just agreed to, and how the hell he was going to deal with it. By staying away from Jessi Brand, that was how. Damn, he'd been sure he would have shaken the Texas dirt off his boots by sundown.

"Sorry, boys, but the pickup is already spoken for." The voice was Chelsea's, and it came from the doorway.

All heads turned in her direction, but it wasn't Chelsea who caused their jaws to drop, one by one. It was Jessi. Chelsea stepped aside to let her walk by into the kitchen, and Lash felt his throat go dry. She looked... Dang...she looked gorgeous. Luscious. Sexy. And *very* grown-up.

Lash's eyes roamed from the low-slung collar of the creamy blouse to the swells of her breasts beneath it. His gaze lowered, following the sleek curves down to legs that would bring a man crashing right down to his trembling knees. Good Lord, he'd had no idea what she was hiding under those jeans and flannel shirts she usually wore.

"Where the hell do you think you're going all gussied up like that, Jessi?" Wes blurted, but even his voice sounded a bit hoarse.

"I have an appointment in town," she said, and her voice drew Lash's gaze back up to her face. Funny how he'd never noticed that her eyes were hypnotic, that her lips were as full and sensual as any Hollywood starlet's. Beyond all that, he noticed that she was nervous. Her eyes were not just incredible and deeper than the velvety brown of a doe's eyes, but wide and darting and glittering. She moistened her lips and went on. "But before I go, I have a little announcement to make."

Lash couldn't take his eyes off her. He lost track of her brothers' reactions, because he couldn't focus on anything but the world-class beauty standing at center stage.

"Go ahead, Jess," Garrett said softly.

Jessi nodded at him, smiling shakily. "Marisella left me everything she had," she said. "Including the house in town, and a sizable chunk of money."

She gave it a second to sink in. Lash saw the brothers focusing on her sharply, lifting their chins, interest lighting their eyes.

"And she left it for a reason," Jessi went on. "She wanted me to set up my veterinary clinic there, and I've decided to do it. I'm going into Quinn today to meet with her attorney and sign the necessary papers."

Wes got out of his chair fast. "Oh, for crying out loud, Jessi, you don't know the first thing about—"

"Weston Brand, you sit down and shut up, because I'm not finished yet."

Lash did manage to look away from her, briefly. Just long enough to see Wes's eyes widen, and his face pale just a bit. He didn't speak.

"I'm a grown woman, with a degree in veterinary medicine. I own my own house and have my own money, soon to be supplemented by the income from my clinic. Now I'm going to say this once, and once only. That house is plenty big enough to support a clinic *and* a home."

This time Garrett was the one who rose, shaking his

head slowly. "Honey...you aren't saying you're... you're moving out?"

"Not yet," she said. Lash noticed that she bit her lower lip, and he suspected that leaving this houseful of Brands would be as traumatic for her as for the rest of them. "But I will if any of you start riding me about this. Marisella believed in me. And so does Chelsea. And I'm not ashamed to tell you that it hurts like hell to know that my own brothers don't. But I'm not going to let it hold me back. Not anymore."

And as the Brand men all started blurting denials at once, Jessi sauntered past them, heels clicking across the floor tiles, and headed right out the front door.

Garrett and Wes both lunged, as if to go after her.

"Don't you even think about it," Chelsea said, and her voice was so loud and so firm that both of them stopped in their tracks. "Just you sit right back down. Jessi might be finished with you, but I haven't even started." Then she came forward and tapped Lash's shoulder. He'd been fixated on watching that little hellcat climb into the pickup, her long legs revealed in their full glory.

"Lash, get your rear end out there. I believe the foreman here gave you a job to do."

"I didn't mean—" Wes began, but a glare from Chelsea stopped him.

"The grain, Lash. Wes told you to take the pickup into town and collect that load of grain."

"My car—" he blurted.

"Isn't big enough, and you know it. Ride with Jess. Go on. Move."

"Then Jess can take my car," Lash said, rushing on.

"Waste of gas." Chelsea put her hands on her hips and nodded her head toward the door. "Git."

She didn't leave much room for argument, and Lash suspected he was being sent away for far different reasons. Chelsea was good and riled about the state these fellows had put their sister in, and she was going to let them have it with both barrels. He ought to be glad to be out of the line of fire. But instead he was sweating bullets.

He nodded once to Chelsea, saw a smile hiding in her eyes, and then headed out the door to jump into the passenger side of the pickup truck before it could get away without him. And as he did he vowed to himself that he wouldn't even *look* at those long legs of Jessi Brand's.

Chapter 3

"What are you doing in here?" Jessi asked him.

Lash told himself not to look at her. He looked at
her anyway. Ah, damn, there were tears brimming in
her eyes again. He hated seeing tears in those pretty
eyes.

"I…uh… Chelsea… I mean, Wes wants me to pick
up a load of feed."

"Oh." She slid the shift easily into gear and eased
up on the clutch. Lash's gaze fixed itself on her legs,
which were parted slightly, of necessity, to reach both
the accelerator and the clutch. Her skirt was riding
high, showing to fullest advantage a pair of thighs so
creamy and smooth he wanted to taste them.

No, he didn't. Damn, if the preacher could see him
now, he'd tell him to memorize ten thousand Bible
verses. At *least!* Old Ezekiel Stanton had always promised Lash they'd come in handy someday.

Exodus 20:17, Lash thought desperately. *Thou shalt*

not covet thy neighbor's wife, nor his manservant, nor his maidservant, nor his ox, nor his ass, nor any thing that is thy neighbor's. Including his sister. Lash recited the verse in his mind, closing his eyes and adding the final sentence, since he was sure it must have been included on the original stone tablet. God wouldn't skip over something this important.

"Lash?"

Swallowing hard, he opened his eyes and faced her. And, dammit, he still coveted.

"Did Garrett ask you to stay on?" she asked, her eyes on the road, instead of on him. Her hands on the wheel, instead of on him.

"Yeah," he croaked. "How did you know?"

"Chelsea filled me in...on the rustling and all." He nodded and said nothing. She glanced his way, and he noticed a tiny smudge of makeup under her eye, right in a spot he bet would be very sensitive, should he press his lips to it. "So? Are you going to?"

"Going to what?"

"Stay on," she said.

"Oh. Yeah, I told him I would."

Her eyes on the road again, she smiled. "I'm glad."

Wonderful. He didn't want her to be glad.

"So what do you think?"

What did he think? He thought he'd better get out of this pickup soon, because she was lifting her beautiful thigh, and then extending it to depress the clutch again, and he was getting turned on.

"About what?"

"My announcement back there," she said. "My clinic."

He smiled at the memory, frankly glad to have something to distract him from thinking about the way she looked. Must be the dress. The stockings. The makeup. He'd only seen her in jeans and work clothes before, and usually with dirt streaked across her face. He'd never looked at her as…well, as a woman. And it was hitting him hard and fast and all at once. It was downright flabbergasting.

"To tell the truth," he said slowly, "I didn't know you had it in you."

"To start a clinic?"

"To stand up to your brothers." Lord knew she'd put Olive Stanton right to shame with that little speech she'd just made. "I was beginning to think you enjoyed having them at your beck and call. Little princess, with her own army of knights protecting her from every threat."

She swung her head around, brown eyes flashing. "That's what you think of me?" Her face flushed with angry color.

"Well…see, I knew a woman like that once, and you were showing all the signs, so I—"

"I oughtta stop this truck and make you walk into town and carry the damned feed home on your back, Lash Monroe!"

She did have a temper. Made her cheeks hot and pink, and her eyes gleam. Made her look like pure fire.

"I didn't say I was right, okay?"

"You didn't say you were wrong, either."

He shrugged. "Maybe I'm reserving judgment."

She glared at him. "So you think you *were* right. You think I'm just some spoiled kid who likes having her brothers treating her like a fragile china doll."

He tilted his head. "Well, you put up with it for this long. Who knows, you go getting all independent now and you might just find you miss having all those men catering to your every need."

"You got a lot to learn about me, Lash. A lot to learn." She shook her head slowly as she said it, and focused on her driving again.

He felt mean. Truth to tell, he was beginning to think he'd been way off base about Jessi Brand. She wasn't turning out to be as much like his foster mother, the helpless and dependent Olive Stanton, as he'd thought she was. But hell, he couldn't very well tell her so, could he? He didn't want her reading anything into it.

"For what it's worth, Jessi, I think you're one hell of a vet."

"For a kid, you mean?"

He didn't answer that loaded question. She turned the truck expertly into the parking lot of the small clapboard law office and killed the motor.

"Look at me, Lash."

Hell, was she nuts? He'd been doing nothing *but* look at her for the whole damned trip. Still, he complied, largely because he couldn't do otherwise.

"My mama was married, with two babies, by the time she was my age. Did you know that?"

He shook his head mutely.

"Do I look like a kid to you?" she asked him point-blank. Right between the eyes. She'd been right awhile back when she'd claimed to be the best shot in the family.

"No, you don't."

Her eyes dipped to focus very briefly on his mouth, and he felt that gaze like a red-hot branding iron. "Well," she said softly. "That's a start."

A start? A start to what?

She opened her door, leaving the keys dangling from

the switch as she climbed out. "You can go ahead and take the pickup to collect that feed, Lash. By the time you get back here, I should be ready to go."

Lash nodded, sliding across the seat to the driver's side. But he didn't leave right away. Instead, he sat there and watched as she walked away from the truck. Watched her hips moving back and forth, those long legs eating up the distance. Lord, but she was something. And he knew that he was in trouble.

But I say unto you that whosoever looketh on a woman to lust after her hath committed adultery with her already in his heart. The preacher's voice echoed in his mind. He could even hear the sound of that fist pounding down on the Bible.

Stop thinking about her, that was the key. Just put Jessi Brand right out of his mind. He could do that, couldn't he?

When she disappeared inside the lawyer's office, Lash started the truck and backed out of the lot. He headed toward the feed store two blocks away, but he was still thinking about Jessi when he got there. He backed up to the loading dock and went inside long enough to request the feed and ask that it be charged to the Texas Brand account. Then he went out back to help with the loading. Maybe a little physical labor would distract his wayward thoughts.

The feed was stacked in hundred-pound burlap bags. Lash slung one over his shoulder, and it emitted a puff of fragrant dust he knew would remain on his shirt all day. He tossed it into the pickup bed and went back for another. Already the sun was sending heat waves down to toast his flesh, and after the third trip he was coated in sweat, as well as feed dust. Fifteen bags later, his back was starting to protest. His heart was thudding in his chest, and he was out of breath. And he was still thinking about Jessi Brand. He dreaded the ride back to the ranch, and hoped it would go quickly. Hoped he could keep his thoughts to himself until they got back. Hoped he could keep his *hands* to himself, as well.

Ah, hell.

He drove back to the law office. And there she was, standing outside, in the sunshine that made her hair gleam like copper. She had a manila envelope in one hand, and a black-and-white cat cradled against her chest. She kept bending to stroke her cheek over the cat's head, and there was something so damned sexy about the act that he almost stalled the truck.

She sauntered over to the passenger side, and Lash leaned across to open the door for her. The cat came first, settling itself down on the seat beside Lash. Jessi climbed in beside the animal and slammed the door. "This is Pedro," she said.

"I knew a Pedro once. Didn't much like him, though. He come with the house?"

Jessi nodded and smiled, but it was a nervous smile. "Yeah. And so did Marisella's old truck." She turned toward him, grimaced, then slowly reached out a hand and brushed the dust from his hair.

Lash didn't know whether to duck away from her touch, or close his eyes and lean into it. Damn, he liked the way her hands felt in his hair.

"You're a mess," she said.

"You got that right." She frowned at him, but he didn't explain his meaning. "So, back to the ranch?"

She chewed her lower lip, then shook her head. "If you're not in a big hurry to get back, Lash, I'd like to stop by Marisella's place. Take a look around."

"Oh." More time alone with her. Great.

"That way I can drive her...my new pickup truck home."

"Or I can tow it home. As I recall, that thing's at least as old as this cat appears to be."

"Older," she said. "But it runs." She turned her attention back to the cat, stroking his head, and Lash felt a twinge of envy.

He ignored it and steered the truck toward the edge of town, and the house Jessi had just inherited.

Lash had never been inside Marisella's house. It was a red adobe cottage, with a matching garage beside it that was nearly as big as the house itself. A front lawn rolled gently between the two buildings and the road, and an even bigger one unfolded in the back.

Jessi took the keys and went to the door, setting the cat gently on the ground as she unlocked it. Lash sat right where he was until she glanced over her shoulder at him, smiled that killer smile of hers, and waved a hand at him to come on. Okay. Everything was okay. He could handle this.

Lash got out of the truck and followed her inside.

The place looked as if Marisella had just left for the day. Pedro followed them through the front door and meowed plaintively for his owner. "Poor thing," Jessi said, speaking in hushed tones. "He doesn't understand where she's gone."

Lash nodded and reached down to pet the cat, but Pedro shot away from him, running through the house, probably in search of Marisella. Jessi looked around the small kitchen area, with its white cupboards and spotless countertop, its small round oak table and matching chairs, its ancient-looking refrigerator.

"I'd have to tear it apart to turn it into a clinic," she said, still speaking very softly. "I'm not sure I can bring myself to do it." She ran a hand over the countertop. "There's so much of Marisella still here. And she was one hell of a lady. I don't want to lose that sense of her."

"Then don't," Lash said. Jessi turned to face him, brows lifted. He shrugged. "I mean...well, the garage is plenty big enough for a clinic," he went on. "Put in a few partitions, do a little wiring in there. It wouldn't be all that difficult."

Her eyes narrowed as she watched him. Then she nodded slowly. "It's a good idea." She turned away then, walking through the kitchen and into the small living room, with its cozy furniture and its countless embroidered samplers decorating the walls. She looked around and nodded. "It really is a good idea. This place should be someone's home, not a sterile clinic, you know? There should be a family here. God, Marisella would love the idea of kids running around her house, getting into mischief, making noise." Her smile was whimsical, as if she were envisioning it all in her mind.

"Thinking of renting it out to some family like that?"

She shook her head. "Thinking of the future, Lash. My own family. My own kids."

Lash felt his brows lift in surprise. "Getting a little ahead of yourself, aren't you?"

She only shrugged. "I don't believe in waiting for what I want," she said. "Maybe it's because my parents died so young and so suddenly, or maybe it's just me. But I've always figured you ought to go after your dreams just as hard and as fast as you possibly can. You never know when fate might step in and take away your chance." She stepped to the window and looked out over a wide, overgrown expanse of grass. "Besides, this backyard was made for children."

Lash almost asked her if she had a husband in mind, but decided against it. He didn't want to know if she was already planning her marriage to some local good ol' boy. He did take a moment to pity the poor fool, whoever he was. Imagine having those overprotective brothers of hers to contend with. Hell, he wouldn't be in that slob's shoes for all the tea in China.

She turned her back to the window, leaning against the sill, and looked at him with a gleam in her eyes that made him squirm clear to his boots.

Lash cleared his throat. "I...er...thought you wanted to keep living out at the ranch."

"For now," she said. "But I know better than to think of staying there forever. Especially if I ever—I mean, *when* I get married. Lord, Lash, can you imagine the way my brothers would feel about the poor guy? They'd probably be as hostile as...as they were with you at first."

He shifted uncomfortably. "Yeah. That's pretty easy to imagine."

"C'mon," she said. "I'll show you the rest. There are two bedrooms, and—"

"I think we oughtta take a look at that garage."

If he'd blurted it too fast, it couldn't be helped. No way was he going anywhere *near* a bedroom with Jessi Brand. Uh-uh. What did she think he was, totally stupid?

She sent him a sidelong glance that said she knew every thought that went through his mind, which was impossible, of course. "Okay," she said.

She scooped up the cat and led the way outside, locking the door behind her. Pedro yowled enough to break a heart, and it looked as if it was breaking Jessi's. She rubbed his head, kissed his face. "It's gonna be all right, kitty. I promise."

The cat settled down some after that. And Lash figured if she'd rubbed *his* head and kissed *his* face like that, he'd probably be lying on his back and purring, as well, by now.

She deposited the animal in the pickup on the way to the garage, then headed there to unlock the overhead door. She tugged on it, too, bending over right in front of Lash and making his pulse rate skyrocket with the thoughts that action invoked. He tapped her shoulder so she'd straighten up and quit torturing him. Then he reached past her to yank the sticky door upward.

And then she groaned audibly.

Marisella's old pickup sat in the only place it possibly could. Around it, the garage was packed full. Piles of boxes and bags loomed higher than Lash's head. There were stacks and stacks of cases and trunks and containers of every shape imaginable.

"Looks like Marisella was a closet pack rat," he observed.

Jessi shook her head slowly and picked her way inside, seeking out a path between the piles. She pulled the flap of one box aside to peer at its contents. "Magazines," she said, turning to face him. "Old ones. I can't imagine why she kept..."

He didn't hear the rest. The box she'd tugged on was in the middle of a ten-foot stack, and that stack was teetering now, tipping, right above her pretty head.

Lash lunged forward as the stack fell. His body hit Jessi's, and they both sailed out of harm's way as the pile of boxes came crashing down right in the spot where she'd been standing.

Only the danger hadn't passed. Not by a long shot.
Because Lash was lying facedown on top of Jessi,
where she'd landed, atop a heap of plastic bags. Every
inch of his body was pressed intimately to every inch
of hers. And his hand had come to rest, for some
damned inexplicable reason, against her firm, nylon-
encased thigh.

He didn't move. Couldn't move, even when he tried
to tell himself he should. He lifted his head and looked
into her eyes, and the heat he saw in those big pools
of melted chocolate seared him right to his toes.
"You...uh...okay?"

"Fine," she said in a deep, sultry whisper. "Maybe
even better than fine. How about you?"

"Um...yeah, I'm okay, too."

She shifted her hips a little, then blinked up at him.
"So, are you carrying a pistol, Lash, or are you just
glad to see me?"

He closed his eyes and grimaced, embarrassed to the
roots of his hair. "You're a mouthy little thing, you
know that?"

She only smiled—a slow, sexy smile that made him
want to groan aloud. "Yeah, I've been told that before." She held his gaze. He couldn't look away. "So,
Lash, what's it gonna be? You gonna get off me, or
kiss me?"

He looked down into her eyes, and it hit him that
she *wanted* him to kiss her. Dammit, wasn't it bad
enough that he was having these bouts of lust for her?
Did she have to go and start having them for him, as
well?

He pushed himself up with his hands.

"Chicken," she said.

"Cut it out, Jessi." He got to his feet, with some

effort, and reached a hand down to help her up, as well. She took it and got up, but he thought she looked a little hurt, or disappointed, or something. He shook his head and heaved a sigh. "Look, just so you know, you don't have to go trying to convince me you're all grown up, okay? I got the message."

"You think that's what I was doing?"

He turned away and began moving boxes aside to clear a path out of the garage. "I know damned well that's what you were doing. And you can save it. I'm convinced already. So you can quit with the nonsense."

He moved one last box and stepped out into the sunlight again.

She stayed where she was. "And what if it wasn't nonsense?"

He went still, feeling a shiver race right up his spine. "That's all it can be, Jessi. I'm leaving here as soon as Garrett and I put a stop to this rustling. Besides that, I'm old enough to be your—"

"My lover?"

He spun around. She shrugged innocently. "Well, you couldn't say 'father,' 'cause it would be bull. And I already have plenty of brothers. Sure don't need another one of those. So what's left?"

"Friend," he said.

"Oh."

He didn't like the look in her eyes, so he averted his own, glancing at the battered old pickup instead of at her face. "How about if I drive this clunker back to the ranch, and you take Garrett's truck?"

"Why?"

She still hadn't moved, and she was still looking at him like a panther looks at an unsuspecting rabbit.

"Well, because I can tell by driving it what kind of work it might need."

"And what makes you think I can't?" she asked him.

He bit his lip. Damn. He supposed he'd underestimated her...again. "Fine, you drive it. I'll follow, in case it breaks down."

"Well, now, isn't that just *friendly* of you." She finally clambered out from between the piles of junk and made her way to the old red pickup truck. She opened the door and climbed behind the wheel. "It's going to run just fine," she told him, inserting the key.

"How can you be so sure?"

She smiled at him. "I want it to. And you know me, right, friend? I'm that spoiled little princess, the darling baby sister of the Brand brothers. I *always* get what I want."

As Lash stood there with his throat going just as dry as the desert sand, Jessi turned the key, and the pickup roared to life like an angry bull. She slipped it into gear and drove it slowly out of the garage, then past him, onto the road heading back toward the ranch.

Lash closed and locked the garage, then returned to Garrett's pickup to follow her. He felt a little sick to his stomach. But he wasn't sure why.

He wants me!

Jessi couldn't stop smiling as she ground the ancient pickup truck into a higher gear and bounced down the road. The thing steered like a tank, and she was leaving a smoke trail behind her that would have choked a horse. But none of that dampened her mood. Lash Monroe had given himself away today. He could deny it till hell froze over, but he couldn't convince her that she'd imagined what had happened between them back there. No way. He'd been turned on. Aroused. Attracted.

She smiled even more. *Hard.*

Yup, he wanted her, all right. But him wanting her was only half the battle. He was going to have to *love* her. And soon, before he and Garrett solved this rustling thing and he got it into his head to go running away from her again. It had to be before that happened.

She settled deeper in her seat and glanced at her own determined eyes in the rearview mirror. "I'm gonna make that man my very own, if it's the last thing I do."

The voice sounded certain, but a hint of doubt crept into her reflection's gaze. Jessi bit her lip as a slight bout of worry assailed her. What if she couldn't do it? What if all Lash felt for her was a physical longing, and nothing more? What if he was too hell-bent on retaining his precious freedom to let himself feel anything else?

Just how in hell did a woman go about making a man fall in love with her? How did she make a confirmed bachelor change his ways? How did she make a drifter decide to settle down?

Lord, she needed a plan. And she needed it quick. Before those damned rustlers were caught and tossed behind bars and Lash flitted off like a goose in winter.

The truck bounded into the driveway and under the arches of the Texas Brand, and Jessi brought it to a whining stop and killed the engine. It died slow, as if it didn't quite want to let go just yet. It coughed, gasped, backfired once, and then finally gave up the ghost. She glanced up to see Garrett on the front porch, shaking his head and waving one hand as if to clear the smoke away, though it was nowhere near him. Chelsea sat on the porch swing beside him, and she gave him a nudge in the ribs with her elbow.

As Jessi got out of the pickup, Garrett rose and came to meet her. "How'd it go?"

"Went fine," she said. "It's gonna be a lot of work, Garrett, but I can do it." She lifted her chin a little as she said it, certain he was going to disagree.

"I know you can."

Jessi blinked. "You do?"

"Hell, you're a Brand, aren't you?"

For now, she thought, and she glanced over her shoulder in time to see Lash behind the wheel of Garrett's pickup, backing the load of grain up to the barn door. Above him, the sky was darkening with ominous-looking clouds. It had been hot and dry for a while now, and she knew too well how dangerous a sudden cloudburst could be. What they needed was a slow, steady rain. The ground-soaking kind. Not a downpour.

"Look, Jess," Garrett said, interrupting her inspection of the horizon, and of the man out near the barn. "I'm sorry if we've given you the feeling that we're not behind you. It's just that...well, you're our baby sister, you know?"

She dragged her attention from the dark clouds and battled the worry skittering up her spine. "How could I not know?"

Garrett smiled a bit sheepishly. "If you're determined to do this, let us help you."

She faced him again, squaring her shoulders. "I don't think so. Look, don't get all offended, big brother, but I want to do this on my own. I don't want anyone thinking I couldn't have made it work without my brothers' help. And besides, you guys have your hands full as it is.''

"But, Jessi—"

Chelsea cleared her throat from the porch, and Garrett cut off his protest.

"Okay, Jess. If that's the way you want it. Just know we're here for you, okay? And don't think that asking for advice is a sign of weakness. That's what family's for, you know.''

"I know," she told him. Then he hugged her hard, and she hugged him back.

When he released her, he stared down at her, searching her face. "Now, about Lash…''

Jessi frowned. "What about Lash?''

Garrett shifted his stance a bit. "I, uh…that is, Wes seems to think there might be…er…''

"Might be…what?''

"Look, Jess, he's a drifter. He's told us all flat out that he's leaving here soon. And besides all that, he's ten years older than you, and—''

"Eleven, Garrett. He's eleven years older than me.''

Garrett just bunched up his eyebrows and tilted his head.

"So, Jessi," Chelsea said loudly, shouldering her way between brother and sister to drape an arm around Jessi's shoulders and begin leading her into the house. "Tell me all about your plans for the clinic. And don't leave anything out.''

Jessi let Chelsea draw her away, but she glanced back over her shoulder at Garrett. "I'm a grown woman now," she said. "I can take care of myself.''

"I just don't want to see you get hurt," he said.

She sighed hard and shook her head. Damn. Things around here would never change.

* * *

Upstairs in her room, Jessi spent some time at her computer, making detailed plans for her clinic. She kept the radio playing, hoping for a weather report, but only half listening. And pretty soon it didn't matter, because she heard the thunder in the distance and saw those clouds rolling in thicker all the time. They were in for a whopper of a storm, and damned if the ground wasn't too parched to absorb it. Could be a mess.

But if there was, they'd deal with it. They always had.

She put the possible repercussions of a storm out of her mind and worked on her plans. She'd added up all the cash she'd inherited and started formulating a budget. She knew more about the costs of equipment for the clinic than she did about the price of construction for the garage, so that was where she began, thumbing through her countless veterinary-supply catalogs and making lists of what she'd need, then subtracting the cost from the available funds. She'd have to earmark most of the rest for the remodeling, she had little doubt of that. There would be none left over for a better vehicle, and she'd need a good pickup truck for this venture.

Well, she'd have to make do. Maybe she could get some work done on the truck she had. It sounded to her as if it could use a new muffler, and probably plugs and points. A little tune-up, an oil change, new filters and belts—heck, she could probably make it run like new again.

Right.

Sighing, she got to her feet and wandered to the window to part the curtains and look outside.

Then she caught her breath and gnawed her lower lip.

Lash was out there by the barn now. He'd stripped off his shirt in deference to the moisture-laden heat, and he was unloading the heavy bags of grain and handing them off to Wes. Wes then carried them a few yards and handed them off to someone else, inside the barn. Elliot or Ben or Garrett. Didn't matter. And it didn't matter that Wes was shirtless as well, or that his rugged Comanche build usually made other men pale in comparison. It was Lash who'd captured her attention. God, but he was a beautiful man. Lean and firm and strong. Not bulging with muscle, but rippling instead. Subtle power slid under his skin, and she sucked a breath through her teeth when she saw the thin sheen of sweat coating his chest. It was dark outside, and the air was heavy and sizzling hot, the approaching storm acting like a woolen blanket, holding the heat beneath it.

"Damn," she muttered.

"Damn, what?" Chelsea asked, popping into the room and coming up to the window beside her. She followed Jessi's gaze and said, "Oh."

"So, what do you think?" Jessi asked.

Chelsea shrugged and leaned against the window. "Not bad. Not bad at all." She looked at Jessi and winked. "So how did the trip into town go?"

"You mean with the lawyer?" Jessi asked innocently.

"You know perfectly well what I mean. Tell me everything."

Jessi grinned. "I thought you'd never ask," she said. "But I'm gonna have to save it for later. I mean, I really oughtta go out there and help my poor brothers unload that heavy grain, don't you think?''

"Not in that outfit, you're not. Talk fast, while you change. Then you can take those poor, hot, sweaty-looking fellas out something cold to drink."

Lash glanced up to see Jessi, back in her usual jeans and a ribbed tank top, making her way across the yard toward the barns with a six-pack of dewy bottles in one hand. He licked his lips, unsure if it was the thought of that icy-cold soda that made him do it, or the way she looked. Lean and curvy and fresh. She didn't look the same way she'd looked before, but suddenly he was seeing her so differently.

She came right up to him, leaned one hip on the pickup's lowered tailgate and freed one of the bottles of soda from the pack. "You're looking..." Her mischievous brown eyes slid all the way down his sweaty chest, pausing on the snap of his jeans and moving slowly back up again. "Hot," she finished.

His throat went three times drier than it had been. "Yeah, it's a scorcher today. Muggy."

"Mmm... I think we're in for a storm." She twisted the cap off the bottle. "You want a drink?"

"Sure, if it's good an' cold." A slow rumble of thunder rolled over them and then faded.

She smiled and held the bottle out. He reached for it, and she moved it quickly past his hand, pressing its chilly glass against his belly. He yelped and jumped back.

"Cold enough?" Damn, she was sparkling like a gemstone today.

"Plenty," he told her, and he couldn't help smiling at her. She wanted to play. He could see that. If her brothers wouldn't take offense, he might just oblige her. Sling her right over his shoulder and haul her butt to the pond to toss her in. Oh, yeah, he could play.

But then she'd stand up, and that little tank shirt she wore would be transparent, it would be so wet. And that cold water would do things to her body. Make him notice it even more than he was already noticing it, and dammit, he was already noticing it way more than he should. And…ah, hell, maybe the pond wasn't such a good idea.

"What's the matter, Lash?"

"Huh?" He met her eyes.

"You were staring at my chest. Just wondering if I had something on me, or—"

He shook his head and averted his eyes, searching for a change of subject and latching on to the first one that came to him. "Garrett's worried about flash flooding. Said it's been known to happen when a big storm rolls in after such a long dry spell."

"Yeah, it has been. But Garrett tends to worry too much." She glanced inside the dim, fragrant barn. "Where is he, anyway?"

Lash sighed. Stupid way to change the subject. Now he had to inform her that they were alone in this big old barn together. Maybe he should just lie.

She held his gaze and drew the truth out of him like mud will draw the stinger out of a bee sting. "He had to go inside to take a phone call. Didn't you hear Chelsea holler for him?"

She shook her head. "No. I was distracted. So, what about the others?"

He licked his lips. "They headed down to that lower pasture that runs alongside the creek. Garrett said he wanted them to move the heifers to higher ground, just in case.''

"Like I said, he worries too much." Her eyes scanned the barn's dark interior, as if to confirm that her brothers were gone.

Lash tried distracting her with a new subject again. "That cat…Pedro…he's in the truck. Best get him out, before he gets too warm in there."

"Okay." She turned and walked away from him. He reached into the truck to haul out the last bag of grain. He hoped Garrett's phone call was a brief one. He was alone out here with Jessi, and he didn't like it.

Or maybe he did. And maybe he shouldn't.

She opened the pickup door, and Pedro shot out so fast he appeared no more than a black-and-white streak. He ran between Lash's feet, shot into the barn and scrambled up through the opening, into the hayloft.

"Damn," Jessi said, slamming the truck's door. She started right through that barn, and stopped at the ladder. "Well, c'mon, Lash," she called. "I'll never catch him by myself. Give me a hand, will you?"

Lash looked at her. Then he looked at the darkness above her, beyond the opening in the ceiling. Darkness and soft, fragrant hay. Silence and solitude. Hot, sultry, sticky air, smelling of fresh hay and Jessi Brand. Oh, man.

She put her foot on the lowest rung of the ladder. Lash set the bag of feed down, and moved as if he had no control over his body. As if he were operating on autopilot or something. His brain was telling him to stay where he was, but his brain was no longer running this show. His libido was, and that part of him wanted nothing more than to follow Jessi Brand up into that hayloft. Hell, that part of him wanted to follow her to the ends of the earth, and all she'd have to do would be to crook her little finger.

Lord, but he was in over his head here. And he was beginning to wonder if there was one damn thing he could do about it.

Chapter 4

Lash got to the ladder just as Jessi started climbing. Her shapely, denim-encased backside moved higher, right past his face, and then disappeared into the darkness above. And he heard her feet moving in the hay, and he heard her calling, "Here, kitty-kitty. Come on, Pedro."

He sighed softly, gripped the ladder and clambered up it after her.

It was dim, but not pitch-dark. The place smelled so strongly of hay that the air felt thick with it. In fact, it probably was slightly thick with it, judging by the dust floating into his lungs. And it was hotter up here than it was below. Hotter than the hellfire he was gonna burn in if he didn't watch himself. Hotter than the combined tempers of the Brand brothers. And dark. Damn, but it was dark. Like dusk, instead of a summer afternoon.

"There he is," Jessi said, and he squinted until he

could see where she was pointing, then followed her
finger. The cat was perched on the top of a stack of
hay. He couldn't have seen the beast well at all, if not
for the white spots. And Jessi headed over to climb up
after him.

Lash was right behind her. "Hold on, now, you'll
pull that whole stack down on top of you."

"Not if I go up on this side. It's solid here."

He examined the stack of bales she proposed to
climb, then gave a tug on them to assure himself of
their stability. "It's also straight up and down, Jess.
There's nothing to climb on here."

"Sure there is." To prove her point, she gripped
high above her, fingers sinking into the hay, and then
she picked up one foot and jammed her toe into the
bale, creating her own toehold. She repeated the process with the other foot, then began moving, hands and
feet alternately higher, like a rock climber, only slower.

"You're gonna break your neck," he warned.

"You're right."

"Huh?"

"I'm gonna fall!" she yelled suddenly.

Lash reached up and pressed his hands to her to keep
her from falling. Only the result was that he ended up
with her firm little backside in the palms of his hands.

Oh, damn. She felt good.

"I've got the cat," she called. "Can you sort of…
lower me down?"

"I don't think so," he said, and the words were
breathless and choked.

"Well, Lash, I can't climb back down. My hands
are full."

"So are mine," he said.

She laughed softly. "That best not have been an insult, pal."

"I'd sooner insult the *Mona Lisa*," he muttered, and he managed to lower her some. Then he moved his hands, one at a time, up to her waist, and brought her down some more. But he hadn't figured on those tight buns of hers sliding so intimately down the front of him.

Lord, he'd never smell hay again and not remember this. The girl was killing him. Slowly. Deliciously. She stood still for a moment, there in front of him. And, holding the cat in her arms, she leaned just slightly back against him.

And Lash bent his head, just a bit. So that his nose hovered really close to her hair, and he could inhale the scent of it. And then he battled the urge to bend even lower and maybe trace his lips over her neck, or taste her tender earlobe. It was bad enough his arms had decided to snug themselves around her waist. As if he were hugging her. Very intimate.

She tipped her head back, so that it rested on his shoulder, and he could see that her eyes were closed. "Damn, Lash, this feels *so* nice," she said softly.

He blinked and gave himself a mental shake. Then he took his arms from around her, though it was hell to let her go. He could have bent over her just now and kissed her. It would have been so easy. So...so good.

She sighed, as if in disappointment. "You really are stubborn," she said.

He didn't reply. Best to let her think he didn't have a clue what she was talking about.

She shook her head hard. "C'mon, then, let's get Pedro in the house before this storm cuts loose," she said in an exasperated tone. "My brothers catch you up here with me, Lash, and they'll think we were—"

"I can imagine what they would think," he said, not wanting to hear whatever colorful euphemism she'd come up with. Fearing that if he heard her say it, he'd see it even more clearly in his mind. As things turned out, he ended up seeing it in his mind anyway, so it was a wasted effort.

The cat stood at one end of the living room, eyeing Blue, who lay at the other end, eyeing the cat. Jessi glanced from one animal to the other, and hoped the two would learn to be friends eventually. So far, they just stared. At least they weren't fighting. They didn't move, and she gave up on them, turning instead to the window to gaze outside.

And she paused there, because she saw Ben. He stood alone, facing the approaching storm, moving in slow, graceful patterns that almost seemed like some ancient dance. She'd had no idea her big lug of a brother could move like that.

"T'ai chi," Elliot whispered in her ear. "When he was off playing hermit in the hills of Tennessee, he studied it. Said it helped, a little. Gave him peace or something."

"Poor Ben," Jessi whispered. "I wish he could get over his grief and move on." She swallowed hard, and reached up to close the curtains. Let Ben have his privacy. Let him mourn in his own way.

Lash was washing up in the kitchen, and Garrett was out there, too, having just finished with a phone call. Apparently it had been business, bad business. Garrett was saying something about another rustling incident at a neighboring ranch. It sounded to Jessi as if he and

Lash would be heading over to investigate shortly.
Damn. There went any excuse she might have had to
spend time with Lash tonight.

Then Garrett popped his head through the arched
doorway into the living room. "You busy, Jess?"

She perked up instantly. "No. Why, you need me
for something?"

"Bar-L had some stock stolen tonight. The boys
rode up on the rustlers and the bastards took a few
shots at them. Hit one of their horses."

"My God, Garrett! The rustlers *shot* at the Loomis
boys? But one of 'em is just a kid!"

Garrett nodded, his face grim. "Yeah. These guys
are dangerous. Luckily, they only hit a horse, but it's
one of their best mounts. Paul Loomis just called, and
I'm headed over there. Can you come?"

"Of course I'm coming. Let me grab some supplies.
You know how bad the animal's hurt?"

Garrett shook his head. "Hurry, okay? It's gonna
storm like crazy tonight, and I'd just as soon you be
safe back home before it hits."

Jessi rolled her eyes at him, but refrained from ar-
guing. Instead, she nodded and raced up the stairs to
haul her bag out of her closet. She rummaged through
the box of supplies she had on hand, and tossed in
anything she thought she might need, including a case
of sterile surgical instruments, a vial of tranquilizer and
a selection of antibiotics. She was very glad to have
already changed back into her jeans. Chelsea's nice
clothes might look great on her, but they were just not
suitable for work. She snapped the bag shut and headed
downstairs again, muttering under her breath about the
heartless bastards who'd shoot a horse, much less try
to harm a teenage boy and his brothers, who were both

around her age, more or less, just to steal a few head of cattle. The jerks would be sorry when Garrett and Lash caught up with them.

She slung her bag into the pickup's bed, then jumped into the front seat beside her brother. Lash got in next to her, and she realized that in her anger and worry over the poor, suffering animal, she'd forgotten all about her plan to seduce him. Didn't matter. Not tonight. This was business. This was what she lived for. She'd worry about roping and branding her man later.

They were barely under way when Garrett hit a bump in the road, and Jessi was jostled tight to Lash's side. She felt a hard bulge beneath his clothes, and bit her lip. Shoot, this time he *was* carrying a gun.

Thunder cracked like a rifle shot, and lightning split the night. In an instant the sky broke loose in a deluge that seemed to Jessi to be of biblical proportions.

Lash handed the heavy bag to Jess and watched as she raced through the pounding rain toward the spot Paul Loomis pointed out. Paul had climbed into the back of Garrett's pickup as soon as it rolled to a stop in his driveway. He'd shouted directions above the noise of the storm as Garrett drove over the rain-wet paths to the distant field. They'd stopped three times to let Paul climb down and open a gate, then close it behind them when they splashed through.

Garrett had been right about the storm. It was a big one, and the ground wasn't absorbing the water. Instead, the rain seemed to be bouncing off the earth, then gathering into miniature streams and running off in a hundred directions.

They'd driven far from the ranch house and the barns. A handful of cattle stood alert and restless, drip-

ping-wet, watching the proceedings, as three young
men knelt around the fallen horse. The mare was a
shadowy shape rising from the dark, rainy field, her
sides rising and falling rapidly with her labored
breathing, steam rising from her wet coat, as well as
her flared nostrils.

Two other horses waited, dancing and pawing occasionally, no more at ease than anyone else. Animals
could sense trouble, and these were no exception.

Garrett and Lash moved forward at a slower pace as
Paul, the father of the three boys, a big man with square
shoulders, a thick mustache and a face that could have
been carved from granite, filled them in on what had
happened.

"The dogs were taking on," he was saying. "The
boys decided to ride out to check on things. I should
have gone with them." He shook his head. "Damn,
Garrett, that could be one of my *sons* lying there with
a bullet in him."

Garrett slapped a hand down on Paul Loomis's
shoulder, splashing rain from the back of his yellow
slicker. "You had no way of knowing what they were
riding into," he said. "Hell, Paul, they've been riding
your place all their lives without you hovering over
them. This isn't your fault."

Paul nodded, as if he knew it, but still felt guilty.
Lightning flashed, illuminating his face, and Lash could
see the horrible "What if?" expression that haunted
his eyes. "They say they came up over this 'ere rise,"
Paul went on, "and saw a half-dozen men or more,
mounted and herding our cattle north."

Lash looked off in the direction Paul indicated,
squinting through the pouring rain, and frowning at
what he saw there. "What, off into that scrub lot?"

"Yep," Paul said. "My guess is, they were heading them through that brush as a shortcut outta here. Only way to move cattle off the place without marching 'em right on past the house. There's an old road out there...been closed for years. But it's the nearest place I can figure where a man could load that many head."

"How many, Paul?" Garrett asked.

The older man shook his head, water beading and rolling from the brim of his hat. "I had a hundred head in this pasture. You can see what's left." He nodded toward the small group of cows in the distance. No more than twenty white-faced cattle remained. "'Course, a few probably scattered when the shootin' started."

Garrett nodded and pulled out a flashlight, snapping it on and shining it on the ground. The beam illuminated the muddy tracks of horses and cows, all mingled together. Garrett lifted the light and moved forward, well past the spot where Jessi was working on the horse. Lash pulled out his own light and followed. Near the scrub lot, he stopped. "Garrett, here's where they went through. The fence has been cut."

Garrett nodded. "I'm gonna follow, see if I can see anything."

"Not alone, you're not," Lash said.

Garrett glanced back at Jessi, then shot a serious look at Lash. "Lash, I don't want her here alone. These bastards haven't been gone all that long, and for all we know, they might not have gone far. Stay with her."

Lash saw the point and nodded. He wasn't about to leave Jessi vulnerable to the type of men they were dealing with. And while there were four Loomis men surrounding her, Lash knew they probably weren't armed. He was. "All right, Garrett. But be careful. You see anything, come back for me."

"Gee, Lash, I'm touched," Garrett quipped.

"Hell, I just don't want to be the one to have to tell that houseful of Brands that I let their brother get hurt."

Garrett smiled, then ducked into the dripping brush and scraggly trees, and soon disappeared from sight.

Lash went back to see if there was anything he could do to help Jessi.

She looked up before he got near, almost as if she could sense him coming toward her. Rain glistened on her cheeks and glimmered like diamonds on her eyelashes. Her hair was plastered to her face, dripping wet. She wore a yellow raincoat, like the rest of them, but she'd let the hood fall back, apparently not even aware of its absence.

"I need you, Lash," she said. Only the words came out chopped and forceful, not slow and sexy, the way he'd like to hear her say them.

Hell, what was he thinking along those lines for?

He hurried close and knelt beside her in the mud. Without a word, he plucked the Stetson from his own head and plopped it down on hers.

She sent him a quick look, the slightest smile acknowledging the hat, then turned her full attention back to the wet, pain-racked horse.

The animal's labored breathing and wide, wild eyes told Lash all he needed to know of its pain and fear. Instinctively, he stroked the smooth, wet neck, and leaned closer to speak soothingly to the horse.

He felt the animal's tense muscles relax a bit under his hand.

Then he felt Jessi's wide eyes on him. He slanted a

glance her way as she shook her head. "I still can't get over it," she muttered.

"What?"

"Just keep doin' what you're doin'." Then she turned to the eldest Loomis brother. "Alan, you hold the light. Keith, Richard, you two stand back. She's liable to kick like a mule."

Lash didn't like the sounds of that. If Jessi went and got herself kicked again, he'd find himself in the uncomfortable position of having to explain to her overprotective brothers just how he'd managed to let her get hurt. It'd be especially uncomfortable since Garrett had left him behind to make sure she didn't.

"Be careful, Jessi," he told her, blinking rainwater from his eyes and pushing his now wet hair off his face.

She grunted, and he was sure she barely heard. Even more sure she would pay no attention to him, whether she'd heard him or not.

"Small-caliber gun, by the size of this hole in her shoulder. Twenty-two, probably. That's good." She fiddled around, and it was tough for Lash to see what she was doing. But he knew a second later, when the mare went rigid and released a choked, surprised sound of protest. Her hind leg jerked forward in a reflex action, and Lash left his post to lean sideways, thrusting his arm between the hoof and the small of Jessi's back.

His reward was a blow to the forearm that would no doubt leave a hoof-shaped bruise.

Jessi withdrew the hypodermic and turned around to frown at him. His arm remained wrapped tight around her, and he realized that it looked as if he were putting the moves on her. Sliding his arm around her waist for a quick cuddle in the midst of chaos. And he didn't want her thinking that. No way did he want her thinking that.

He moved his arm away. "She almost kicked you," he said, by way of explanation.

She offered him a slight smile. "No need to make up excuses, darlin'." Then she winked.

"I— Jess, I wasn't—"

She gave her head a quick shake and returned her attention to her patient. The mirth quickly faded from her eyes. They seemed troubled now, instead of mischievous. "If I can't stop the bleeding, we'll lose her." She nodded toward the mare's head. "How's she doing?"

Lash dragged his eyes away from Jessi, and returned to his position beside the horse's head just as the animal let it fall gently to the short, scraggly bed of wet grass. Her eyes closed, opened slowly, then closed again.

"Oh, Lord, is she dying?" the youngest Loomis cried. Lash thought his name was Keith, and he appeared to be around sixteen.

"It's just a tranquilizer," Jessi soothed.

"It's working, Jess," Lash told her. "She's relaxed now."

"Good. Lift that light higher, Alan. No, to the right. Yes, right there." She dug in her bag again, and raindrops glistened from the black leather as Alan shone the light down on it for her. "Lash, keep her calm. The tranquilizer will help some, but I don't dare give her too much just now. I have to get this bleeding stopped, and it's gonna hurt."

"Damn," Lash said, but he stroked and soothed and made soft sounds that the animal seemed to respond to. Jessi probed with some instrument, and the horse occasionally stiffened or jerked, but for the most part she remained still.

"How's he do that?" Alan Loomis asked.

"Has a way with women," Jessi replied, and Lash heard the two younger boys chuckle nervously. Good for Jessi, relieving their stress a little, even if it was at his expense. Then, Jessi said, "Okay, I've got it. The bullet's right here, wedged against bone. If I can get it out…" Surgical steel clanged as she changed tools, and then the horse went rigid again, its eyes flying open.

"Easy, girl, hold on now. It's gonna be just fine. Yeah. That's it." Lash stroked and spoke softly.

"I've got it!"

There was more clattering as she dropped the bullet into a waiting receptacle. By the time Garrett came back toward them, boots slapping the rain-wet ground to announce his presence, Jessi had already stitched up the wound and was applying thick layers of bandages to the mare's front shoulder. She finished and got to her feet, holding her bloodied gloves up in front of her.

"There's a stream where you can clean up a little," Alan Loomis offered. He took Jessi's arm and led her away into the darkness.

"You be careful near that stream," Garrett called after them. "This rain keeps up like this, and we're gonna be seeing trouble."

"Don't you worry, Garrett," Alan called. "I ain't gonna let nothing happen to this one."

Lash didn't like the friendly hand the man placed at the small of Jessi's back, or the way he could hear Alan's gushing compliments on her talents…then her beauty…as they walked away in the downpour.

"The mare?" Garrett asked, drawing Lash back to attention.

"Er...yeah. Right. Jess got the bullet out and stopped the bleeding. I think she'll be okay." He heard a soft laugh, and glanced off into the rainy darkness where Jessi had gone with that cow-eyed cowboy.

"Paul's theory was right," Garrett said. "Looks like they herded the cattle through that scrub lot to the old dirt road on the far side. There are tire tracks in the mud out there. Dualies."

"Dualies?" Lash echoed.

"Dual tires," Garrett clarified. "Had a semi out there. Maybe two."

"Damn. This is no small-time operation then."

"Nope. These boys are serious."

Voices carried on a stray wet breeze, and Lash heard Alan Loomis clearly. "The boys and I would be thrilled to come help you clean out that garage of Marisella's, sugar. We owe you for this."

Sugar?

"Thanks, Alan. And I won't be taking any pay for tending to the mare. You guys help me clean out that garage, and we'll call it even."

"You bet," he said. And this time, as they strolled into view, the jerk's arm was around her middle, and he turned to give her a big manly cowboy sort of hug. With them both wearing raincoats, it shouldn't have seemed as intimate as it did, but it still made Lash grate his teeth. "That mare's my pride and joy, hon. And I'd have lost her if it hadn't been for you."

Hon?

"That's my job, Alan."

Lash cleared his throat, and then wished he hadn't. It not only got Jessi's attention, it got her big brother's, as well. Garrett was looking at him a little strangely.

"Isn't it time we get going?" Lash asked.

Jessi frowned at him. Garrett saved him, though. "Lash is right. I gotta get into town and alert the Rangers to be on the lookout for a couple of tractor-trailers full of prime beefers. Sooner the better."

Jessi nodded. "She shouldn't be walking on that leg at all," she told Paul. "And you have to get her in out of this rain. She needs to be warm and dry. I have a sling at home for lifting downed animals, if you—"

"We got one, too, Jessi. This ain't the first mishap we've had with a critter too big to toss over your shoulder. We'll bring out a wagon, and get her back to the stables nice and gentle. Don't you worry."

"I'll come by tomorrow to check on her," she said. "She'll need another shot of antibiotics, and clean bandages."

Alan grinned...in anticipation, Lash thought. "I'll be here, Jessi. You can show me how to take proper care of that wound until it heals."

Jessi nodded.

"Yeah," Lash said, without even realizing his mouth was running without brakes. "And I'll come along, too, in case you need any more help." Everyone looked at him. He cleared his throat. "I'd...er...like to get a look at this crime scene in daylight."

Garrett who'd rejoined the group shook his head, sent Lash a worried glance and then climbed into the pickup, which he'd left running. "I'll do everything I can to get those cows back to you, Paul."

"I know you will, Garrett. If there's anything I can do to help, you know where to find me."

Garrett touched the brim of his hat and turned the wipers up a notch as Jessi and Lash climbed in the passenger side. Garrett didn't head back toward the ranch, but into the town of Quinn, and his office, instead. The rain just kept coming, and the creek was already running alarmingly high when they crossed the bridge just outside town. As they drove, Lash heard thunder rolling constantly, like the thundering hooves of a thousand stampeding cattle. The wind was picking up now, as well, adding to the chaos outside. It whipped tree limbs and weeds viciously, and sent the raindrops into a horizontal, slashing pattern. Those slate-dark clouds had thickened over the face of the moon until they obliterated it.

"Hell of a storm," Garrett observed. "I don't like it."

"I hope they get the mare inside fast." Jessi looked over her shoulder, as if she could still see the Loomis ranch, which of course she couldn't. "And they'd better remember to rub her down till she's completely dry," she went on. "Damn, I should have stayed."

"You couldn't do anything more, Jess," Lash said, hating the worry he heard in her tone. "They'll do right by the horse. Hell, Alan seemed as smitten with that animal as he is with you."

Jessi blinked twice and turned wide eyes on him. "What kind of an asinine remark is that?"

Lash shrugged. "Just an observation."

Garrett made a sound that was half grunt, half growl. "Jessi ain't interested in Alan Loomis."

Now Jessi glared at her brother instead of Lash. "Who says I'm not?"

"Hell, Jess, he drinks. Everybody knows that. And when he drinks he gets ornery." Garrett steered around a deep-looking puddle. The wipers slapped in time with the conversation.

"Well, maybe I like 'em ornery."

Garrett's jaw twitched, and Lash thought he was

grating his teeth behind his thin lips. "He's trouble. Understand, Jessi? Trouble. You stay away from him."

"Or what?" she snapped, eyes flashing fire.

"Or I'll break his arm off at the shoulder and beat him over the head with it, hon." For some reason, Garrett's words made Lash grimace. Too damned visual. "The guy's got a mean streak, and I don't aim to see it turned loose on you."

"Garrett Brand, I'm a grown woman, and it's high time you stop treating me like a little girl. I'll see any man I want, you understand? Sooner or later I'm gonna marry someone, and I hate to be the one to tell you this, honey, but you and the boys *don't* get the privilege of picking him out for me. You aren't going to have any say at all, matter of fact."

Garrett grimaced and pulled into the small space in front of the sheriff's office. Rain was streaming from the eaves like rivers. "I know you're a grown woman, and I know you're gonna see men. Hell, Jess, it's tough for me to see fellas looking at you...the way they been lately. But I'll get used to it, I suppose. Still and all, that doesn't mean I can stand by and watch you make a mistake that could get you hurt. Please, hon. Tell me you ain't carrying a torch for that Loomis fella. He ain't good enough for you."

"Then who is?" She crossed her arms over her chest, leaned back in the seat and stared straight through the window. "Let's see, what about his brothers? Richard or Keith?"

"Richard's lazy. He'll never amount to anything. And Keith's too young for you, Jessi. You know that."

She shook her head. "So what about Freddy Ortega?"

"Freddy? The *bartender?* C'mon, Jess, you can do better than—''

"Bobby Joe Hawthorne?" she asked, interrupting him.

"That fool? Gambles away every nickel he earns, and—''

"Sam Bonander?"

"Sam's a womanizer. You watch out for that—''

"Lash Monroe?" she shouted.

Garrett stopped talking and just gaped at her. Lash's throat went so dry he couldn't have swallowed if he tried. Then Garrett looked at him, almost accusingly, and then he looked back at his sister in disbelief.

"Lash is too old for you," Garrett said, very softly. "And besides that, he's a drifter. He's gonna be leaving here soon." He looked past her again, at Lash. "Right, Lash?"

"Right. Absolutely. I always hated being in one place for too long, and—''

"So basically, big brother, you've eliminated just about every single Quinn male between the ages of eighteen and eighty. What you're saying is that no man in this town is good enough for me, right? So maybe I should join a convent, or turn gay, or something."

"Jess!"

She turned her back to Lash to poke her brother in the chest with her forefinger. "Let me tell you something, Garrett Brand. No one is going to pick my man for me, because I've already picked one out all by myself. You aren't going to have anything to say about it."

"What man?" Garrett asked. "Who?"

She tossed her head, turned the other way, and poked Lash's chest, as well. "And neither are you!"

"Hey, I'm just along for the ride, Jessi! This isn't my fight."

"The hell it isn't," she muttered. Then she leaned across him, and she was warm and close and soft. Damn. But all she was doing was shoving his door open and glaring at him as she waited to be let out. He stared at her face in the glow of the dash lights, eyes flashing, cheeks red, lips parted. She was looking at him from underneath his too-big hat, her skin still rain-water fresh, and he thought he'd never known a woman who could compare. Not ever.

He got out, and held the door for her while the rain pummeled him. He couldn't take his eyes off her as she dashed to the front steps. He just stood there like an idiot, getting soaked to the skin.

Garrett tapped him on the shoulder, snapping him out of his little trance, and searched his face with a curious expression. Curious, and maybe a little bit worried.

Lash felt his face heat under Garrett's probing stare.

"Stop looking at me like that, Garrett. I don't have any more clue what she's talking about than you do."

"Yeah, well, let's hope it stays that way. Otherwise...you and I are gonna have some serious talkin' to do."

"Talking, huh?" Lash refrained from rubbing his nose as he recalled the last time Garrett Brand had felt "serious talkin'" was called for.

Garrett frowned at him one last time, and then gave his head a shake and lit out, racing through the deluge to the office door, where his sister stood waiting, sheltered by the eaves. Lash followed, and only got himself more thoroughly soaked for his trouble by the time he ducked inside behind the other two. He could hear the rain drumming against the roof and slashing over the windows. The wind had taken to howling like a banshee.

Garrett reached for the thermostat on one wall and cranked it up. The tiny furnace hidden away in the small office-slash-jailhouse rattled and clanked to life, and in a few seconds Lash dared to peel off his yellow raincoat, shake some of the water off it and hang it on a hook near the door. Jessi and Garrett did likewise. Lash took the chance to venture up beside Jessi where she stood warming herself over the baseboard register.

Garrett had plopped down behind the desk and put in a call to the nearest Ranger station, asking them to set up roadblocks and keep an eye out for cattle trucks with questionable manifests. He reached out to turn on his computer.

Jessi marched across the room, letting Lash have the heat all to himself while she reached out to turn the computer off.

"What the—"

"You big lug, you can't go using a PC during a thunderstorm," she told her brother.

"I have a surge protector," he countered, turning it on again.

"Which is useless against lightning," she said. "You get zapped and you'll be spending precious time shipping this thing off to be repaired."

Sighing heavily, Garrett switched the monitor off once more. "For a little chicken, you sure do a good job of playing the mother hen. Fine, you win. I'll do this the old-fashioned way." He reached for the file drawer, removed several folders, then armed himself with a pen.

"So what can I do to help?" Lash offered, stepping

closer to the desk to see that the files were those on each rustling incident in the area over the past six months. Garrett was apparently going to review them.

Garrett divided the stack in half and handed one pile to Lash. "Gotta go over these cases until we know 'em by heart, Lash. There has to be something connecting them, some clue or *something* we're missing."

Lash nodded, pulled up a wooden chair and bent over the files. He sat on the opposite side of the desk from Garrett, and he read until his eyes burned.

Sometime later, the aroma of fresh coffee tickled his nostrils and made his mouth water. Jessi leaned over him to set a steaming mug down on the desk. She handed a second mug to her brother. Lash looked up at her, noting the damp spots on her shirt and the darker color of her jeans below the knees. Her hair had dried a little, but damn, she had to be freezing. He was chilled himself.

"Anything else I can do to help here?" she asked.

Before Garrett could answer, Jessi went on. "'Cause if there isn't, and it's all the same to you two, I'm thinkin' I'd just as soon head home."

"I don't think so, Jess." Garrett's tone was gentle, but his words didn't sit any better with his sister for that.

"Why not?" she asked. "I can send one of the boys back with your pickup, so it isn't like I'd be leaving you stranded. Elliot's been dying to get involved in this case, anyway. He'd be glad to come—"

"You won't be leaving me stranded, kiddo, 'cause you won't be leaving me at all. Not in this." Garrett nodded toward the nearest window. As if to punctuate his warning, the lightning chose that moment to flash again, and the thunderclap that followed shook the entire building.

"It's just a thunderstorm. Jeez, Garrett, I've driven in worse."

"If you have, this is the first I've heard of it."

"Surprise, big brother—I don't tell you everything."

He glared. She glared right back.

"Garrett, I have so much to do. Lists to make, supplies to order—"

Sighing hard, Garrett shook his head. Then he looked at Lash, who felt like a spectator at a close boxing match. "You mind running her home for me, Lash?"

Jessi sputtered, as if to argue, then bit her lower lip as if to halt the words from coming forth. And Lash knew damn well she was furious at her brother for thinking she needed a chaperon to get home safely. Which made him wonder why she'd bitten back her fury.

She slid a sideways glance at Lash, and he could see the wheels turning behind those cunning, sexy-as-hell eyes. What was she up to?

"Oh, all right," she finally said. "If you insist, Garrett, I'll let Lash drive me home."

Garrett had noticed the change in her attitude, as well, it seemed, because he narrowed his eyes on her, then shifted his meaningful gaze to Lash. "Take my truck, see she gets safely inside, and then meet me back here. Shouldn't take you more than—" he glanced at his watch "—an hour. *At the most.*"

Lash nodded, getting the full gist of the man's message. No pulling off the road into some secluded, rain-veiled glen for a little one-on-one with Garrett's baby sister. Right. As if he needed that warning.

"Forty-five minutes, tops," Lash said, taking the keys from Garrett's outstretched hand.

Jessi stood looking from one to the other, and if Lash wasn't mistaken, the best word for the look she sent them was *glower*.

Lash went to the hook near the door and retrieved their yellow vinyl slickers. He handed one to Jessi and pulled the other over his head, poncho-style. It was still damp, and he winced at the chill.

With a final nod to Garrett, Lash dropped his hat on his head, reached out to yank Jessi's hood up so that it covered hers, opened the door and made a dash for the pickup. When he jumped in behind the wheel and slammed his door, Jessi was already clambering in the other side and slamming hers. Quick as a fox and twice as clever, he thought, turning the key, switching on the headlights and wipers. Then he watched her push her yellow hood down and swipe the droplets from her face with a delicate brush of her hand. She missed some. Her lashes still glistened with a diamond or two. The dash lights made them glow magically, made him want to kiss them away...

"Lash, you gonna sit there looking at me all night, or drive? I'm sure Garrett's set some kind of timer by now."

Lash blinked, cleared his throat, then tore his gaze away from her. He shifted the truck into reverse and backed carefully out of the parking space. There was no traffic in town tonight. The weather had worsened dramatically while they'd been inside going over files. Even though a while ago, Lash wouldn't have thought it could get much worse. Only a lunatic would be out in this nasty weather. He had to drive slowly, and even then he could barely see. God, he hadn't realized it from inside Garrett's safe, dry office, but the storm was probably the most severe he'd ever seen. The rain came down in sheets over the windshield. The wipers, slapping at their highest speed, were barely effective at all.

"This is ridiculous," he muttered.

"Oh, I don't know. I think it's kinda nice," she said. She reached out a hand and flicked the radio on, fiddling with the buttons until a slow country song came wafting in to fill the space between them. Didn't seem to bother her in the least that the song was interrupted by crackling static with every flash of lightning. He could feel her eyes on him. But he didn't dare look at her. And it wasn't just because he was afraid to take his eyes off the road.

"It's getting worse," he announced, though he was sure she could see that perfectly well without being told. Lightning split the sky, and the radio crackled again before returning to its crooning melody.

"You can always pull off and wait for it to let up a little," she suggested.

Yeah, right. That would be brilliant. Take little Jessi Brand out parking in a thunderstorm. He kept driving. It took fifteen minutes to leave the town behind them, and the weather only worsened. He realized a short while later that he'd have been better off listening to her, because at least then they'd have been in town, with houses nearby, and maybe a phone to call Garrett from. Now they were on the long, deserted, muddy stretch of road that led back to the ranch, creeping along at a snail's pace. He glanced at his watch's luminous dial and groaned inwardly. Thirty minutes had passed. He wasn't going to make Garrett's deadline. Lord knew what the big cowboy would be thinking.

They approached the tiny bridge that spanned the

usually small and slow-running creek. Lash noted with alarm that the water was high, way higher than normal, and way higher than it had been a couple of hours ago, when they drove in. He slowed the truck even further.

"It'll be fine," she said. "That bridge has held up during flooding before."

"You sure?" he asked.

"Sure I'm sure. Just go over it quickly. Gun it, Lash."

He stepped down on the accelerator, and the pickup lurched forward onto the surface of the bridge. Then Jessi screamed, "Stop!"

He jammed the brakes in a knee-jerk reaction to her shout, and looked at her to ask what the hell she was shouting about. But Jessi was already jumping out of the truck. Lash was baffled until he looked through the windshield again. There, huddled right in the center of the bridge, was a shivering, dripping-wet animal that appeared to be mostly made of rainwater and brown legs. Rolling his eyes and cussing, Lash got out of the truck, as well. Rain pounded him, and rivers of it ran down the sides of the poncho he wore, soaking his jeans and his boots in a matter of seconds. When he reached Jess, she was slowly creeping closer to the trembling fawn. She reached out for it, but it sprang to its spindly legs and stumbled backward, eyes wide, rainwater rolling from its sides. Jessi held out her hands. "Easy, now. Are you hurt, little one? Or just cold and afraid? There now. I'm not gonna hurt you."

Lash came up slowly beside her, and wanted to scold her for jumping out in the rain like that, but he couldn't. She was too beautiful, even dripping-wet. The fawn had stopped retreating now. Its white-spotted coat twitched as it shivered, though, and the animal stared with eyes huge and afraid.

Those big brown eyes were heartbreaking.

"She's beautiful," Jess was saying. "Oh, yes, you are. You're beautiful."

"Prettiest drowned rat I've ever seen," Lash said. He had to speak loudly to be heard over the rain, and the animal flinched in response to his voice. "Let's just grab her and put her in the truck, Jess, and get out of here."

She nodded, but just as she stepped close enough to make a grab at the fawn, the animal's head came up and turned to the right. Its delicate ears perked forward, and its baby-size tail flashed up straight. It whirled and ran gracefully off the bridge, disappearing into the rain-drenched woods on the far side. Jessi squinted off in the direction it had gone, then pointed, smiling. Lash saw the flash of a larger tail running along beside the little one. Nodding, he met Jessi's eyes. "Looks like she found her mama," he said. He took her arm, turning her toward the pickup. Then he paused, because there was a roar in his ears. Different from the howl of the wind, and definitely not thunder. "What the—"

He turned his head in the direction the sound seemed to be coming from, and then frowned, because he wasn't sure what he was seeing. It looked like...

"Flash flood!" Jessi shouted.

Lash reached out for her just as the wall of water unleashed its fury on the tiny bridge. His hand caught hers. A torrent flooded over them, slamming into his side and washing up around his waist, the current fierce and pulling at him, pulling at her, as if determined to snatch her away from his grip. Lash held tight to her hand, yelling at her to hold on. He tried to hold his footing, tried to back off the damned bridge and onto solid ground before it was too late, but the force of the water just kept shoving at him, trying to knock him off balance.

He sought for something to hold on to, something to grab to pull them both to safety, but there was only Jessi's cold, wet hand in his, and the roar of the water, and the pressure of it. And her eyes meeting his, filled with a terror that made his stomach clench.

There was a cracking sound as the bridge gave way, and the wood under his feet dissolved beneath the onslaught. He and Jessi were hurled forward, pitched into the frigid turmoil of the flood, tossed up and sucked back under the waves again and again as they were dragged downstream. He managed to get an arm around Jessi, then another, and he held tight to her as he struggled to get their heads above water. But it was no use. He was at the mercy of the flood. He only hoped they'd both survive.

Chapter 5

Garrett looked at his watch for the tenth time in as many minutes. The hour he'd given Lash to get back to the office was up, and then some. Of course, the rain had gotten worse. Weather might be holding them up. But he just couldn't shake the nagging feeling that something was up. And though he'd told Wes he didn't believe his suspicion about Jessi having a crush on Lash, he couldn't get the thought out of his mind now.

If Lash so much as—

The telephone on his desk interrupted his thoughts with a soft bleat, and Garrett snatched it up.

"Oh, good, you're still there."

It was Chelsea's voice and, as always, it put a dreamy smile on his face. He settled back in his chair, the worry fading. "That's not good at all," he told her. "I'd rather be home with you."

"Yes, but I'm glad I caught you all the same. We just got a bulletin over the radio. There are flash flood warnings posted for Sycamore creek. So you'd best take the long way home.''

His smile died a sudden death. "Honey, did Jessi and Lash make it back there yet?''

Silence.

"Honey?''

"No. Garrett, were they taking—''

"They're fine,'' he said, hearing the panic in her voice. "I'm sure they're fine. Look, just to be safe, why don't you send the boys out? I'll meet them at the bridge. All right?''

"Garrett, you don't think—''

"Don't worry, darlin'.'' But she was worried. He knew her too well to think otherwise. And he was worried, too. "Send the boys. I'll call you as soon as we find them.''

"Be careful, Garrett.''

"Always,'' he told her. "I love you, Chelsea.''

"Me too.''

Garrett put the phone down, and looked again at the rain slashing against the windows. "Damn.'' He grabbed a raincoat and a flashlight, then headed out to borrow a car from the first person he could rouse.

Jessi clung to Lash with everything in her, stark terror giving her additional strength. The cold water filled her nose and mouth and blinded her eyes, dragging her into its tumultuous depths again and again, despite her struggles. The two of them pitched and rolled at the whim of the waves, and there was nothing she could do but hold on and wait it out. Each time the current forced her to the surface, she dragged in desperate gulps of precious air, only to be sucked beneath the frigid, filthy waters once more. More than once she was slammed against debris, and she never knew for sure just what had hit her—logs or limbs or what. And each time her body was yanked forcefully, Lash would only tighten his grip on her. He refused to let go. No matter what hit them, he refused to let her go.

The weight of the raincoat was tugging her down, and it seemed Lash knew. Somehow he wrested it away from her and let the current carry it off. He'd lost his, as well, she realized, or maybe he'd shed it deliberately.

They were battered and dragged and pounded in the water's fury for what seemed like hours, though it could have only been minutes. And then, suddenly, the force eased, and it was Lash who was pulling her, tugging her through the still-rushing water. She was barely aware of the shallows, the stony bottom dragging beneath her legs, the lack of water over her head, the rain pounding down on her. Still drenched by the floodwaters, it took a full minute for her to realize that she was no longer immersed in them. Instead, she was stretched out on the muddy bank, Lash lying beside her, raised up on one elbow to bend over her, his face inches from her own. Water dripped from his chin into the hollow of her neck as she blinked her eyes open and met his. She shivered. God, she'd never been so cold.

"Jessi? God, Jessi, are you all right? Come on, darlin', talk to me. Tell me you're okay."

She closed her eyes, coughed, and nodded slowly.

Lash sighed loudly, and it was as if his body melted, in relief or in exhaustion. She wasn't sure which. Maybe a combination of the two. But the result was the same. His upper body lowered to rest atop hers, his arms anchored around her as if they were still clinging to one another for dear life. She slipped her arms around his waist, feeling the water squeeze from his shirt in response to the pressure of her embrace. "I thought we... God, Lash, I've never been so frightened in my life."

"I know," he whispered, his fingers threading through her wet hair. She could feel his warmth seeping through their wet clothing, infusing her chilled flesh, and she clung tighter when he moved as if to get up.

"Don't," she told him. "Please, Lash, don't go running away from me this time. Just hold me...just for a minute."

Head lifted, he stared down into her eyes. He didn't want to get up. She could see that very clearly.

"I'm cold, Lash. I'm freezing."

"Me too."

"You didn't let me go," she whispered, blinking up into his eyes. "I can't believe you didn't let me go."

"I'd have to be nuts to let you go," he replied, and seemed as surprised to be blurting out those words as she was to be hearing them.

He touched her face, just a slight caress of his chilled fingertips across her cheek. And it was so intimate, so honest, that touch. It was her undoing.

"Will you kiss me this time, Lash?"

Very slowly, he lowered his mouth to hers. Gently, he kissed her, and she could taste the cold water on his lips. She parted her own, and felt him tremble. She wondered if it was from the cold, or something else. Something like the finger of heat that was sending tremors of longing through her.

When he would have lifted his head away, she slipped her hands up over his wet shoulders, higher, into his hair, and pressed her mouth tighter to his. With her tongue, she touched his lips, and when they parted she slipped inside the inviting warmth of his mouth.

He groaned softly, deeply, and his weight shifted, his body moving to cover hers completely. Instinctively, she moved her hips against his, and felt the answering motion of his, arching against her. His hands slid under her, then down to cup her buttocks, and he squeezed and pressed her tight to him, moving intimately. She parted her thighs to bring him to the place where she longed for him to be. She shuddered, clinging, kissing, moaning softly as her hips moved with his in the age-old rhythm of woman and man. The rain pounded down on their heated bodies as they mimicked the act of lovemaking, fully clothed, pressing urgently against one another without consummating their desire.

But she knew it was going to happen. And she wanted it to happen. And she knew he wanted it, too. The hardness pressing insistently between her legs was more than he could deny this time. And she didn't think he'd even try.

He ground against her, his mouth devouring hers as if he were starving for the taste of her. Jessi pulled her hands from around him, and slipped them between their bodies, pulling the snap and zipper of her jeans until they came open, tugging at the buttons of her shirt until they tore free.

Lash stiffened, and slowly lifted his head. And then his body, up and away from hers, leaving her cold and alone. He stared down at her—blouse gaping, breasts naked and tingling beneath his heated gaze, jeans parted as if in invitation. He stared down at her, and with one trembling hand, he reached out, touched her breast, his thumb running slowly over the aching peak. Jessi closed her eyes and arched her back.

The hand moved away.

"I can't do this, Jessi."

It was like a slap in the face.

Her eyes flashed open, and she felt her cheeks warm. He was still kneeling beside her, staring down at her, and she felt vulnerable and exposed to those eyes, instead of aroused and caressed by them, as before. "I d-don't understand." It was difficult to speak. She was breathless, her heart hammering against her ribs so loudly he had to hear it. She'd never been this aroused. Never.

"Jessi…" He shook his head, then averted his eyes. "I can't. Look, this is just stress. The aftermath of damned near drowning together. Understand? This isn't—"

"Liar!"

He shook his head, keeping his eyes averted.

"Look at me, dammit."

He did. He turned his head, slowly, and looked at her, and his gaze dropped from her eyes to her lips, to her still-uncovered breasts. She shivered at the chill touch of the wind on her nipples. "Jesus, Jessi, fix your shirt." But his gaze didn't change its focus.

She sat up, leaning back on her hands, leaving her blouse just the way it was. "You want me just as much as I want you, Lash Monroe. Admit it."

Lash licked his lips. He shook his head in denial, but continued staring. "It isn't right, Jessi."

"Feels right to me." She got up onto her knees, bringing her exposed chest up to eye level for him. Let him deny it now, she thought. "You're gonna say it's wrong because you're older, aren't you?"

Eyes transfixed, he nodded.

"But ten years isn't all that much older. And you know that as well as I do."

"It's not just that."

"No?"

His tongue darted out to moisten his lips again. "I'm a drifter, Jessi. You know that. I can't stay—"

"I didn't ask you to stay," she whispered, and she reached down to slip her fingers into his hair. He moved his head a little closer, closed his eyes, bit his lip.

"Please fix your shirt, Jessi. I'm begging—"

"Tell me you want me," she told him.

"You're killing me."

She leaned in, just enough. Her taut nipple brushed his lips, and then she backed away again.

Lash's eyes flew open, and they blazed. His hands clasped her waist, hard and without warning, and he jerked her close, capturing her breast in his mouth as he trembled from head to toe. Jessi clutched handfuls of his hair as his tongue flayed her nipple, his lips capturing it, suckling it. His teeth catching it and pinching with delicious pressure. She closed her eyes and let her head fall backward, pulling him closer, holding him to her breast and craving things she'd never even thought about before.

"Jessi! Lash!"

At the sounds of male voices shouting their names, Jessi's eyes flew open, and Lash jerked away from her as if he'd been electrocuted.

His eyes met hers, unspoken need flashing from their pale, silver-blue depths. She released a shuddering sigh, got to her feet, and righted her clothes as best she could. She could easily have screamed in frustration, but she resisted the impulse. Barely.

She heard a low barking, and turned to see Ol' Blue's tall, sagging shape loping toward them from farther up the slope. Behind it, bobbing beams of light showed the location of her brothers. She waved half-heartedly, knowing they'd be worried, and knowing she had to reassure them. And yet wishing she could take Lash by the hand and run off into the night where no one could find them. No one could stop them. Damn, she'd been so close!

"Here," she called. "We're here. We're all right."

"Jessi!"

The beams of light bobbed faster, and then her brothers ran into view. Wes reached her first, sweeping her into his arms and hugging the breath out of her. He kissed her wet hair and held her tight, while Ol' Blue barked at her and raced around her legs, moving more enthusiastically than she'd ever seen him move. He'd be exhausted when he got home. And chilled through, as well. She stroked his wet fur. "You're too old to be playing hero, Blue."

"You okay?" Wes asked.

"Yeah," she breathed. "Lash pulled me out. If he hadn't..." She lowered her eyes, shaking her head.

Elliot slammed Lash's shoulder. "Good man," he announced. Jessi looked at Lash and saw the horrible guilt on his face. It was eating him alive. "Hell," Elliot went on, "Garrett will probably even forgive you for the pickup."

Lash looked at Elliot, brows lifted in an unspoken question, and Jessi, too, frowned at her brother. "I kind of lost track of the truck," Lash said. "Is it—?"

"Nose down in the creek, a mile upstream," Ben

said softly. "When we spotted it, we thought…" He didn't finish. Instead, he pried Jessi from Wes's arms and hugged her himself.

"There's Garrett," Wes said, pointing to another flashlight beam on the opposite bank. Cupping his hands around his mouth, he shouted, "Garrett! We found them! They're okay!"

The beam of light on the other side stopped moving, then lifted in an effort to reach them. Wes shone his light on Jessi so that Garrett could see for himself that she was in one piece. Then Garrett's voice drifted across the rapid water. "Take them home. I'll meet you there."

Jessi bit her lip, and hoped no one would notice the missing buttons on her blouse. The old hound dog barked once more, and she looked down to see Blue sitting at her feet, looking up at her with a question in his big brown eyes. "Yes," she said. "You done good, old boy." And she stroked his ears and whispered, "But your timing could have been better."

Lash's head came around, and his eyes met hers, letting her know he'd heard that remark. She held his gaze, and wished to God she could tell what he was thinking. But she couldn't read the man. He was better at hiding his feelings than anyone she'd ever known.

Damn. Was he regretting the untimely interruption? Or maybe regretting that he'd lost his stoic resistance to her for just a moment?

Jessi was soaking in a hot bath, and Lash knew she'd be all right. Chelsea was dancing attendance on her, as if she were a fragile little china doll in danger of shattering in a strong wind. Ol' Blue had taken up residence in Jessi's room, and he was convinced the hound had decided to watch over her until *he* assured himself she was okay. Damn dog was close to human. And as protective of Jess as if he were one of her brothers.

She didn't need their help, though. Lash was only just beginning to get a feel for the real Jessi Brand. And she was tougher than he'd given her credit for.

Smarter, too. There was no longer any doubt in Lash's mind about what Jessi had meant when she told her brother that she had chosen her own man. She'd meant *him*. It scared the hell out of him. Especially when he thought about certain other remarks she'd dropped his way lately. Like that one about her always getting what she wanted.

Damn. If the boys hadn't come along when they had, he'd have...he'd have...

Damn.

Walk in the Spirit, and ye shall not fulfil the lust of the flesh, he thought to himself. It didn't help. He still lusted. And Jessi was right, ten years or so wasn't all that big an age difference. But for crying out loud, Lash Monroe had known what he wanted all his life. Freedom. Solitude. He wanted to be untethered, able to roam where the wind took him, whenever he pleased. He didn't want a relationship, and he knew better than to think Jessi had a casual fling on her mind. No, she'd want more. She'd want commitment. Imagine, Lash thought, just imagine being crazy enough to plunk himself down in the midst of another big family. A family chock-full of older brothers, all of whom would hate his guts for soiling their baby sister with his unworthy touch. Imagine the tension, the arguments. Damn, this thing with Jessi would end up making *all* of them miserable, himself included.

Besides, it wasn't as if he loved her. Any red-blooded male would respond to her. She was gorgeous, and sexy as hell, and clearly attracted to him. And damned if he could figure where she'd managed to learn it, with her brothers as guard dogs, but she sure as hell knew what she was doing.

So, he wasn't acting illogically to want her. He was only human. Hell, Saint Francis of Assisi would want her! But that was as far as it went. And Lash needed to keep that in mind. Maybe find himself a casual fling in town to relieve the pressure. And keep his distance from Jessi Brand at all costs.

He thought then about the women he'd met while he'd been here in Quinn. Beautiful sloe-eyed Mexican women who could keep a man awake nights. Blue-eyed Texas girls with big hair and bright smiles and bodies to die for. He thought hard about those girls. And he felt cold inside. Couldn't even work up enough interest to dwell on any one of them for more than a second.

Who the hell was he kidding? He didn't want any other woman. He wanted this one. He'd never been hit as forcefully with desire's hammer until right now. He felt as if he were under some sort of spell, one that wouldn't let go.

But he owed Garrett. Owed him a lot. And Lash wasn't the kind of man who could pay back his debt by committing what would be seen as the ultimate betrayal.

And that was final. Even if it killed him.

He resolved not to think any more about what it might be like to make love to Jessi Brand, to hold her hot, naked body close to his own. To run his hands along those firm thighs, and taste, just once more, those round, luscious breasts, and kiss those plump lips.

He shifted in his seat, and tried real hard to bring

his attention back to the conversation taking place around him.

"Might as well spend the night here, Lash," Garrett was saying. "No sense trying to drive back to town now."

Lash swallowed hard. Maybe he ought to *walk* back into town. "I'm real sorry about your pickup. I never would have stopped on that bridge, Garrett, but there was this baby deer lying there, and—"

"I know. You've already explained all that." Garrett smiled crookedly and dropped a big hand onto Lash's shoulder. "The pickup's insured, Lash. I don't give a damn about that. Jessi said you could have probably dragged yourself out of the current a hell of a lot sooner, just by letting go of her. But you didn't, Lash." The hand on Lash's shoulder squeezed. "You saved my sister's life. And I think you know that there's not much on this planet I hold closer to my heart than that hellcat baby sister of mine. You're one hell of a good friend. Feel free to drown my pickup any old time."

Lash couldn't look Garrett in the eye. His stomach twisted up in knots, and guilt washed over him just as forcefully as that flash flood had done. Damn.

"Consider yourself part of the family from here on in," Elliot said.

"Anything you need, Lash," Ben added. "Anytime, anywhere, you call on us. You hear?"

Lash forced himself to meet their gazes, one by one, and he nodded. Last, he faced Wes. His dark onyx eyes were glinting.

Wes took a step forward, drew a thoughtful breath, and finally extended a hand. Lash blinked in surprise, but took it, and returned Wes's firm shake. Wes never said a word. But he didn't have to.

Lash felt ill. These men were not the bullies of his childhood, out to cause him trouble and make him miserable. These were good, honest men who thought of him as a friend, welcomed him into their midst, treated him like a brother, for God's sake. They *trusted* him.

The telephone rang. Garrett picked it up and spoke softly, then glanced toward Lash and held it out. "You have an aunt Kate?"

"My foster mother's sister," Lash muttered, and took the phone, feeling his self-appointed aunt couldn't have picked a worse time to call.

He covered the receiver with one hand and glanced at the brothers. "Sorry for the interruption. This might be a while. She feels it's her civic duty to check on every one of us periodically and grill us about every aspect of our lives. No matter where I go, she manages to track me down."

"I'm heading up to bed anyway," Garrett said. "Why don't you take Adam's old bedroom, Lash? There are some of his clothes in the closet, so you can get dry. They oughtta fit."

"Thanks," Lash said, eager to get out from under their grateful eyes. Adam was the one missing brother, the one still living in New York and working for an international bank. But with Lash's luck, he'd show up in time for the lynching. He watched the brothers head toward the stairs, then covered the phone again, briefly. "Which room would that be?"

"Second to the last one on the right," Elliot said. "Right between mine and Jessi's."

Lash's heart tripped over itself, and he felt heat creep up his neck and into his ears. "Oh."

He dragged his gaze from theirs, though he could still feel their eyes on him as they marched up the stairs. Then he drew the phone to his ear. "Hello, Aunt Kate," he said.

He could still hear the Brand brothers talking upstairs. Extolling his virtues and his heroism, he imagined, groaning. Damn, if they knew the truth...

He answered Kate's questions without thinking. Told her he really wasn't interested in hearing what his so-called "brothers" were up to, and finally put the phone down.

It didn't matter that the Brands didn't know the truth, he thought, because he wasn't going to so much as *think* about touching Jessi again. It was simple. Mind over matter. Willpower. He could do this.

He sat there a long time, telling himself just how easy it would be. Then he headed up to his assigned bedroom, took a long, hot shower, changed into some dry duds and crawled into the welcome warmth of the bed. And thought about Jessi lying in her own bed, naked, maybe, thinking of him, maybe. Touching herself gently and closing her eyes and whispering his name. Just a wall away from him.

Lord!

When he finally fell asleep, his willpower dissolved along with his consciousness.

The dream spun its seductive web around him. He was on that same bank with Jessi, only this time it was grassy and lush instead of mud-slick and cold. The creek ran calm, and glittered beneath a blazing white sun. But the storm raging inside him was a fierce one. They were naked, the two of them, arms and legs twined as they undulated in a chaos of passion. He could feel her body tight around the length of him, and he was so close...so close...

And then a lasso settled around his neck from some

unseen place, and yanked him away from her. He heard Jessi cry out…and he stared back at her…but she faded, slowly, like a damp mist evaporating in the sun. And then he saw himself, sitting atop a great black horse. And he was dressed oddly…like some saddle tramp from an old western flick. The horse stood still beneath a giant oak tree, and Lash forced himself to look up at the sturdy branch that stretched above his head. A noose dangled from it, swaying softly in the breeze.

It lowered to eye level. He wanted to bat it away, but his hands were bound behind his back. The ghostly noose settled itself around his neck, pulled itself tight with a sudden jerk that left him gasping.

He lowered his gaze, tried to swallow and couldn't.

Around him, the Brand brothers—all five of them, even the missing Adam—sat their mounts. They wore long, time-yellowed dusters and had six-shooters strapped to their hips. None of them had taken the time to shave this morning, by the looks of them.

Garrett puffed on a hand-rolled smoke, then flicked it to the ground. "Any last words, Monroe?"

Lash tried to speak, but couldn't. The damned noose was too tight.

"Didn't think so," Garrett said. Then he nudged his horse up beside Lash's, leaned over and raised up a hand. He slapped the rump of Lash's mount hard, and the horse reared beneath him, and then bolted right out from under him.

Lash felt himself falling and he closed his eyes, waiting for the snap of his neck that would come when he reached the end of this rope. Falling, falling, falling…

He jerked upright in the bed, gasping for air and

clawing at his neck. But there was no rope there, and no lynching tree in sight.

There was only Jessi Brand, smiling sweetly behind her seductress's eyes. He blinked to clear the dream away, but she remained. He was awake. And she was here, in his bedroom.

"It just occurred to me," she said, very softly. "I never thanked you properly...for saving my life."

Chapter 6

"You shouldn't be in here," he said. His voice was hoarse, but he attributed that to last night's cold water, and the fact that he'd just dreamed of slow strangulation. "Your brothers—"

"It's morning, Lash. Garrett and Wes have gone to see about the pickup and to help the crew repairing the bridge. Garrett had to return the car he borrowed in town to come home last night, too. Elliot and Ben are out checking the stock, and Chelsea took the baby into town for his checkup." She moved closer and sat on the edge of the bed. "She had to take the long way around."

Lash swallowed hard and slid toward the other side.

"When you didn't get up in time for breakfast, I was afraid something might be wrong," she whispered. She reached up, as if to untie the sash of the satiny pink robe she wore. But instead, she just toyed with the dangling ends of it, arousing him more than if she'd yanked it off and sat there naked.

"Guess I was tired," Lash stammered. Dammit, he couldn't stand much more of this. He could see she wasn't wearing a thing beneath that robe. Her breasts were perfect, and he could taste them again just by looking at their shape, so clearly outlined in the thin fabric. If she crawled into this bed...if she touched him...

"Yeah, me too," she said with a careless shrug. "I don't know, though, it seems I haven't been sleeping much at all lately."

Damn. He hadn't been sleeping well, either, and he knew she was well aware of that fact. She had to be. She was the cause of it. And he'd pretty much revealed the direction of his thoughts last night.

He cleared his throat. "So, uh, how are you?"

"Bruised in all the places I can see, and it feels even worse in the places I can't." She smiled at him, a devilish look in her eyes. "But I'd have been a heck of a lot worse off if it hadn't been for you."

"I didn't do anything any other man wouldn't have done."

"Only if the other man were one of my brothers." She turned around and leaned her back against his headboard, drawing her knees up so that she could wrap her arms around them. "I think that's why I'm so drawn to you, Lash. 'Cause I never expected to find any man who could measure up to those brothers of mine. But then I met you, and you do it in spades."

He sensed she was being sincere with him. Not laying it on to soften him up. And it touched him, in spite of himself. "That's probably the nicest compliment anyone's ever given me," he told her. "Especially since I think so highly of your brothers, Jessi."

She nodded. "I know you do. That makes all this kinda hard on you, doesn't it?"

Damn. Straight to the point, again. She sure didn't pull punches or play games. "Yeah, it does. Friendship is something sacred, Jessi. A person would be foolish to let something as fleeting as...as lust get in the way of it."

"So you're pretty sure that's all there is between us? Just...lust? Just two people who can't stop thinking about tearing each other's clothes off and—"

"Don't." He met her big brown eyes and felt it again. Desire, rushing through him like some internal brand of hellfire. Searing-hot.

"I love my brothers, too, you know," she told him, holding his gaze trapped in her own. "But not enough to let them run my life, Lash. And I can't quite swallow that you care more for my brothers than even I do. So I'm thinking there's something else bothering you."

He drew a breath, then looked away.

"You wanna tell me about it?"

He shook his head, but heard himself talking to her all the same. "I was raised by a foster family, Jessi. A great big oversize family, just like this one."

"And it was terrible?"

"No, it wasn't terrible," he said quickly, but he lowered his head when he said it.

She dipped her head, searching his face.

"Okay, parts of it were pretty awful, but parts were okay. It's just that it was enough to convince me that a settled-down life with a dependent little wife and a bunch of relatives tripping over each other wasn't what I wanted. I want freedom, Jess. I want to be able to sling my stuff in a bag and take off whenever the urge hits me. Go wherever my feet feel like taking me. No guilt trips or balls and chains dragging me down. No anchors holding me still.''

"That all sounds real nice.''

He nodded. "It has been.''

"So you think I'm looking to hook myself around your throat like an anchor, Lash? You think I'm gonna cry to my brothers if you and I do what we both want to do, and then you up and walk away?'' She pierced him with her eyes. "C'mon, do you really think I'd do that to you?''

He spoke, but his voice was so hoarse his words came out unintelligible. He cleared his throat and tried again. "I don't know. I guess...I guess I don't think you'd do that. But—''

"And you want me, right?''

He closed his eyes. "One of the good things about being raised by the Reverend Mr. Stanton, Jess, was that he taught me right from wrong.''

"And you think making love to me would be wrong?''

"I know it would.''

She drew a breath, then let it out all at once. "You know something, Lash, I don't think I believe you. I think you're afraid of me. Afraid that once wouldn't be enough, and that being with me might just smash that drifter's way of life right to smithereens.''

His eyes widened, and he felt as if she'd hit him between the eyes with a mallet. Could she be—? No. No way in hell. She wasn't even close to the truth.

She got slowly to her feet, straightened her robe, and started back to the door, but paused there, facing him again. "But I'll tell you this much. I know it's real, because I feel it in my gut. It's going to happen, Lash. If not now, then later. You know it as well as I do. I want you, and I'm not ashamed to admit it. You want me, too, though you're having a little more trouble accepting it. We're both adults, and you don't have one thing to be afraid of. Not me, and not my brothers. I think what you're really scared of is yourself. But this thing between us isn't gonna go away, you know, no matter how much you try to ignore it.'' Her hand touched the knob, like a caress. He couldn't breathe. "When you're ready for me, Lash, you just let me know. But don't wait too long, 'cause I'm not going to.''

Then she slipped away and he managed to breathe again. Damn, he was in trouble here. Deep trouble. It would take a saint to resist that woman.

And Lash Monroe was no saint.

She was wearing him down. She sensed it.

The morning sun had burned off the dark clouds of the night before, and dried the rain-ravaged ground. Jessi was grateful to be alone in the house as she washed up the breakfast dishes and did a load of laundry. The boys had refused to let her work in the barns today, insisting she sleep late and take it easy after her episode last night. So she'd just make up for it by doing some of the indoor chores. It was hot already. The coming day was going to be the scorcher after the storm, she predicted, and she dressed accordingly: cut-off shorts and a sleeveless tank that hugged her curves. Funny, she'd never noticed whether her clothes hugged her curves before. It was Lash, she decided. He made her feel like...like a woman. A sexy, desirable woman. And the reason he made her feel that way was that he wanted her. He wanted her so much it scared him wit-less. Wanted her even though he was determined not to. Wanted her so much he wasn't sleeping nights thinking about it.

Oh, yeah, she knew. She couldn't help but know. It was in his eyes every time he looked at her, and getting more and more evident all the time. Hell, it was going to be obvious to everyone in the house pretty soon.

She was at the sink, drying coffee mugs with a dish towel, when she sensed him behind her. She took her time about turning to acknowledge his presence. Let him look his fill, she thought, feeling a little trill of excitement sing through her veins. She *liked* this feel-ing. It was so new, so thrilling.

He cleared his throat, so she finally glanced over her shoulder at him. "Oh. You're up."

"Your brothers will skin you for dressing like that," he observed.

Jessi frowned at him. "It's how I always dress when it's hot outside. Gee, Lash, you've seen me in shorts before."

His gaze slid down her legs, slowly, and came back up again. "Maybe I have," he muttered.

"Maybe it's different now that you know you want me, though."

"Jessi, don't—"

The screen door banged and Elliot traipsed in, fol-lowed closely by Ben. They looked at Jessi, then at Lash, then at each other. Ben shrugged. Elliot grinned, and came forward to take the dish towel away from her.

"Thought we told you to take it easy today, sis. You never could follow an order."

"And probably never will," she said, but she filled

a cup with the fresh coffee she'd made and sauntered to the table, electing to sit before one of them told her to, in which case she'd be forced to remain standing, just on principle. "Have you heard from Garrett?"

"Yeah, he called from the office. Damage to the bridge wasn't as bad as they thought, and the repairs ought to be finished by tomorrow. Meanwhile, he got a loaner from the dealer, so he has wheels again while he waits for the insurance company to settle up on his pickup." Elliot's grin was infectious.

"What's so funny about that?" Jessi asked.

Elliot shook his head. It was Ben who said, "The loaner is a little bit of a car that looks, according to Garrett, like a toaster on wheels. He can barely sit upright in it."

Jessi laughed out loud at the image, and Elliot did, as well. A low hissing sound came from the living room, and Jessi frowned and went to check it out. "Uh-oh. Look at this, you guys."

Her brothers and Lash followed her, and paused at the sight of the scene being played out on the floor. The old cat, Pedro, was poised, rear end in the air, chest to the floor, hissing and batting a paw at Ol' Blue. The big hound lifted one eyebrow, then closed his eyes again with a tired sigh.

"Blue, you lazy dog, he wants to play," Jessi said.

Blue made a groaning sound and didn't stir.

"Either that or he wants to fight," Elliot said. "You sure that old cat isn't gonna claw Blue's eyes out?"

"He's just feeling him out, seeing how much he'll put up with," Jessi told him. She walked into the living room, coffee mug in hand, to bend down and stroke the hound dog's head. "Blue, how come you're ignoring Pedro?"

Blue lifted his head high enough to reach up and lick her face.

"Hell, Jessi, I think Blue's just jealous. He never showed you so much affection until you came lugging that cat home," Elliot said.

"Could be that he knows how close he came to losing you in that flood last night," Ben put in, speaking low and soft. She knew he was thinking about his wife, and how much it hurt to lose someone you loved. But her brain quickly jumped back to what Elliot had said. About Blue loving her more now because of the competition. Maybe that thought merited some more study.

"Well, guys, I have to leave you now. Keep an eye on these two for me, will you?"

The three of them frowned. It was Lash who spoke. "Where to?"

"Marisella's house...my house, I mean. The Loomis boys are supposed to help me hoe out that garage today to pay me back for taking care of that mare. And I have a contractor coming at noon to check the place out and give me an estimate on the remodeling. I'll be out most of the day. I want to check on the Loomises' mare while I'm at it. And if it gets too late, I'll probably just spend the night at my soon-to-be new clinic. So if I don't come home, don't go calling out the National Guard, okay?" She paused near the door, where her overnight bag was packed and waiting.

Ben shook his head. "You had a rough night, Jess. Maybe you ought—"

"I had a wonderful night," she said. "Damn near a perfect one." Her gaze slanted deliberately toward Lash, but he quickly looked away.

"Nearly drowning agrees with you, huh, sis?" Elliot asked.

"*Not* drowning is what agrees with me. I could have died last night, but I didn't. And today I feel like a new woman."

"And I suppose you're taking that old clunker of a truck," Ben asked.

"That's what it's for, brother dear."

"You...um...oughtta change first."

She paused on her way to the door to stare at Lash, who seemed to be rather surprised that he'd just blurted what he had. As if he had any right to express an opinion about what she wore. "Why would I want to change? It'll be ninety-five by noon."

Lash shrugged. "You want those Loomis boys concentrating on what they're doing, don't you?"

She smiled. Maybe Elliot had been right. "I think I'll take that as a compliment. See you guys later." And she would. She'd see Lash later, at least. Because she had let him know she'd be there, alone, all night, in Marisella's house. Or at least she knew she'd be there alone. He might wonder. Maybe enough to stop by later, just to check in and reassure himself. Lord, she could only hope.

Lash fixed fence, counted cattle and repaired a loose shingle on the barn roof. Then he took his own car into town—the long way around, since the bridge wasn't fixed yet—and spent the afternoon going over the rustling incidents with Garrett in his office. They pieced together the bits of information until they had a pretty good picture of the men responsible. It was a big-time operation, judging by the hundreds of head that had been stolen over the past weeks. And in order to make such an operation profitable, there had to be a steady market for the stolen cattle. One not so far away as to make transporting them too costly. All signs pointed south. Garrett suspected the cows were being smuggled across the border and marketed in Mexico. But where, and by whom?

Though Lash fought hard to keep his mind on the case, he couldn't stop thinking about Jessi, and the way she'd looked when she left the ranch this morning. She'd changed in the past few days. It was as if all of a sudden she knew just how attractive she was, and it seemed to make her giddy with the power of it. She used to look innocent and cute in cutoff shorts and tank tops. Now she looked like some man's secret fantasy. Beguiling. Seductive. A siren. A fox.

Or...maybe she only looked that way to him. Maybe he was the one who'd changed. He'd certainly become aware of her as more than his boss's baby sister.

Thing was, he had a feeling those Loomis boys had noticed that about her a long time ago. And he didn't like the notion of their eyes feasting on those long, gorgeous legs of hers, or of the thoughts that might be racing through their minds. Suppose one of them put his hands on her? Suppose she didn't object? Hell, she was going to be in that damned empty house all alone tonight.

Waiting for him. He'd received her message this morning loud and clear. Kept seeing it flashing in her big, sultry eyes, over and over again. Hearing it in her voice. Damn.

"You with me, Lash?" Garrett asked, breaking into his thoughts. Lash looked up fast. "You seem... distracted."

"Sorry." Lash jerked himself away from the window he'd been staring absently through, and turned to cross the office. There was another desk now. An old, dark wooden one that looked as if it belonged in a one-room schoolhouse from days gone by. He ran one hand over the gleaming, freshly polished wood, feeling guilty as hell. "It was nice of you, dragging this desk in here for me, the way you did," he said.

"Hell, it was sitting home in the attic collecting dust. I figured it might as well get some use. No big deal."

But it was a big deal. The desk had belonged to Maria Brand, Garrett's mother, and it was most certainly a big deal. Lash didn't imagine the Brand brothers would consent to letting just anyone use it. And someone had taken pains to restore the gleam to that wood.

They treated him like family. Especially Garrett.

"You okay, Lash?"

Lash gave his head a shake. "Just wondering how you managed to haul this thing over here without your truck."

When Garrett didn't answer, Lash looked up to see him grinning and shaking his head. "That damn toaster-car is a hatchback. I drove over here with the desk half in, half out, and the rear end squatting so low I think we were throwing sparks from the back bumper." Garrett closed the file folder he had been perusing and slipped it into its spot in the drawer. "What say we call it a night? It's getting late, anyway. The boys probably have chores finished by now."

Lash glanced at his watch, noting the late hour with surprise. *Time flies when you're obsessing*, he thought.

"Okay. Guess I'll head home, then." *Sure you will*, he thought miserably.

"You can come to supper if you want. Chelsea's making her fried chicken tonight."

He thought of the last time he'd joined the Brands

for fried chicken. Sitting across the table from Jessi, watching her lick her fingers. Lash compressed his lips into a hard line. "No, thanks. I'm beat. Think I'll turn in early."

"Okay. See you in the morning, then?"

"Sure." Lash snatched his hat from the back of his chair and headed out. He drove his noisy black convertible back to his lonely apartment in town. His haven of solitude.

It was waiting there for him, empty and dark. He shoved his door open, stepped inside, and the thought flitted through his mind that the place was as quiet as a graveyard. And then he frowned. "Since when did quiet bother me? Hell, I *like* quiet."

He went inside and tried to enjoy the quiet. One of the best parts of his freedom, he reminded himself over a solitary dinner consisting of a cold meat sandwich and a beer. But the quiet got on his nerves tonight. He found himself flicking on the little portable TV set he barely ever watched, turning the volume up loud. But the tinny voices and canned laughter didn't do the trick. Damn those Brands. He must be getting so used to being around them, being immersed in that big familial den of chaos, that he actually missed it when he wasn't. Imagine that.

Maybe he oughtta get a dog.

He tossed his paper plate into the trash, drained his beer and opened a second. He carried the can with him into the living room to sink onto the little easy chair and stare sightlessly at the television.

Was this what he truly wanted out of life? Endless nights like this one? Alone, bored.

"But free," he muttered, and lifted his can in a mocking toast to freedom.

It was that damned Jessi, making him feel restless and frustrated and itchy. Her and all her suggestive glances.

Her and her hot kisses. Her and her talk about the clinic and the house and the family she'd have there one day.

He didn't want that, dammit.

But he did want her.

His shower that night was a cool one. He dived into bed still wet, hoping the dampness would keep the oppressive heat from smothering him. And after a third beer, he fell into a jerky, restless sleep.

But she didn't leave him alone then, either. She was there, haunting his dreams, touching him, kissing him, teasing him, as he lay there paralyzed and unable to reciprocate. He thrashed in agony, his head whipping back and forth, his body coated in sweat. Invisible chains held him immobile as Jessi leaned over him, trailing her fingers slowly up and down his body, touching lightly, and moving away. Repeating the torture with her lips. Laughing at him for his helplessness.

He woke shouting her name. And then he blinked the dream away and sat in his bed, shuddering with need, coated in a cold sweat. The phone was ringing. And he knew better than to pick it up. But he picked it up anyway.

"Are you ready yet, Lash?"

"Jessi?" He frowned into the receiver, and then her words registered, and he started sweating all over again.

"You sound sleepy. Were you sleeping? I haven't been able to."

"No?" he asked, telling himself to put the phone down now.

"No," she breathed. "It's so hot, and I'm just...I don't know, jittery, I guess."

"Jittery," he repeated. "And hot."

"Mmmm... Every time I slide between the cool sheets and close my eyes, all I can see is...you. The way we were on the bank of Sycamore Creek. The way your mouth felt when you—"

"Why won't you leave me alone, Jess?" He asked it softly, feeling desperation clog his throat.

"I thought you'd stop by tonight. I'm here, you know. I'm alone. And I've been waiting. Damn, Lash, when are you going to quit disappointing me?"

"I'm hanging up the phone now," he told her. But he didn't do it.

"I'm sorry if I'm making this hard on you," she whispered. "Maybe I ought to be ashamed of myself, but I'm not, you know. I want you so much I can't—"

"I'm human," he muttered. "Dammit to hell, I'm only human." He slammed the phone down, flung back the covers and reached for his jeans.

Jessi had replaced the receiver, and sighed. He wasn't coming. Okay. She could live with that...for now. But she sure as hell couldn't sleep.

So now she was balanced precariously on a rickety step ladder, screwing a new light bulb into an old socket in the now empty garage. The Loomis boys had worked like wild men for her today, and between the three of them, they'd had the entire contents of the garage sorted, packed and hauled away to a storage shed on their ranch—which they'd insisted she use for as long as she needed—in a matter of a few hours. They were grateful to her, and they showed it. The mare was on her feet today, and doing well. Jessi had gone out to their spread at lunchtime to check on her. She'd be all right. Jessi felt good about that.

She also felt perfectly all right about the little stop she'd made on her way back here. At Mr. Henry's Drug Store. She'd gathered up her courage, and for the first time in her life, she'd purchased condoms. No easy task, what with a mischievous-looking nine-year-old boy peering at her and giggling every few seconds, with his carrot-colored curls and his faceful of freckles. But he was too young to know what the little foil packets were. She hoped. She had bought three, individually wrapped, and had silently hoped Lash would come to her...tonight. Well, he hadn't, but he would. Soon. And when he did, she'd be prepared.

She'd fully expected him to come to her tonight, and her disappointment burned. She wouldn't sleep before dawn, she was sure of it. It was still early. But if he hadn't shown by now, he wasn't going to.

She'd been so ready for tonight. She'd thought of everything. The peach-colored silk teddy still hugged her secretly beneath the robe she'd pulled over it when it became obvious Lash wasn't going to come over. The condoms were still in the robe's pocket. She'd soaked in a scented bath that left her skin silky-soft and smelling faintly of honeysuckle. In the bedroom, she'd had soft music playing, and candles glowing. But he hadn't come to her. Even her little wake-up call hadn't convinced him. And dammit, she'd been too wound up to sleep. So she'd come out here to get some work done.

Beginning with new light bulbs.

The garage was pretty much empty now. Aside from the ladder on which she stood, there were only a few items scattered around—things she'd decided to keep for her own use. The rusty toolbox in the corner containing a valuable selection of tools that were in surprisingly good condition. A brass magazine rack she planned to use in the clinic's waiting room. A box full of antique books.

She reached overhead to twist the new bulb in tighter. The ladder wobbled. Her balance faltered. And two strong hands clasped around her waist to steady her.

She knew those hands. Knew the familiar warm pressure of each callused fingertip. "Lash," she breathed.

He didn't say anything. Just lifted her gently, and lowered her to the floor. Her body brushed his on the way down. Her knees felt weak, and when she was standing, she leaned back against him, feeling the heat of him, relaxing against him. His arms hesitated, then slowly slid around her waist. His head bowed, and he spoke softly, very close to her ear. "What the hell am I ever going to do with you, Jess?"

She turned in his arms, tipped her head back, stared up into his eyes. "You know the answer to that just as well as I do."

"You're driving me crazy," he whispered, his eyes roaming over her face. "I can't sleep nights anymore. You're like a siren, Jessi, and I think you know it. I think you're actually *trying* to drive me right out of my mind."

"No, Lash. I only want to drive you into my arms."

He threaded his fingers in her hair, touching it, rubbing locks of it, bringing it to his face to inhale its scent. "Dammit, Jess, I don't want—"

"Yeah, you do," she said. "You know perfectly well you do, Lash. Just as much as I do. So why don't you just shut up and kiss me?"

Chapter 7

He shook his head slowly, slightly, and he searched her eyes. Then he kissed her. And she knew that her plan was going to work. He was going to make love to her. He was going to see how perfect they were together. He wouldn't be able to stay away from her after this. And when his job with Garrett was finished, and it came time for him to leave, he'd realize that he had fallen in love with her. He'd decide he had to stay. He was going to love her. It was going to work.

"I can't stay," he muttered between kisses. "You have to know that up front, Jessi. I'm not a settling-down kind of guy."

"I didn't ask you to stay," she told him. "Just this. Just tonight. This is all I want," she lied.

He lifted his head, probing her eyes, and she knew that he knew she was lying. For just an instant, she saw the hesitation—the second thoughts clouding his eyes. So she took a single step backward, pulling out of his arms, and she parted the robe she wore, letting it slide from her shoulders, down her arms, to pool around her feet.

And Lash's lips parted and his eyes widened and his Adam's apple swelled and receded again as he swallowed hard. His gaze moved slowly down the silky teddy, back up again. He drew a shallow breath. "Mercy," he muttered, and she thought maybe he meant it.

Too bad if he did. She wasn't going to show him *any* mercy tonight.

She moved close to him again, pressed her body to his, caught both of his hands in hers, and kissed him. And when she finished, he was shuddering and shivering and sweating. Best of all, he was kissing her back. He trailed his lips over her chin, down to her throat, and then her shoulder, pushing the teddy's silken strap aside with his mouth as he did. His hands kneaded her buttocks, pulling her tight to him as he arched against her. Her fingers sifted his hair, urging his head lower, until he worked her breast free of its confines to suckle it thoroughly.

He was hers. All hers now. She knew it a second later, when he let go of her, eyes blazing, and tore his shirt open, struggling out of it hurriedly. She smiled softly when he reached for the button fly of his jeans, as well.

But her smile died when he paused. "Dammit, what the hell am I thinking?"

"Don't think," she whispered. "You think way too much as it is, Lash. This isn't about thinking. It's about *feeling*, Lash."

He gave his head a shake. "We can't do this," he muttered, turning slowly away from her, pushing one hand through his hair and messing it up endearingly. "I didn't bring... I don't have..."

"Oh," she said. "You don't have...protection? Is that what you mean?" Jessi crouched and slipped her hand into the pocket of her robe, emerging with one of the small foil packets and holding it up. "But I do."

He blinked, eyes narrowing. "You were that sure of yourself, were you?"

She shrugged and tossed him the packet. He caught it, still staring at her. Still having second thoughts, she was afraid. So she pushed the straps of the teddy the rest of the way down, and let it fall to her feet. She stepped out of it, catching the peach silk on the end of one toe and flinging that at him, too.

He didn't catch it, though. The teddy hit him in the center of his glorious chest, and fell to the garage floor, forgotten. Lash didn't seem to notice it. His gaze slid, very slowly, all the way down her naked body, and then up again. And then he whispered, "I'm gonna burn in hell, Jessi Brand, but not until I've loved every inch of you."

He pulled her against him, kissing her deeply, hungrily, and lowering her to the floor atop her soft robe. He pushed her down on her back, and held her arms at her sides, and kissed her all over. It was incredible, the way he made her feel. And all Jessi wanted was more of this magic. She didn't let herself tremble, even when a tiny whisper of fear—fear of the unknown—tiptoed through her mind. Instead she played the role of seductress, the one she'd written and then cast herself in, to the hilt. She kissed him and trailed her hands down his hard back. She touched him everywhere, and when he sucked air through his teeth, she knew she was doing it right.

His fingers dipped and probed and parted her, and Jessi shivered with a forbidden pleasure as she parted her thighs for him. "Now, Lash," she whispered. "We've waited long enough. Do it now."

She wrapped her legs around him, moved her hips against him, and he did what she asked. She felt him nudging his way inside her, bit by bit. And then she felt filled and stretched, and there was a brief stab of pain that made her go stiff all over and had her eyes flying wide open.

He stilled. "Jessi?"

No, he wasn't going to stop. Not now. She closed her hands on his firm buttocks and pulled him to her, and into her, and she moved against him, and in a few seconds he was hers again. All hers. No second thoughts about repercussions could hold him the way she could. He was hers, dammit. And he might as well get used to the idea, because he was going to stay hers.

It wouldn't be long. *Couldn't* be. Not if he was feeling a tenth of what she was right now. It was as if...as if they'd become one.

When he moved inside her, she arched to receive him. When he turned his head in search of her mouth, he found it there, waiting for his kiss. No words, no signals—nothing was needed, because the connection between them was so strong. He held her hard and tight, as if he'd never let her go, and she wished it could go on forever.

And then her mind whirled out of the realm of cognizance, as the feelings he was stirring took over. Sensation enveloped her. There was nothing else, only pleasure, mounting pleasure, pleasure so intense she wanted to scream with it.

And then she did scream with it, words tumbling

from her lips in a rush, driven by a passion so intense she wasn't even sure what she was saying.

He bucked harder and then drove into her, holding her tight to take him. He shuddered, and she did, as well. And it was a long time before he relaxed enough to move again. A long time before she came back to earth and realized what she'd shouted when the climax swept her away.

She closed her eyes and prayed she hadn't ruined everything. Maybe…maybe he'd been too carried away to notice the words she said.

Or…maybe not.

Jessi had curled into his arms, pulling his discarded flannel shirt over her. She lay relaxed and warm and sated against him. Flesh to flesh. Body to body. And he couldn't deny that it had been incredible. The best sex he'd ever had in his life.

And it had also been, he realized, the biggest mistake.

Lash relived the experience, knowing the precise moment when he should have stopped. He should be horsewhipped. He wouldn't blame her brothers for lynching him now. He wouldn't blame them a bit.

He stared down at the scarlet proof of what he should have known all along, staining the pale pink satin of Jessi's crumpled robe. The pink of a tea rose. The pink of innocence.

"You should have told me," he said, and his voice was strained.

She snuggled closer to his side, tugging at him as if she wanted him to lie down again. "Told you what?"

"Dammit, Jessi, you were… I was…"

"You were my first," she said, and she smiled up

at him. It was a sleepy, sexy smile in the too-bright light of the single bare bulb. "And if you'd get back down here with me, you could be my second...and my third and m—"

"Dammit," he muttered again, and this time he eased himself out of her embrace and got to his feet. He pulled his jeans on hurriedly, while she looked on, her doe eyes round and hurting. Of course she was hurting. He was a bastard.

He averted his eyes and paced the barren garage in broad strides, sweeping his hand through his hair. "I never would have...if I'd known...we shouldn't..."

She sat up, tilting her head to one side. "Don't tell me you thought I was in the habit of—" she glanced down at the robe, the dirty floor, her fallen teddy "—of this."

"Well, hell, Jess, you were too good at it to be an amateur. I didn't stand a chance, once you set your mind to—" He bit off the rest when he met her gaze by accident and saw fresh pain flash in her eyes. But it vanished fast.

Chased away by anger.

"Forgive me," she said. "I kinda got the idea that you were willing."

"You know damn well what I meant. I didn't want this... I mean, I *did,* but I wouldn't have...not if you'd left me the hell alone when I told you to. Damn, Jessi, what the hell am I supposed to do now?"

She got slowly to her feet, pulling his shirtsleeves over her arms, jerking it closed in the front. "You can always have me arrested," she snapped. "Charge me with rape, seeing as how I gave you no choice and ignored you a while ago when you were screaming no. Hell, you probably have a good case, right? So you decide, Lash. Meanwhile, why don't you get the hell out of my garage, off my property and out of my life.''

"Gladly." He snatched up his boots, put them on haphazardly and fled. As if the devil himself were on his heels, Lash stomped to his car, slammed the door and spit gravel in his wake when he headed home. But he couldn't run fast enough or far enough. He'd been raised better than this. The Reverend Mr. Stanton had taught him far, far better than this. But even so, he'd given in to his baser urges. He'd told himself they were two consenting adults and that so long as she understood up front that this meant nothing, it would be all right. Hell, she'd even had condoms on hand.

But he'd been wrong. She was an innocent, no matter how effective her seduction. *An innocent.* She didn't know anything about sex or men or…

What should he do? What the hell should he do? He pulled the car into the spot in front of his apartment, killed the engine and sat there cursing himself. He closed his eyes and saw Reverend Stanton at the pulpit, fist slamming down on the open Bible, fire and brimstone in his eyes. "You have to marry her, boy! It's the only honorable thing you *can* do. You sullied an innocent, defiled her, deflowered her. And, boy, the blame for that is only half hers, and you know it."

"You're right," Lash muttered. And he knew it was true. Sure, she'd acted as if she knew what was what. But if he'd searched his soul, he'd have known it was all bluster. All an act.

She'd told him she loved him. She was an innocent young girl who thought she was in love with him. And if he hadn't been so busy lusting after her, he'd have seen love shining from those big brown eyes. He'd have seen it and he'd have run like hell. She thought

she loved him. And because of that, she'd given him
something more precious than gold, and she'd sure as
hell regret it some day.

He owed her. He owed her brothers. He had to do
what was right.

Jessi was stunned.

After what they'd shared, she'd thought he'd have
to know they were meant for each other. How could
he not know it, after that? How?

She closed her eyes. God, it had been…it had been
like nothing she'd ever dreamed of. The way they fit
together. They'd been so close, so insane with wanting
and giving and feeling. How could he still not know?

Jessi sighed and pulled his shirt tighter around her,
hugging her waist. She'd thought he would understand
that they were meant to be together once they made
love. But she'd been wrong. He hadn't understood anything. He'd acted angry, instead of moved. Instead of
in love, he'd been in what looked and felt like mortal
fear of her.

Were all men this dense, or only Lash?

Or maybe…maybe she was the one who wasn't getting it. Lash had been with other women. Maybe being
with her hadn't been anything so special for him.
Maybe it had been just like the rest, and not the earth-
shattering experience it had been for her.

That thought made more sense than any other.
Maybe she was the one who'd been a total fool. She
picked up her bathrobe, balled it up and carried it under
her arm. Her chin lowered to her chest, she walked
through the darkness back into the house and stuffed it
into her overnight bag. Then she showered, letting
steaming-hot water pound her sore body, telling herself

to let it rinse away this heartache that had settled over her like a heavy shroud.

It didn't. And the quiet of the empty house only made it worse. She didn't want to be alone tonight. If she were, she'd just spend the night bawling like some weak-kneed female, and she *hated* women like that. No, better to find some distraction. Something else to think about.

She threw on some fresh jeans, snatched up her bag and headed to the one place where she knew she could always find comfort. And love. And chaos. Home. The Texas Brand. Even if she slipped up to her room without seeing anyone, just being there would be enough. Just hearing all that noise, feeling the warmth that big house was always filled with, would be enough. It would be better to lick her wounds there than here, alone. And maybe then she could make some sense out of all of these strange feelings swirling around in her heart, and decide what she was supposed to do next.

There was an unfamiliar car in the driveway when she arrived, and she figured someone had company. Part of her wanted to creep into the house through the back door and sneak unseen up to her room. Most of her, though, wanted to shake this dark cloud from over her head and march in with her head held high. She had nothing to be ashamed of. Lash should have been happy to learn he was her first. He should have been thrilled. And if he had half a brain, he'd have understood what an honor it was that she'd bestowed on him. She'd wanted him to be her first. She'd waited all her life for him.

And he'd been furious about it.

"Well, to hell with him."

She was hurt, but there was a lot more to it than that.

She was mad as hell. And sniveling her way through the house as if she had something to be ashamed of was not her way of dealing with it. Because she wasn't ashamed. She'd done nothing wrong.

Besides, her brothers would sense something was up if she didn't act like her usual self. So she did.

She burst through the front door, small bag in her hand, plastering a smile on her face and acting as if she were on top of the world. But she paused when she saw a harried-looking woman who seemed to be on her way out. The woman had a boy in tow. A carrot-topped, freckle-faced little boy. Jessi recognized him at once and frowned, wondering what on earth was going on. Her first thought was that the kid *had* known what those foil packets were, and that he'd ratted her out to her older brothers. And the bottom fell out of her stomach as she looked up at Garrett.

But Garrett was smiling as he and Chelsea saw the woman and the boy off. "Don't let it happen again, you hear? And Mrs. Peterson, don't you worry about the late hour. I'm glad you came to me, and you did the right thing by letting Mr. Henry know right away. I'm sure no harm's been done."

The woman nodded, red-faced, never quite meeting Garrett's eyes. "I just can't imagine what came over him, Sheriff Brand. But I was always taught confession is good for the soul. Now that he's owned up to it and you had that little talk with him, I'm sure he'll mend his ways."

"Don't be too hard on him, ma'am. Boys tend toward mischief, you know. They can't help it much."

The woman scowled at her son and hustled him out of the house to their waiting car.

Jessi stood just inside the screen door, watching as

the two left. When they were gone, she looked at her brother, frowning. "What was all that about?"

"Hardened criminal," Garrett said. "His mom caught him in the act and made him confess to the sheriff." He shook his head, grinning. "I gave him a talkin'-to. I don't think he's gonna mess up again."

"Oh." Jessi nodded. "I heard you mention Mr. Henry. What did the kid do, shoplift something from the drugstore?"

Garrett shook his head, and she could see that he was battling a gut-deep chuckle. Chelsea elbowed him in the ribs. "It's not one bit funny, you big lug."

He sobered. "You're right, of course. I was just wondering if little Bubba's gonna be as much of a heller as that one is. Thank goodness his mama caught him and let ol' Mr. Henry know what he'd done."

"That bad, huh?" Jessi asked.

"You bet," Garrett said. "His mama caught him in the prophylactic aisle with a sewing needle in his hand. Seems his friends dared him to poke holes in the condoms."

Jessi's blood rushed to her feet so fast she felt dizzy. "P-poke...*holes?*" Her hand clenched tighter around the handle of her small bag.

"Little feller annihilated a dozen or more before she caught him. Seems he was at it all afternoon."

Jessi put one hand on her belly to calm it. This was just silly. She was just being silly. What were the odds that the ones she'd bought had been—?

"Well, I hope he's learned his lesson," she said, but her voice lacked conviction, and it cracked a little. She wanted to chase the woman down and wring her child's freckled neck. "I'm heading upstairs. I'm tired out."

"But, Jess, you didn't tell us about the garage. How'd it go today? You get much done?"

She kept walking, speaking softly as she went, not turning around. She was operating on autopilot right now, while her brain reeled from the shock. The very thought... "Fine. It's coming along fine."

"Now what the heck do you suppose is ailing her?" she heard her brother mutter.

She hurried to her room, closed the door, turned the lock and raced to her bed, shaking the contents of her overnight bag onto the comforter. She grasped her robe when it rolled onto the bed, and shook it.

The two remaining foil packets spilled out in front of her, and her hands were trembling when she picked one of them up. She scanned the little sucker, front and back, straining her eyes. But there were no punctures. The packet was fine.

She dropped it, sighing in relief and grabbing up the second one. She'd been afraid for nothing. There'd been no reason to think that...

"Oh, my God."

She swallowed hard and stared at the series of tiny holes in the second packet, willing them to disappear. But they remained.

"Oh, my God, this is like Russian roulette. What about the third one? The one we...used?"

No way to tell. Lash had disposed of it, wrapper and all, though she had no idea what he'd done with it. She only knew she'd looked around the floor after he left, wanting to leave no telltale signs for her snoopy brothers to stumble upon. And she'd found nothing there. She'd be damned before she asked Lash what he'd done with it. She'd be damned before she even mentioned any of this to him.

She closed her eyes and pressed her palm to her forehead. Oh, God, what if…what if…?

No. It couldn't happen. It couldn't.

But there was no way she was going to stop worrying about it until she knew. And she couldn't know. Not yet. All she could do was wait…and try not to let her panic show in her eyes in the meantime.

Because if the worst *had* happened tonight… She closed her eyes, chewed her lower lip… Damn. Her brothers were going to skin Lash alive.

He knew what he *ought* to do, he just wasn't quite sure he could bring himself to go through with it. He hadn't heard a word from Jessi in three days, and he'd managed to avoid her so far. It might do to give her some time to get over him, he thought. After all, she might decide she wasn't in love with him, after all, and maybe she'd be okay, and he wouldn't have to sacrifice his freedom on the altar of her lost innocence.

He ought to be ashamed of himself. He really should. Hell, he *was*. He told himself, though, that it was better for Jessi not to rush into anything. To cool down and think it through first. And he figured he'd get a pretty good handle on how she was dealing with all of this any minute now. This morning Garrett had called to ask Lash to be at the ranch for breakfast. Said he wanted to get an early start as they headed out to a ranch forty miles east where another rustling incident had taken place recently. It would be easier if they left from the ranch in one vehicle.

And if every excuse Lash could think of hadn't sounded so lame in his mind, he might have tried using one or two of them.

He sat at the table in the Brand's kitchen, feeling

like Judas at the Last Supper. And maybe it was just him, but there seemed to be a pall hanging over all of them. Lash was used to Ben's solemn face and sad eyes. But it wasn't just Ben. Wes sat across from him, looking preoccupied. Elliot wasn't cracking jokes or grinning. Garrett rarely stopped frowning. Even Chelsea was unusually quiet.

He didn't think they knew. Hell, if they knew, he wouldn't be sitting here and they wouldn't be moping. He'd be running for his life and they'd be chasing him with blood in their eyes, more than likely. He cleared his throat and decided to face it head-on. "Why's everybody so glum?"

Garrett shook himself. "Hell, Lash, I forgot you haven't been out here for a few days."

"Nope," Wes said, and then his black eyes narrowed. "In fact, he hasn't been around since Jessi first started acting so strangely."

Chelsea's head came up, her eyes widening. "Wes, she told you, it's just a stomach bug. Flu, probably. It'll pass. She'll be fine."

Wes grunted, and Lash swallowed hard. "So something's wrong with Jessi?" he asked.

"Don't worry about it," Chelsea replied. And her eyes pierced his. "She's too tough to let any insignificant little *bug* keep her down."

Lash flinched. Damn, if no one else knew, it was obvious Chelsea at least had a pretty good idea of what was bothering Jess. He felt about two inches high. But he was worried. "Is she—"

"Here she comes," Elliot said. "See for yourself."

No sooner had he said it than Jessi sailed into the kitchen, chin high, overly bright smile on her face.

"Overslept again," she sang. "You guys should have woke me."

"Heard you up pacing till after midnight," Ben said softly. "Thought if you were finally sleeping, we oughtta let you have at it."

She smiled even harder, then caught sight of Lash, and her face froze, the smile dying slowly.

"Morning, Jessi," he managed.

She blinked the emotions from her eyes and turned her back to pour herself a cup of coffee. "Morning," she muttered.

When she faced them again, her smile was back in place, and every bit as phony as before. Maybe even a little bit more so now.

Something was sure as hell bothering her. She wouldn't look him in the eye, barely spoke more than a syllable in his direction at a time. She looked pale, and there were dark rings surrounding her eyes. From lack of sleep, no doubt. Up pacing till after midnight, indeed.

She picked at her food. Normally, that bundle of energy had an appetite like a horse, but this morning— and maybe for the past several mornings, judging by her family's worry—she pushed the food around on her plate, looking at it as if it held no appeal whatsoever. And Lash knew he wasn't imagining the haunted look in her eyes.

Looking at her, Lash lost his appetite, as well. She was a mess. Trying hard to hide it, but a mess all the same. Lash couldn't avoid the consequences of his actions. Not anymore. It was clear he'd hurt her. Hurt her bad. If he'd known she was a virgin, he'd never have assumed she could deal with a casual one-night stand. And he should have known. Thing was, he thought, he just plain hadn't wanted to know. He'd wanted her, and he'd had her, and now the poor little thing was devastated.

Probably she'd been harboring some fantasy about how it would all play out. Probably she'd thought he'd fall madly in love with her after having her once, and that he'd be hers forever. She was still in love with him, and he'd broken her innocent heart all to hell. Poor thing, falling apart over him.

Lord, but he'd messed up good this time.

She sipped her coffee, leaned back in her chair. "So you two are heading out to the Bar Z today?" She addressed her question to Garrett, acting as if Lash weren't even in the room.

"Yeah," Garrett said. "The rustling spree out their way last year bears some similarities to ours."

"That's great," she said. "Maybe you'll break this case wide open."

"That would be nice," Garrett said. "I'm sick of working on this thing into the wee hours night after night."

"You aren't the only one," Lash said.

Jessi looked right at him, those brown eyes locking on to his like laser beams. "That's right," she said. "Once this thing is over, you can be on your way. I know you can't wait."

Lash took the blow she dealt and didn't even rock backward under the impact, which he thought was admirable. "Actually," he said slowly, forcing the words out, "I was thinking about staying on."

There was, in that instant, a flicker in her eyes. Lash thought it might have been hope, or joy, or something. He thought maybe he'd caused it.

But it died quickly, and the sadness was back in her

eyes, or worry, or stress, or whatever it was. Darkness. That was what he saw. And she said, "Sure you are. And I'm thinking of running for mayor."

Lash gave his head a shake. "You don't believe me," he stated flatly.

"You shouldn't say things you don't mean, Lash."

"I meant it."

She held his gaze for a long moment, and Lash couldn't look away, even when he felt curious gazes on him. Speculative eyes. Hostile ones.

Finally, Jessi broke eye contact with a shrug. "Hell, it doesn't matter to me one way or another."

But it did. And he knew, dammit, he knew what he had to do.

"We'd best get a move on, Lash," Garrett said, pushing away from the table and snatching up his hat.

Lash nodded, his eyes on his boss's baby sister. "I'll see you later, Jessi," he said. Hoping she'd get the message. They had to talk. He had to do right by her.

But Jessi refused to so much as look at him as he stood near the door with his hat in his hand. And he had to give up, because he didn't want to have to deal with her brothers until after he'd fixed that pretty little heart he'd stupidly managed to break. And he was being pretty obvious here.

He plunked the hat on his head, nodded to the others and headed out the door.

Chapter 8

He tried to put the pain he'd seen in her eyes out of his mind by throwing himself into the rustling investigation up to his eyeballs. He and Garrett interviewed ranchers from one end of the county to the other. They examined tire tracks and hoof tracks, and Lash had an impromptu lesson from Garrett in making plaster molds of them for future reference. Almost as if Garrett might be taking seriously Lash's words about sticking around.

Hell.

He knew Jessi was doing the same, throwing herself into her work. By the time Lash and Garrett got back that night, the contractor she'd hired was out at her place in town. The guy was already raising hell with that garage. When Lash drove by on his way home, he saw crews of men. Muscular types, working shirtless. All of them tanned and rippling, the bastards. Jessi stood nearby, overseeing their progress, and never hesitated to correct them or boss them around. The lawn was a mess of lumber and sawhorses and pickup trucks and power tools and extension cords. These guys were pros, and they were going to town on the clinic. All of which made Lash suspect Jessi was deliberately hurrying the process along, just to divert her mind from the way he'd broken her poor, innocent heart.

He was truly a slug.

He pulled over, not really thinking about what he was doing or why. He sat in his car for a very long time, parked right across the street from her new place, and stared at the activity as the sun went down—like a kid hoping for a glimpse of a sweet at a candy store, but without the wherewithal to go inside. And all the while, the preacher's voice rang in his mind with Bible verses telling him the right thing to do.

No matter how tempting Jessi's advances had been, this was his own fault. He wasn't an animal. He could have said no, done the honorable thing and walked away from her. He'd wanted her as badly as she wanted him. Thing was, he was experienced, and she was innocent. He was older, and supposedly wiser. He was the man, she the woman. His role should have been to protect her, watch out for her, not to take advantage of her innocent feelings for him.

He'd crushed her. And no matter how he looked at it, there was only one way to fix this mess. Hell, marrying and settling down wasn't the way he'd planned to live his life, but it wouldn't be so bad. He liked Jessi. She was attractive—no, she was gorgeous—and smart. Fabulous in bed. God, more than fabulous. For a while there, she'd robbed him of his will to live without her body wrapped around his. And Quinn, Texas, wasn't such a terrible place to settle down, if a man was forced to settle down somewhere. And her brothers—hell, they'd come around. It wouldn't be so bad.

He sat there. She'd seen him, he knew that, but she pointedly ignored his presence. After a while, the contractors packed up their equipment, leaving the bigger items in the garage, then cleared out.

Jessi glanced across the way at him, shook her head, almost as if she were exasperated, and turned to walk into her house. It was time. Taking a deep breath and stiffening his spine, Lash wrenched open the door of his car and strode purposefully across the street and up the walk to the little house, eyeing it the way a newly condemned man eyes his prison cell. Silently he said goodbye to his dreams of roaming free and unfettered, wherever the wind would take him, and resigned himself to the mundane life of a married man. He felt pretty damned proud of himself for making this supreme sacrifice.

He knocked on the little door, knowing in his heart that the joy in Jessi's pretty eyes when he told her what he'd decided to do was going to be all the reward he needed.

Jessi opened the door and saw Lash standing there, looking at her as if she were a kid with a boo-boo and he had the only Band-Aid in town. She frowned, tilting her head to one side.

"Look, Lash, you said it was a one-night stand, and I agreed, okay? I don't remember offering seconds."

He lowered his eyes. "I just want to talk."

Her eyes narrowed suspiciously. "Talk, then."

"Can I come in?"

She heaved a sigh, shrugged and stepped back, away from the door, so that he could come inside. He did, looking around the place and nodding in approval. "Wow. You've been busy."

And she had. She'd scrubbed the place spotless, hung new curtains, had the furniture professionally cleaned, stored most of Marisella's personal things and moved in a whole lot of her own. She'd decided not to rent the house to strangers after all. She'd use it herself when she felt like it. And she'd stay at the ranch when she didn't. So there. In fact, she was going to do exactly what she wanted, when she wanted, where she wanted, from now until she died a spinster at eighty-something.

Mostly, though, all the work had been to pass the time until she could get rid of this gnawing worry over the possibly faulty condom. It would be two weeks before a pregnancy test could give any sort of accurate results. Once she got past that, and the stupid thing read negative—as it most certainly would—she'd be rid of this nervous energy. Until then, all she could do was direct it into something constructive, just to burn it off. It was the only way she could sleep at night. And even then, she tossed and turned, and slept in fits and starts.

The cottage was hers now. She'd made it hers. Forest-green curtains matched the new slipcovers on the sofa and chair. White throw pillows with green ruffles littered the sofa, and there were matching throw rugs on the hardwood floors, for accents. She'd placed a few of her treasures around the room. Knickknacks she'd collected over the years. Bowls full of flowers here and there. The shelves on the wall where Marisella used to pile her collection of trinkets were now Jessi's bookshelves, lined with most of her veterinary books. She'd even brought her PC over and installed it on its own desk, in the corner near the window that overlooked the front yard. That way she could work on her plans and budgeting and still be close enough to keep track of the workers outside.

She watched Lash look around the place, saw the approval in his eyes, and thought he'd better blurt the apology he'd been practicing, beg her forgiveness on bended knee and ask for the chance to start over with her pretty darned fast, or he'd find himself out on his ear.

"I've been worried about you," he said.

"No need for that. I'm just fine." She paced to the small sofa and sat down. Might as well resign herself to the fact that he would only get to his apology in his own good time.

"You don't look fine," he told her, and he stood in front of where she sat, looking down at her almost worriedly. But it was a paternal, or big-brotherly, sort of worry. "You've lost weight, haven't you?"

She shrugged and averted her eyes. Worry would do that. It was only three or four pounds. Nothing to get excited about. In fact, it was rather reassuring. Pregnant women *gained* weight, right? That she'd lost weight only added credence to her firm belief that she couldn't possibly be carrying Lash Monroe's baby.

Lash cleared his throat, drawing her gaze back to his again. He was holding his hat in his hand, now. Worrying the brim with kneading fingers. Ah, the apology must be forthcoming, she thought. Maybe she ought to make him kneel.

"I wasn't fair to you before, Jess. I mean, it would have been different if you were...you know, experienced, but you weren't, and I should have known that."

She shrugged and wondered when he'd get around to apologizing and asking for a second chance.

He turned slowly, taking a deep breath and paced to a nearby chair, one right across from her. Finally, he sat down and met her gaze again. "I take full responsibility for what happened between us, and I've decided to do the honorable thing and face up to the consequences."

She drew a swift gulp of air and lifted her brows. He couldn't possibly know about the condoms, could he? "Consequences?"

"Yes," he said, nodding firmly. "Look, just because I never intended to settle down, doesn't mean I can shirk my responsibilities. I screwed up, and I have no one to blame for that but myself."

Jessi frowned at him. "You act like you robbed a bank. We had sex, Lash. Pretty incredible sex, actually. Last I knew, incredible sex wasn't a capital crime."

He lowered his chin and his eyes simultaneously.

"Did you come here thinking you had to do some sort of penance?"

He nodded. "Something like that."

Jessi sighed hard and shook her head. "You're confusing the hell out of me. Just say what you came here to say, all right?"

"All right. I will." He stood up, took her hands in his and drew her to her feet. "Jessi, I'm going to marry you. It's really the only thing I can do to make this right, and I'm willing to do it."

She blinked in shock, feeling as if he'd slapped her. Her jaw dropped. She snapped it closed, drew a breath, resisted the urge to slam him upside the head and gave her own head a shake to clear out the confusion. "Let me get this straight," she managed. "You made a mistake by sleeping with a virgin. You feel guilty about it, and figure you have to pay for your crime. And marrying me is your sentence?''

"W-well, I don't know if I'd put it like that—''

"But that's the way you did put it, Lash. That is *exactly* the way you put it."

"No, I didn't. What I meant was—''

"What about your precious freedom? What about you not being a 'settling-down kind of guy'?''

He shook his head, looking confused. "I'll give all of that up, Jess. Look, I know I broke your heart, and I'm just trying to make it right."

"*You* broke *my* heart?'' She blinked up at him, then shook her head and turned to pace away. "Gee, it's the first I've heard of it. But thanks for being willing to sacrifice your life out of guilt, and thanks all to hell for being so very generous in offering to do hard time as my husband to make up for it." She whirled on him, hands clenched into trembling fists at her sides. "I oughtta knock your teeth out, you arrogant, pious, self-righteous snake in the grass!"

"I— I—''

"What makes you think for one minute that Jessi Brand would even *consider* marrying a man who sees her as some kind of punishment? Hmm? What makes you think I'd settle for a man who doesn't love me?''

"But, Jessi, I thought—''

"Well, here's your answer, Lash. I wouldn't marry you if you were the last mammal on the planet. I wouldn't marry you if I were ninety years old and still single. I wouldn't marry you if you got down on your damned knees and begged! Now get the hell out of here before I throw you out.''

He took a step toward her. "Jessi, you don't understand what I—"

"Get out!" Her hand closed around the nearest item handy, which turned out to be a fake Aztec vase, and she hurled it at his head. He ducked, and the vase smashed against the wall beyond him. Jessi spun around in search of more ammunition.

"Just think about it, okay?" he said, heading for the door. "Just give yourself some time to calm down and think—"

A second item sailed over his head, a porcelain figurine of some sort. It sailed by him and smashed into the door. He yanked the door open before all the pieces hit the floor, ducked outside and closed it fast behind him.

"Damn you, Lash," she muttered. Then she sank onto the sofa, and lowered her head into her hands. To think she'd believed such an insensitive, dense S.O.B. could actually fall in love with her. God, she'd been an idiot!

She shook her head and refused to allow the tears burning in her eyes to spill over. "You're the one who's the fool, Lash," she whispered. "You could have had the best damned woman north of the Rio Grande, and you blew it, you jerk. You blew it all to hell."

Lash sat in his rather battered convertible, feeling as if he'd just been through a war, but with no idea what the fight was about, or on which side he was supposed to be fighting.

What the hell was wrong with Jessi? Why wasn't she glad he wanted to do the right thing by her?

Hell. Nothing was going the way he'd expected.

Even his own feelings were out of whack. He ought to be relieved that she'd let him off the hook. Relieved that he wouldn't have to make the supreme sacrifice after all, that he could continue with the freewheeling life-style he held so dear. That she wouldn't marry him if he was the last mammal on the planet.

So why was he feeling such an acute sense of disappointment? And why was he getting this urge to go back there and try everything he could think of to make her change her mind?

This was insane. Made no sense whatsoever. None. She was supposed to melt into his arms, maybe cry a little bit with joy. She was supposed to kiss him and tell him how happy he'd made her, and how miserable she'd been these past few days.

And she *had* been miserable. The rings around her eyes, the weight loss that made her cheeks slightly hollow, the sleepless nights and lack of appetite and fake smile, all pointed to that. But maybe she had some other reason to be upset besides him. Maybe he hadn't broken her little heart after all.

So if he hadn't, then what was wrong?

Jessi went back to the ranch that night. The next day was Sunday, so she didn't expect her construction crew to come around. And it was good to spend the day at home with her family. She felt a little battle-scarred, but maybe wiser than before. And she knew that the way she was feeling was partly her own fault. She'd seduced a man, thinking she could change him.

And that was always a mistake. Hadn't she seen enough talk shows to know that by now? She guessed a woman had to live it to really understand. You can't make someone love you. You can't change a drifter into a devoted husband just by luring him into your bed. It can't happen. Men don't change.

Breakfast was the usual boisterous occasion, with Ethan making a mess of his food, dropping lots of scraps to the floor, where Ol' Blue waited, frowning when the quick cat got to the bits of food before him. He was going to have to mend his lazy ways if he hoped to compete for table scraps with Pedro around.

"Goggy!" Ethan chirped, flailing his hands excitedly and aiming his crumbs at Blue, or so it seemed.

Blue shifted his position so that he was lying under the table beneath Ethan's feet, big brown eyes pleading for sustenance. When Ethan only stared back, the irritated old dog actually barked. Ethan laughed out loud. "Goggy eeet!" He tossed more scraps. Blue caught them as they came down, and it was the cat's turn to look irritated.

"There's more color in your cheeks this morning, Jess," Wes observed. "You feeling better?"

"Sure. It was just a bug. It's practically gone."

He nodded. "Glad to hear it. I was getting worried."

"You guys always worry about me. It's wasted energy. I'm tougher than any of you."

"Hell, Jess," Elliot said, "I'm beginning to believe it. Have you guys seen what she's done to that place of Marisella's?"

"I stopped by there yesterday," Garrett said. "It's looking great."

"I knew you could do it," Chelsea said.

Ben, quiet as always, got up from the table to go into the living room. When he returned, he carried a very large, flat cardboard box with a huge bow on top. He set it in front of Jessi.

"What's this?"

He shrugged. "I got to thinking, if Penny were here, this is exactly what she'd have done. So I did it for her."

Jessi blinked fast, so she wouldn't cry. Poor Ben was still hurting so much. And there didn't seem to be any way she could help him get over the pain of losing his young wife. It was always in his eyes, even on those rare occasions when he smiled.

She took the cover from the box and set in on the floor beside her chair. Then she pawed aside the tissue paper. Inside was a hand-tooled hardwood sign, gleaming with layers of painstakingly applied shellac. It was arched in exactly the shape of the big wooden arch over the ranch's driveway, and the lettering was the same, as well. The words Texas Brand curved across the arched top, and in the area beneath it read Veterinary Clinic. Another line below the first two read, "Jessica Lynn Brand, D.V.M."

Jessi's eyes brimmed and the tears she'd been battling spilled over. "Oh, Ben…"

"I figured if you couldn't have the clinic here on the ranch, you could take a little bit of the Texas Brand to the clinic."

She set the precious gift aside, pushed her chair away from the table and slung her arms around her big blond brother, hugging him hard. "You're the sweetest man alive, Ben."

"Just love my kid sister, is all," he said.

She stepped away from him, searching his sad eyes, and wishing with everything in her that he could find the happiness he so richly deserved. Someday, maybe… "I love you, too," she told him. "Thanks, Ben."

He nodded, and reached for his hat. "Gotta go," he

said, and headed out the door. Same as he'd done every Sunday since he came back from his year of solitude in the hills of Tennessee. He spent Sunday mornings at the cemetery where his young wife was buried. It was enough to make a grown woman bawl like a newborn calf.

Wes rose, breaking into her thoughts. "I'm headed out, too. Be back in time for chores tonight." He didn't offer any explanations, just left.

"Now what is he up to?" Garrett asked.

Chelsea tilted her head. "I know, but if you tell him I found out, I'll wring your neck." She sat back and sipped her coffee. "He's been spending time out near the Comanche reservation where he was born."

"Really?" Jessi was surprised. She'd never known Wes to show any inkling at all toward getting in touch with his roots on his mother's side. Hell, he'd lived here on the ranch since he was seven. Maria Brand had treated him as if he were her own child, and never once let him feel an outcast just because he was the product of her husband's infidelity.

Chelsea nodded and slipped a hand over Garrett's. "Don't be upset by this. I've said all along that Wes has something missing inside him, and you know as well as I do he needs to do this."

Garrett nodded. "I'm not upset, darlin'. Just amazed at how right you always manage to be." He leaned over and kissed her. "C'mon, Elliot. Looks like it's you and me riding the fencelines this morning."

Elliot wolfed down another sausage patty on his way out the door, slamming his hat on with his free hand. "Fine by me," he said around the food. "I can practice roping a few head."

Garrett shook his head in mock exasperation, with

just a hint of indulgence, and the two left. Minutes later, Jessi heard the gentle slapping of hooves as they rode away. She started clearing the table, with Pedro rubbing around her calves in a shameless effort to extract more scraps.

"So what's really been wrong with you these past few days?" Chelsea asked.

Jessi drew a breath. She'd known this was coming. But she wasn't going to tell Chelsea about the very slim chance she might be pregnant, because it was so very unlikely that there was no sense in worrying her. "I don't know," she said, instead. "I guess Lash just isn't the man I thought he was."

"Disappointed you, did he?"

Jess nodded.

"I know how that goes. Hell, I'll never forget your big lug of a brother trying to romance me just to keep me from leaving here and putting myself in danger. When I found out, I was sure that everything he was pretending to feel for me was only a part of his act. Of course, at the time, he thought so, too."

Jessi tilted her head. "Is there supposed to be some lesson in this tale for me?"

"Yeah," Chelsea said. "Men can be pretty stupid when it comes to matters of the heart, Jess. They can tell themselves all sorts of things, make up all kinds of excuses for the feelings they just don't understand. But in the end, they figure it out." She frowned. "Sometimes it takes clubbing them over the head, though."

Jessi laughed out loud for the first time in days. Clubbing Lash over the head held a wonderful appeal to her right now.

Their laughter was interrupted by a knock at the screen door, and to Jessi's surprise, Ol' Blue got up from his nap under the kitchen table, faced the door and growled.

On the other side of the door, a bulky man with beady little black button eyes and a bit of a paunch around his middle peered at them. "This the Brand ranch?"

"Sure is," Jessi replied, moving to the door, but not opening it. She didn't want Blue to up and bite the stranger. "Can I help you with something?"

"I sure hope so." He smiled broadly. "Name's Zane, ma'am. I'm Lash Monroe's brother...well, foster brother, anyway."

Lash's foster brother? Jessi returned the smile and stepped out onto the porch, closing the door on the still-snarling hound dog and taking the beefy hand the man offered. "Well, I'll be. Lash never mentioned you. I'm Jessi Brand, Lash's...friend." She stumbled a little over the last word, then gave her head a shake and motioned the man to take a seat on the porch swing. "Can I get you a drink? Coffee, iced tea?"

"No, no, I'm fine, but thank you kindly. I was hoping to find Lash. Been a long time, you know."

No, she didn't know. "Sorry, but he's not here today. He's in town, probably at the sheriff's office. You can check there. Or...I could call him and tell him you're here."

"Naw, no need to bother him if he's busy. You say he's with the sheriff? That Lash. He always was one to get himself in trouble. I should have known he'd be in hot water."

Jessi blinked and, despite her anger at Lash, felt her hackles rise just a little. "Lash isn't in any trouble, Mr....uh...Zane. He's working as a deputy." Had her chin lifted just a little as she said that? "He's helping my brother Garrett—Garrett's the sheriff here—to solve a rash of cattle rustling in the area.''

"Well, I'll be! Lash is a lawman? Imagine that.''

"Doesn't seem so hard to imagine to me,'' she muttered.

The man chuckled. "Well, you didn't know him when I did. Close as two peas in a pod, we were. I adored the little runt. Damn, I'm sorry I missed him, but I just found out he was in town, and I couldn't resist the urge to stop by and find out what he's been doin' with himself. Heard he was working here on the ranch.''

"Well, yes, he does that, too.''

"Busy fella,'' Zane said. He stretched his arms along the back of the porch swing while gazing out at the horizon. "This looks like a mighty big spread. You run many cattle?''

"A thousand head,'' she said proudly.

"Well, now, I musta missed all those cattle driving in. I seen only a dozen or so heifers out in the pasture.'' He pointed. "Sure is a beautiful ranch, though.''

He was a friendly, talkative sort, Jessi decided. And hell, so long as he was Lash's brother, she figured she ought to be friendly.

"A thousand head,'' he said, sighing and shaking his head in wonder. "Now that is one sight I'd give just about anything to see. Always wanted a ranch, myself. Maybe someday...''

"Do you ride, Zane?'' she asked impulsively.

He smiled brightly, and gave her a nod.

It was a nice long chat they had as they rode side by side at a comfortable walk, and Jessi showed Zane around the ranch. He was so very polite, and genuinely interested in everything about the ranch, and her brothers, and her clinic. He seemed to hang on her every word, asking lots of questions, wanting to know everything about his brother's life of late. Jessi wondered why Lash had never mentioned him before.

When they finally said goodbye at the front porch, Jessi found herself inviting Zane back to visit anytime. She wished later that he'd talked more about himself and his childhood with Lash. Maybe she could have learned more about Zane's pigheaded foster brother that way. Ah, well, she thought, waving to the stranger as he drove away, maybe next time he visited he'd volunteer more.

He'd asked her to dinner. Flattering, but not a very attractive offer. She'd eased out of it with a noncommittal reply. But maybe if she accepted, she could get him to talk about Lash. Maybe she could figure out just why it was he was so damned hung up on freedom, and roaming, and so deathly against being tied down by anything or anyone.

Maybe she ought to go ahead and have that dinner with Zane. She'd think on it. It irked her to realize, that despite her claims to the contrary, she still hadn't given up on her hopelessly thickheaded drifter.

Not by a long shot.

Chapter 9

Lash leaned over the polished hardwood bar, nursing a beer and a headache brought on by thinking too much. He couldn't figure Jessi out, and he'd decided it was high time he quit trying. She didn't want him. Fine. He'd just consider it a narrow escape and get on with his life. The best thing to do, the way he figured it, was to avoid her as best he could until he and Garrett wrapped up this investigation, and then get the hell outta Dodge.

Unfortunately, all of those things were easier to decide, than to actually do. He still wanted her. Every time he saw that girl, he ached with wanting her. The memory of that one time he'd been with her haunted him. Bits of it, feelings, sensations, hearing her heartfelt declaration of love, in a voice rough and loud with passion, the way she'd touched him, the way it had *felt* to be inside her—all of it—drifted through his dreams at night, and kept his mind so stirred up by day that he couldn't think about anything else.

The longer he stayed away from her, the more he missed her. And yet, he avoided her. Because he didn't understand any of this. And to tell the truth, it scared him.

Garrett had told him Jessi was spending Sunday at the ranch when Lash stopped in that morning. He'd run into Garrett out near the pasture, saddling up to ride the fencelines, so he'd decided to avoid the house. He'd helped with the various tasks that needed doing around the place, and then he'd headed back into town, never once venturing near the house, where he might run into her. He didn't want a repeat of the other night being played out in front of her family. Vases sailing at his head might make them start asking questions.

Jessi had spent today at the clinic. Yeah, okay, he'd been keeping track of her. Avoiding her like the plague but for some reason unable to stop watching her without her knowing it. He was behaving like some crazed stalker, and he couldn't for the life of him figure out why he had this morbid need to look at her all the time. It only made him crave her touch all the more.

God, he couldn't believe how very badly he wanted to kiss her again!

Lash had seen the contractors packing up their gear, and most of them had left by noon today, with one or two men remaining to finish up with details. And then, early tonight, there had been a van backed up to the door with the name of a veterinary supply company painted on the side.

The garage no longer resembled a garage. The overhead door was gone, replaced by a wide front window. The smaller door served as the main entrance. Lash was dying to see the inside of the place, but didn't figure that would be a very good idea. But he had managed to come up with excuses to drive by often enough to keep tabs on its progress. And on Jessi.

He couldn't help but be worried about her. In fact, his concern for her was on his mind almost as much as his desire for her. He knew something was bothering her, something besides the fact that she'd decided he was the scum of the earth, that is. He'd thought it was a broken heart, but if it wasn't that, then it must be something else. And he was still—vainly, perhaps—convinced that whatever it was, it was his fault. The idea that he might have nothing to do with her odd mood bothered him too much even to consider.

He took another sip from the foamy mug, and nearly choked on the brew when a voice from the past drifted over the jukebox's country twang and the clink of glasses. "Well, well, if it isn't my kid brother."

Very carefully, Lash set the beer down, centering it in the damp ring it had left on the hardwood. He turned, telling himself that his worst nightmare from childhood hadn't just caught up with him. But it had. Zane smiled at him, but the grin didn't meet his piggish eyes as he sauntered forward to take a stool beside him.

"Been a long time, Lash."

"Not long enough," Lash said, and there was a prickling sensation dancing along his nape.

"Oh, hell, can't we let bygones be bygones, brother?"

"You're no brother of mine."

Zane shook his head slowly, clicking his tongue. "Crying shame, that. 'Cause let me tell you, Lash, that little kitten over at the Texas Brand would make one fantasy of a sister-in-law."

Lash's fists clenched, where they rested on the bar. "Maybe you'd like to tell me what the hell you're talking about?"

"Why, Miss Jessi Brand, of course. She gets that look in her eyes when your name comes up. Then again, you always did have a way with the females."

Teeth grated, Lash willed himself calm. "So, you've met Jessi."

"Ah, well, yeah, I suppose you would be curious about that, now wouldn't you? Smart fella. I spent several hours with her Sunday morning, just sitting in that porch swing beside her and chatting like old pals. And then that sweet little thing invited me to go ridin' with her, and of course, being a red-blooded male, I took her up on it."

Lash swallowed the sand in his throat.

"I always did have a knack for taking things that were yours, little brother."

"What the hell are you doing here, Zane?"

Zane just shrugged. "Missed you. Wanted to catch up. But you don't need to say much, because that pretty little thing filled me in nice and thorough. We rode all over that sprawling ranch of hers...all alone. Just the two of us. 'Course, she did most of the talking. I was mostly enjoying the view."

Lash stood up fast.

Zane held up his hands. "Now, Lash, no need getting all excited. I didn't lay a finger on that pretty little thing." He tilted his head. "Not yet, anyway. Have you?"

"You're slime, Zane, and I'm going to have to kick your ass for that. But before I do, maybe you'd like to tell me just what the hell you're really doing here. More importantly, are you gonna get out of town under

your own steam, or am I gonna have to see to it that
you leave in a pine box?''

Zane smiled, got to his feet, and swallowed the shot
he'd ordered in one quick gulp. "I'm here on business.
Won't be for long. A few more days at most. So do
you have any claims on the woman or not, Lash? I
really need to know, 'cause you know, I think she
kinda likes me. I asked her out—dinner's how I put it,
but we both know it isn't food I'm gonna be devouring.
Man, I can't remember when I've seen such a sweet,
tight little—''

Lash's fist flashed out, connected with Zane's face,
and the larger man rocked backward, falling over his
stool to the floor. He gave his head a shake, rubbed his
nose, then looked up at Lash and smiled. "Then you
do return the lady's feelings. Hell, all the more reason
for me to show her how a real man would feel when
he—''

Lash gripped the bastard's shirt and hauled him to
his feet. "Don't let me catch you anywhere near her,
you son of a bitch!''

Grinning, Zane shook his head. Then he sucker-
punched Lash in the belly. Lash released him and doubled over, but came up swinging.

"Sheriff Brand! Hurry up! There's trouble at La Cucaracha!''

Garrett shot up from behind the desk, grabbed his
hat and headed out. He'd been working late in the office, again. This damned case was baffling him. He'd
sent Lash home early, mostly because it was fairly obvious his mind wasn't on his work, anyway. Something
was bothering his deputy. Lash wasn't himself at all.

Seemed distracted and brooding all the time. But Garrett supposed it was none of his business.

Well, maybe there was a silver lining in his being stuck here at the office late, yet again. He'd been close by to see to whatever little crisis had cropped up at the local bar.

He strode down the cracked sidewalk, ignoring the shiny new pickup, nearly identical to his old one, that sat outside his office. The insurance company had finally come through. And Garrett didn't miss the little toaster-car one bit. His long strides ate up the distance between his office and the bar. Then he walked inside the smoky room, heard glass smashing, and looked up to see his deputy holding his own in a brawling match with a man twice his size. Both men looked pretty bad, though, and Garrett shook his head slowly, battling a smile of admiration for Lash's spunk. He headed over to break it up.

He damn near took a fist to the head for his trouble. Ducking fast, Garrett spun around and caught the stranger's fist in his hand. "Care to explain what you're doing using my deputy for a punching bag, stranger?"

The big guy stopped, glanced down at the badge pinned to Garrett's chest and lowered his hand, panting, sweaty and bleeding from several locations on his face. Behind him, Lash stood in much the same condition. "He started it," the big guy said. "You ask anybody in here, Sheriff. Lash here hit me first."

Brows lifted, Garrett glanced at Freddy Ortega for confirmation.

The bartender piped up. "Yup, Garrett. I seen it all. Lash started the whole fight." He stood behind mahogany ridge, wiping glasses with a towel and acting utterly unruffled. "Right after this 'ere stranger insulted your baby sister, wasn't it?" he asked the beefy man.

Garrett's brows lifted. "My sister, huh? Well, hell, didn't you know that's illegal here in Quinn?"

"Wha—"

"Hey, everybody, tell this fella about that law. How's it go again? Article four, section two. Hell, I oughtta have it memorized, seeing as how I just wrote it myself, right this minute." He spun the man around, twisting one arm behind his back, then pulled the other one to join it and snapped on a pair of handcuffs. Paul Loomis was sitting at a corner table, fighting a smile, and Garrett motioned to him. "Paul, you mind taking this pile of garbage on over to the jail and shoving him in a cell for me? I need to talk with my deputy."

Paul touched the brim of his hat, and got to his feet, gripping the guy's elbow and leading him out of the bar. The big guy didn't resist, just sent a menacing glance over his shoulder at Lash. Then he glanced at Garrett. "You can't hold me for anything more serious than disorderly conduct," he called.

"Try assaulting an officer," Garrett told him as he was marched out the door.

As if on cue, the murmur of conversation and the clinking of ice in glasses resumed. Garrett turned to Lash. "That forehead of yours will need stitching. You can tell me about this little incident on the way to Doc's office."

"Doc's out of town tonight," the bartender called. "Best take him on over to the clinic. Jessi's stitched up her brothers often enough to take care of that little cut."

A chuckle went up from the patrons close enough to

hear. "Been hanging around them Brands so long, he's getting to be just like 'em," one said.

"Yep. Durn fool stranger ought to know better than to mess with that bunch." More hearty laughter followed as Garrett led Lash outside and along the sidewalk to the new pickup in front of the office.

Lash argued, but it did little good. He could feel the blood trickling down the side of his face from the deep cut just above his eyebrow, and he knew it needed stitching, but damn, he didn't want to see Jessi. Not like this.

Garrett took him inside the little house, since the clinic was still a jumble of unpacked boxes and equipment. He hollered for Jess, and she came out of the living room, took one look at Lash and scowled.

"Garrett, how could you!" she cried.

Garrett frowned, and Lash caught Jessi's eyes and shook his head slightly.

"How could I what?" Garrett asked.

Jessi's eyes narrowed. "You didn't do that to him?" she asked her brother.

Garrett blinked. "'Course not. Why would I—"

"What happened?"

"Some stranger insulted you, little sister. And since there were no Brand brothers at the bar to defend your honor, Lash stood in for us."

Jessi's eyes widened, and her hard expression softened as she searched Lash's face. He felt the touch of those big brown eyes on him. "You did that?" And she smiled just a little, and reached out to brush the hair away from the cut on his forehead. "You got this defending me?"

Lash nodded, then winced as Garrett slapped a hand

on his shoulder. "I gotta go see to my prisoner. You take care of that gash for him, okay, Jess?"

"Yeah," she muttered, and damned if she didn't look a little worried as she took Lash by the arm and led him to a kitchen chair.

Garrett hurried out. Lash had told him who Zane was on the way over. Now, he supposed, he'd have to repeat the whole damned story to Jessi.

She leaned over him, pushing the hair away from his forehead and examining the cut. She was touching him. Damn, but he liked her touching him. "Are you all right?" she asked him.

"Fine."

"You sure? No, just stay there. Sit. I'll get my bag. You look awful."

"Zane looks a lot worse than I do." It was male pride that made him say it, but he didn't take it back.

She had turned to retrieve her bag, but she paused with her back to him. While he could no longer see her face, he *felt* the warmth drain out of her. She wasn't soft toward him now. That straight spine spoke volumes. "You were duking it out with your *brother?*"

"Make no mistake, Jessi, that slimebag is no brother of mine."

"I can't believe you would beat up your own brother!" She fetched the bag and returned, tearing open alcohol wipes with her teeth. Then she began cleaning the cut, and it stung like crazy. Which was good, because it kept him from enjoying having her hands on him so much. Lash sucked in a breath and pulled his head away, but she caught it in one hand and held him still. "Why did you do it?" she asked. "Just because he asked me out to dinner?"

"He really did that?"

"Sure he did. And what's it to you, anyway?"

Lash shook his head, catching her arm in one hand and stilling her. "You stay away from him, Jessi." He stared up into her eyes, making his own hard and his voice firm. "He's trouble, you understand? Don't you go anywhere near him."

"I'll go near him if I want to, Lash Monroe. Since when did you decide you were one of my brothers? Don't I have enough men trying to run my life without you joining the ranks?"

"But, Jessi—"

"No buts. You don't want me for yourself, but you don't want any other man anywhere near me, either, is that it?"

"What the hell do you mean, I don't want you for myself? I offered to marry you, didn't I?"

"Lucky me," she snapped.

"Jessi, Zane's a bastard. He only wants you because of me," he stated.

Jessi stepped away, blinking down at him as if she'd never seen him before, and Lash knew he'd said the wrong thing, yet again.

"Gee, thanks for the compliment. I don't suppose it's even in the realm of reason that he might want me because of me, is it? No, of course not. So tell me, Lash, what is it about you that makes your brother— I'm sorry, *foster* brother—want me?"

"Because making me miserable is his reason for living," he said, shaking his head slowly. "Always has been. He thinks you mean something to me, so—"

"Oh. Well, then, there's no problem, is there? Because I *don't* mean anything to you. He's dead wrong about that. No harm, no foul, Lash. You beat him up for nothing. All you had to do was tell him that I was no more to you than a roll around the garage floor, and he'd have left me alone.''

"Dammit, Jessi, you know that isn't the way it is!''

She tilted her head, staring down at him. ''No? Suppose you tell me just what way it is, then, 'cause I sure as hell don't know.''

"I...I don't know. I don't know, Jessi. If I did...I'd tell you. But...hell, if nothing else, we're friends, aren't we? Or, hell, I thought we were.''

Her eyes fell closed, but not before he saw the little flash of pain that came into them. Hell, he'd gone and hurt her again.

"I got plenty of friends, Lash. I don't need another one.''

"Jess—''

"Just sit still. This is gonna hurt.''

He had no doubt she intended to make sure it hurt as much as possible. He grated his teeth while she readied some needles and silk thread.

"He came to the ranch, didn't he?'' he asked, to distract himself from the inevitable. Not the pain of the stitches she administered, but the pain of wanting nothing more than to pull her into his arms and kiss her senseless. Of wanting to scoop her up into his arms and carry her into that bedroom and love her...

Love her?

"Sure he did,'' she was saying as he blinked in shock and tried real hard to figure out why such a turn of phrase would pop into his mind. ''Sunday. We had a nice talk.''

"About what?''

She shrugged. ''Nothing in particular. Ranching, cattle. He didn't tell me any of your secrets, Lash. Maybe he'll get to that when I have dinner with him, though.''

"Dammit, Jessi, I told you—"

She pinched the edges of the cut together and jabbed the needle through his flesh. He winced. "I don't give a damn what you told me," she said. She tied off the stitch, snipped the thread with a tiny pair of scissors, then prepared to install another.

He looked up and met her eyes. "Don't do this," he whispered.

"Give me one good reason why I shouldn't." And there was something in her eyes, something that should have told him what he was supposed to say, but he couldn't read it quite clearly.

He searched his mind, sought for the right words to convince her. "He'll hurt you," he said. "I don't want to see you get hurt, Jess."

Her chin lowered, and her eyes fell away from his. "Wrong reason," she told him, and then she put in another stitch.

A week later, she was still every bit as miserable as she'd been the night she stitched up Lash. He had avoided her as if she carried some deadly plague, and she told herself she didn't really care. She did, though. She must be a hundred kinds of fool, but she did. She hadn't had dinner with Zane, who'd spent one long night in Garrett's jail before her big brother turned him loose and told him he had one week to get out of town. She might have gone, if she'd had the time, just to see if it would make Lash realize that he belonged with her. But with the clinic coming together so fast, there hadn't been a free night yet. And today was her grand opening.

Chelsea had been helping her plan for this all week long. Lord knew she had plenty of time on her hands,

what with Garrett so busy trying to track down the
rustlers. There hadn't been another incident all week,
and Jessi was of the opinion that the creeps had left to
go prey on some other cow town, but her stubborn
brother refused to let it go.

Monday morning came far too early. But Jessi
couldn't have slept anyway, it being the biggest day of
her life and all. She dressed quickly, and drove her
smoke-belching pickup over to the clinic. The deco-
rations were already in place. She and Chelsea had
done all of that last night. Balloons and streamers
danced in the early-morning breeze. Picnic tables lined
the lawn out front, and that beautiful sign Ben had
given her hung proudly over the clinic's front door.
Jessi parked in the driveway, and walked slowly past
the house, unlocked her clinic and stepped inside to
take it in. Her dream come true.

The reception area was lined with chairs and a potted
plant Elliot had brought over. A wide counter sectioned
off the area where the receptionist would work, once
she hired one. Meanwhile, she'd handle that job on her
own. The phones were hooked up, lights had been installed, everything was done.

She had two treatment rooms, their cabinets stocked
with supplies. She had a surgery room, with sterile instruments at the ready. She had a kennel area with pens
of various sizes for overnight guests. And she had an
office of her very own. Situated right on the spot where
she and Lash had made love. Some demon had com-
pelled her to put her own private space there, not wanting to share it with anyone else. It was her own precious memory, and she'd keep it here, safe.

Damn the man.

Jessi had also had a big metal box installed in the

old pickup truck's bed, its dozens of drawers and compartments filled with still more tools of her trade. Most of her work would be with large animals, and it would be done from that truck, at the homes of her neighbors. But there would be plenty of business here, as well. Cats and dogs, mostly, she figured. And it would all begin today. In a couple of hours, half the town would start showing up with food for the celebration picnic. Freddy from La Cucaracha had promised to bring a keg of beer over. Chelsea would be hauling in the salads and casseroles she'd made. People would come to admire the clinic while eating, drinking and making merry.

She really ought to be happy. She really, really ought to be.

But there were a couple of things still undermining her happiness. One was Lash's indifference, of course. That was the main one. The second was the home pregnancy test she had tucked away in the bottom of her purse. She hadn't bought it at the local drugstore. She'd gone out of town for it yesterday, because Lord knew how tongues would have wagged around here if she was seen making such a purchase. Garrett would have known about it within the hour, she'd bet.

She hadn't used the thing yet. Hadn't been able to work up the nerve last night, and she'd told herself that she'd just go ahead and enjoy today's festivities first. That she'd rather not know the results until later. She'd been wrong, of course. She was only going to worry until she had the answer. It was cowardice that was keeping her from doing it right now and having it over with.

"The place looks great."

She sucked in a breath and turned fast. Lash leaned

in the doorway, studying her. She felt the same old rush she always felt when he looked at her that way. Scanning her, head to toe, and maybe liking what he saw. At least he hadn't gone back to looking at her as a kid. Maybe he was even remembering...how it had been. She hoped he was. She hoped he wanted her so badly his teeth ached with it.

"And so do you," he said, finally. "Look great, that is."

She didn't. She knew damn well she didn't. She was pale and tired-looking, and she couldn't seem to keep those dark circles under her eyes from growing on a daily basis. But all that would change once she used the stupid kit in her purse and got the negative result she knew was inevitable. It was the not knowing that was getting to her. That kernel of doubt.

"So you showed up after all," she said.

"What, you didn't think I would?"

"The way you've been avoiding me, Lash, I figured you'd hole up in that stupid apartment of yours and stay there until the festivities were over and done."

He shrugged, his gaze falling away from her accusing one. "I thought it was for the best."

"Sure you did."

"Every time I see you, it seems like I say something that hurts you. I don't like hurting you, Jess."

"You don't care one way or the other, and we both know it."

"You're dead wrong on that score. Hell, I proposed to you, didn't I?"

"Yeah. As penance. It's real flattering to be considered the wages of sin, you know that? All that ol' Pharaoh got for his crimes against Israel were plagues and locusts. But you—you must be a far worse sinner than he was to think God would sentence you to something as horrible as marriage.'' She turned away from him as she spoke, but felt his hand on her shoulder a second later, pulling her around to face him again.

''If it sounded that way to you, Jess, then I'm sorry. It's not how I meant it.''

''No? Suppose you tell me just how you did mean it, then?''

He stared down into her eyes, and she could see the confusion in his. His hand eased on her arm, his palm rubbing the spot he'd been gripping before. ''You're like that apple must have been to Adam, you know that?''

''Lord, but we're full of biblical references today, aren't we?'' Her words lacked the acid she'd intended them to carry. It was the look in his eyes that was making them come out soft and whispery, instead of harsh and condemning.

''I still want you, Jess. Dammit, I know it's wrong. Your brothers have treated me like family. They trust me, and I'm surely gonna burn in hell for it, but I can't stop thinking about you...the way it was with us that night...''

His eyes closed. She saw the battle he was waging, saw the guilt in the little lines between his brows and at the corners of his mouth. And, like an idiot, she leaned up, and pressed her lips to his. Lash shuddered, and his arms slipped around her waist. He pulled her close, tight to his body, and he kissed her, long and slow. And Jessi thought there might still be a chance for them. The damn fool had to care a little. He must. He couldn't kiss her like this, hold her like this, if he didn't. He was just too dense to realize it, was all. And right now she didn't know whether to start tearing off his clothes, or smack him upside the head.

His hips arched against hers, and she leaned toward him. She could smack him later.

God, he tasted good. And his arms around her felt right. Strong and sure, as if they belonged there. Always. He tasted her with his tongue, threaded his fingers in her hair to tip her head to just the right angle as he fed from her mouth.

And then a horn sounded, followed shortly by the slamming of a car door. Lash straightened and moved away from her, albeit reluctantly. And as he did, he looked at her, confusion clouding his eyes. She just barely resisted the urge to say, "You're falling in love with me, you big dope. Don't worry, it's not fatal." But she said nothing. Because she wasn't at all sure that was the case, and besides, even if it was, he was going to have to realize it on his own.

The door opened and Garrett stepped inside. He stared from one to the other, and frowned.

"You're early," Jessi said, because it was the only thing that popped into her head to say.

"I'm right on time," he replied. "Apparently Lash is the one who's early."

"He just got here." She dragged her gaze from Lash's, and battled the insane surge of hope she felt trying to wash her sense of reality down the drain.

"Well, people are startin' to arrive, Jess. You ought to be outside to greet 'em."

She plastered a smile on her face and nodded at her brother. Then she went outside to join the festivities. As soon as she exited the clinic, she was hit full in the face with the cheerful noise of a mariachi band. They struck up the second they saw her. She smiled. A person couldn't help but smile when a mariachi band was playing in her face. And she turned to Garrett, blinking in surprise. "Where'd they come from?"

Garrett shrugged. So she glanced to her right, where Lash stood, looking slightly sheepish. "Surprise," he muttered.

Her heart felt as if some big hand were squeezing it. "I didn't know you had it in you to be so sweet," she said. "I can't believe you did this."

"Neither can I," Garrett put in, but the suspicion in his tone didn't break the hold Jessi's gaze had on Lash's, and if he saw the tiny tear that came to her eye, well, she couldn't help it, could she? It was a sweet gesture that touched her—probably a little more than it should.

And maybe she was reading more into his actions today than she should, but it seemed that maybe his heart was finally giving his brain a wake-up call.

Lash reached out to take her hand in his, and as soon as he did, the mariachis changed to a slower tune. And then he actually pulled her into his arms, and danced with her. Right there on the lawn in front of her clinic, with the entire town, and all her brothers, watching. He danced with her, and he leaned close and whispered in her ear, "Don't give up on me just yet, okay, Jessi?"

She tried to swallow and couldn't. "If you think I'm planning to give up, you don't know me very well."

He spun her around the grass until Freddy Ortega cut in. After that she danced with each of the Loomis boys, and then her brothers, except for Elliot, because Elliot hated to dance. And then she danced with Lash again.

The food was put out on the tables, and the music ended as everyone headed that way to eat. And Lash sat beside her during that picnic lunch. As if he belonged there. As if they were a couple or something.

Lord, if he was getting her hopes up like this only to let her down again, she'd never forgive him. Or herself. She had to be realistic here. She had to remember that he felt strongly about marrying her because he'd taken her virginity. And she'd turned him down, so maybe all of this was just his attempt at getting her to change her mind. So he could do the right thing and clear his conscience.

Or maybe…just maybe…he was falling in love with her after all.

It might not mean anything at all, this attention he was suddenly paying her. She told herself that over and over. But for some reason, she just couldn't quite make herself believe it.

At any rate, the party itself was a huge success. The entire town turned out. But Jessi noted one absence that disappointed her right to the toes of her boots. She'd made a point of inviting Zane to this event, having made up her mind that even a foster brother was a brother of sorts. He was the only family Lash had, so far as she knew. And Jessi felt strongly that no family should remain estranged when there was a Brand around to help fix things. She'd run into Zane in town one day, and she'd told him all about the party, talked it up as big as she could, hoping to entice him to attend so that she could try to help him and Lash patch things up at long last. They'd obviously been estranged for quite a while now. Too long, in Jessi's opinion.

She could just picture it all so clearly in her mind. The joyful reunion. The manly hug. Lash's undying gratitude to her for intervening and saving his relationship with Zane after all these years.

She sighed, and kept watching each new group of people that arrived, looking for Lash's foster brother. But Zane never showed. And it wasn't until they all returned to the ranch much later that night that she finally understood exactly why.

The worst part was, she had no one to blame but herself.

Chapter 10

Lash knew something was wrong before he even hopped out of his car. It was obvious. Garrett's pickup had pulled in ahead of him, and Jessi's rolled in behind. And one by one they piled out of the vehicles and stood there, shaking their heads, brows furrowed in blatant confusion and dawning understanding. The barn doors were wide open, the gate to the south pasture was gaping, and the ground was scarred by tire tracks. Lash just stood there for a moment, gaping in disbelief as his eyes picked out the trail of flattened grass that led as far as the eye could see, without veering once, all the way to the pasture where the young stock grazed. Only he had a feeling they weren't grazing there now.

Jessi raced past him as her brothers swore in turns. It seemed to take the rest of them a second longer to convince their bodies to move. Chelsea—with little Ethan anchored on her hip—and the boys followed where Jessi led, and stood around the spot where she crouched.

"Dual tires," Jessi muttered. "Semis, and more than one. Been gone for at least a couple of hours by now. Maybe longer."

Wes swiped his black Stetson from his head and slammed it against his thigh. "Damn it straight to hell! Look at those tracks! It's like they knew exactly where they were going."

"More than that," Garrett said. "They knew exactly when we'd all be away from the ranch at the same time. I mean, come on. They drove right past the house, bold as brass. They wouldn't have done that if they'd thought anyone was home."

"But everyone in town was at the party," Elliot said. "Who could—"

"Not everyone," Jessi put in. And she turned remorseful eyes on Lash, and he knew right then what she was going to say. "I'm really sorry if I'm wrong about this, Lash, but...I think it was your brother."

"Foster brother, and it wouldn't surprise me. I told you he was trouble."

"But what makes you so suspicious of him, Jessi?" Garrett asked.

She closed her pretty eyes and sighed as if her heart was going to break. "God, Garrett, this is all my fault. He came over here last Sunday, all full of questions about the ranch and the cattle—how many head we ran and how the pastures were growing and how big our spread was. I thought he was just curious about us because Lash worked here, but I should have known. Jeez, I was stupid. I told him everything, even took him on a tour of the ranch and showed him the pastures where the beefers graze. Pointed out the young stock, showed off the prize bull…''

"And you told him about the party?" Chelsea asked.

Jessi nodded, then slowly lowered her head. "I thought if I could get him to come to the grand opening, he and Lash might be able to patch things up." She lifted her gaze, meeting his eyes. "I didn't know how bad it was, Lash. I really didn't. I should've kept my nose out of your business. I'm so sorry."

"You were only trying to help," he said. "I should have figured you'd try something like that. Jessi, this isn't your fault. I should have been more clear about Zane when I tried to warn you about him, but I was just too damned jea—" He broke off. Holy cow, he'd nearly said he was jealous. What was wrong with him?

Oh, Lord, it was worse than he'd thought. Now that he considered it, it was true. He actually *had* been jealous.

Jessi pressed her palms to her cheeks and stared out toward the pasture. "Lord, this could ruin us."

Wes put a hand on her shoulder. "Hey, come on, kiddo, we can always mortgage your clinic to recoup the losses." She looked up at him, and he winked. "C'mon, Ben," he said to the big, quiet Brand who just stood musing. "Let's saddle up and see what the damage is."

Ben nodded. "Let's hope those trucks spooked the cattle so that at least a few of them ran off before they could herd them into the trailers."

"Yeah." Wes headed for the house instead of the barns, and when Ben asked why, he said, "Figure we'd better take a couple of shotguns, just in case."

"Make it one," Ben said. "I don't plan to kill a

man unless I have no choice, and if that's the case, my hands are all I need."

Everyone just stared at Ben for a moment, but the shocked reaction passed and was swallowed by the buzz of activity. Lash could hear the phone jangling insistently from inside the house. Chelsea went running off to answer it, the baby bouncing on her hip. Elliot joined Ben and Wes in checking on what cattle remained. And Jessi just stood there, her gorgeous face twisted into a mask of regret. Lash took a step toward her, with every intention of pulling her close to him and holding her and making her feel better any way he could—only to feel Garrett's heavy hand fall on his shoulder.

"She's gonna be just fine, Lash. We need to talk, you and I."

Lash swallowed hard. It almost sounded as if Garrett knew. "I never meant to hurt her," he managed.

Garrett frowned. "It's not your fault this Zane character robbed us blind. He's the one who hurt her—hurt all of us. Hell, Lash, you can't think we'd blame you for this."

A three-hundred-watt bulb flashed on above Lash's head then, and he realized it wasn't Jessi Garrett he wanted to have a talk with him about. It was Zane. He did his best to recover his fumble, and followed Garrett into the house.

Before they got through the door, Chelsea was holding the phone out toward Garrett. "It's Jimmy Rodriguez from the Circle-Bar-T. They got hit, too. Before he called, I heard from the Double Horseshoe. And, Garrett, the machine is blinking like crazy. I'll check the tape, but it looks to me like the bastards wiped out half the county."

Garrett closed his eyes. "Take down the details, dar-lin', and tell Jimmy I'm doing all I can."

Lash grated his teeth. "I might be able to find out something, Garrett, if I can make a few phone calls."

He nodded. "Looks like our line's gonna be tied up all night. And I'm afraid the phones in the office will be just as bad. Let's head over to your place and see what we can turn up."

Lash nodded and turned to Jessi as Garrett headed for his pickup truck. "Jess, honey, you gonna be okay?"

She met his eyes and blinked—maybe at what he'd just called her, because it had surprised him, too, to hear the endearment roll naturally off his tongue. "I'm fine. You go on."

He reached out to enfold her hand in his, squeezed it gently, and turned to join Garrett.

But what they turned up about Zane through the long hours of the night was definitely not good news. Turned out the bully had been a busy boy for the past twenty-odd years. No small-time larceny, either. He'd turned cattle rustling into big business, and he was wanted in five states. Garrett had the FBI fax him the information they had, and the theory the Feds devel-oped was that he was smuggling the stolen cattle by the truckload over the border into Mexico. There the trail ended. No one knew who his Mexican buyer was or where he might be located. The Texas Rangers had an APB out on the big rigs, but if Jessi's tracking skills were as good as she claimed, those trucks were long since over the border.

But Lash had an idea.

"You know, Garrett," he said later as they sat over hot coffee in his apartment, wondering what the hell to do next. "I learned a little bit about this slob, being raised in the same house with him."

"You have my sympathies," Garrett muttered.

"He's a coward," Lash said. "Always loved trouble, but never had the balls to stir it up all by himself. He needed egging on. Needed a few other lowlifes around to show off for, or it wasn't worth the effort. Plus, when it was time to pay the piper, he could always be sure to have a scapegoat."

Garrett was sitting up a little straighter now. "So, you think you know who else might be involved?"

"This might be a long shot, but in those days it was always Jack and Peter who helped him pull his nonsense. Now, Peter's given name was Pedro Gonzales. The preacher—"

"The *preacher?*"

"Our foster father," Lash clarified. "He saw fit to give Pedro a more 'American'-sounding name. But as I recall, Pedro used to like to brag about his relatives in Mexico."

"So it's safe to assume he might have connections there," Garrett said.

"I can make a couple of phone calls."

"To your preacher?"

"No, he's gone now. No doubt thumping Bibles in that big pulpit in the sky, and probably ordering little angels to memorize verses when their wings are wrinkled. But his wife's sister is still living in Illinois, and she always did have a knack for keeping up on the family business."

"Don't tell me," Garrett said, "aunt Kate."

"You got it." Lash picked up the phone and dialed the string of numbers he knew by heart.

* * *

An hour later, Lash was packing his belongings.
Then he slung his bag in the back of his beat-up convertible, thinking that it was almost as if he were drifting on to the next great adventure. Only this time, the
idea didn't appeal to him in the least.

Garrett leaned on the driver's-side door, shaking his
head. "I don't like this, Lash."

"Look, I'm not going to do anything. I'll just check
it out. If Petey inherited his rich uncle's meat-packing
business like aunt Kate says, then chances are that's
where all the cattle are ending up. I'll call you as soon
as I see for myself what's going on."

"You could get in over your head, Lash."

"But you understand it, don't you, Garrett? This is
a family thing. An old grudge between Zane and me
that goes back as far as I can remember. It's my fight,
and I have to settle it on my own."

Garrett scowled, but nodded. "Yeah, I understand."

"I need to ask you a favor, Garrett. And it's a big
one."

Garrett lifted his brows and waited.

"Don't tell Jessi I've left town, and even if she
somehow finds out I'm gone, don't tell her where I
went or why."

Garrett tilted his head. "You're gonna have to explain that one to me, Lash. Now, I been letting a lot
of stuff between you and my sister slide lately, but
this—"

"You know her," Lash said. "You know how she
dives into trouble headfirst, without a thought about her
own safety. Rushes in where angels fear to tread, right?
If she finds out, Garrett, she's liable to decide I need
help and come charging down there after me. And I

don't want her anywhere near my slimebag foster brother. More than that, I just don't want her getting hurt."

Garrett nodded. "All right, you make a good point. I won't tell her. But, Lash, we're going to have to talk about this…this whatever-it-is with you and Jessi—"

"When I get back," he said. "Promise."

Garrett scanned Lash's face, eyes narrowed, but eventually he nodded, and clasped Lash's hand. "Okay. You just be sure you come back in one piece so you can keep that promise."

"I will. And, Garrett, don't tell your brothers about this, either, okay? I don't want one of them doing something foolish, or slipping up and telling Jessi. This is just between you and me."

"You have my word on it. Call me when you get down there. And I mean the minute you get down there, Lash, so you can tell me where you're staying and how I can reach you."

Lash nodded. "Best set a time, so I can be sure you're the one who answers the phone." The thought of having to explain himself to Jessi didn't appeal to him. He wouldn't be any damned good at lying to her. He'd be seeing those big brown eyes in his mind, all hurt and damp and loving.

"Midnight tomorrow?" Garrett asked. "That give you enough time to get down there and find a phone?"

"Midnight tomorrow," Lash repeated. "Thanks, Garrett. For everything."

Garrett stood in the darkness, staring after him, as Lash pulled away.

Jessi couldn't stop pacing back and forth, endlessly, across the front porch. The telephone kept ringing inside, but Chelsea was covering the calls like a pro. Little Ethan was having a much-needed nap. Wes, Elliot and Ben were out checking on the cattle. And Lash was at his place with Garrett, chasing down leads. But they'd been gone quite a while now, and though she squinted into the distance, willing them to show up, there was no sign of them yet.

Lash had squeezed her hand before he left. He'd called her honey.

She gnawed her lower lip and wondered what she was supposed to make of that.

"You okay?" Chelsea asked softly from beyond the screen door. The phone had finally decided to give its ringer a break.

"Restless," Jessi replied. "I think I'm gonna take a drive. Look around."

"Heading south, by any chance?" Chelsea had crossed her arms over her chest and was looking her over thoroughly.

"Just driving. Not tracking rustlers. Hell, Chels, I wouldn't know where to begin."

"If you're not back in an hour, I'll send your brothers looking."

Jessi rolled her eyes. "You're ruthless, you know that?"

Chelsea only smiled and waved Jessi on her way. Jessi jumped into her pickup, then took a shortcut to reach Route 10. Her plan was to head south from there, until she found the most likely bridge for a half-dozen semis to use to cross the Rio Grande. The idea was stupid. There wasn't going to be any sign of the cattle trucks by now. But then again, she wasn't doing any good sitting at home, either. So she bounced and rattled over the dirt-road shortcut, turned onto the paved stretch that would get her to Route 10, then frowned into her rearview mirror.

The car coming up fast behind her looked like— Hell, it didn't just look like it, it was— Lash's old black convertible.

But he was supposed to be back in Quinn with Garrett and— She slammed the door on the thoughts that tried to come to her then. She wouldn't jump to conclusions. It was a bad habit she'd been meaning to break for quite a while, and now seemed like a good time to start. She blew her horn, and watched him in her rearview mirror. He flashed his headlights to let her know he'd recognized her. Okay, time to figure things out. Jessi put on her right turn signal and pulled off onto the shoulder. She watched as Lash did the same.

Then she got out of her truck. They were close to the highway. She could hear the traffic, even see the glow of headlights moving in the distance. But this side road was all but deserted. If a car passed once every half hour, it would be a busy night.

Thrusting her hands into her jeans pockets, she walked back toward Lash's car as he got out. The convertible's top was down. It was a beautiful night for a drive with the wind in your hair, she thought, and wished she'd been riding in there with him.

Lash shut his door and took a step toward her. Then, as if he'd just thought of something, turned to reach into the back seat. Frowning, Jessi saw him quickly toss a jacket over the suitcase that rested there. And her eager footsteps came to a halt.

So this was it. They knew who was behind the rustling, and he and Garrett had probably turned the whole case over to some higher authority. The Texas Rangers or the FBI or someone like that. And now that his job with Garrett was done, Lash was keeping his promise. He was leaving town, just like the drifter he'd claimed to be. He was moving on, just the way he'd warned her he would.

And he hadn't even said goodbye. Probably figured it would be easier on her this way. Hell, he knew she loved him. It wasn't his fault he didn't feel the same.

She was glad she hadn't told him about the damaged condoms, or the home pregnancy test she'd bought. At least he was doing what he wanted to do. At least this was honest. Real. Not that obligatory thing he was trying to foist on her before. Not his stupid, overdeveloped sense of duty.

She sighed as he turned to face her again. Hell, if this was the way he wanted to do it, fine. Let him go on thinking she hadn't seen that suitcase in the back. Let him slip away without having to face her and tell her he was leaving. What did she care?

She plastered a smile on her face and started walking toward him again, stopping when they stood toe-to-toe.

"What're you doing out here, Jessi?" he asked her, his voice low and soft. And his eyes were probing hers, seeing way more than she wanted them to.

"Just felt like a drive," she said. "You?"

"Following up on a lead. It shouldn't take long."

She closed her eyes, because his white lie hurt so much he'd have to see it reflected there. "Sure," she said. "A lead."

"I'm glad I ran into you, though," he told her. "We have to talk, Jess."

To say goodbye? she wondered. Was he going to tell her how he was leaving tonight, and how he'd probably never see her again?

Lash took her hand in his, and pulled her with him

as he walked back to his car. He opened the passenger door for her, and she got in, steadfastly refusing to glance into the back seat. Then he got in the driver's side and closed the door. The top was still down, so the night air surrounded them. She could hear crickets starting up their nightly thrum, and gradually competing with the sounds of the highway not far away. Lash turned toward her, took off his hat and tossed it in the back before pushing one hand through his hair.

"I think you misunderstood me before," he began.

"I understood you just fine, Lash. You told me the truth, right from the start. I'm a big girl. I can handle it."

"That's not what I meant, Jessi."

She blinked when her eyes tried to fill, then lifted one hand to touch his face. "I don't want to do this," she whispered. "I don't want to talk." Not if talking meant telling him goodbye. She was strong, but she didn't think she was strong enough to do that.

"But, Jess, I—"

She leaned forward, and pressed her lips to his. And it was only an instant before she felt him beginning to respond. His mouth softened, his hands slipped around her neck, his fingers cradling her head so gently it made her want to cry. Those same fingers threaded upward, into her hair.

He lifted his mouth from hers. His eyes had turned to molten silver. "You're just about the sweetest thing I ever tasted," he murmured.

"Then taste me again, Lash."

He closed his eyes. "Damn, woman. I must've been out of my mind to think..."

"Shh..." she whispered. "No talking, Lash. Not tonight. Not when..." She stopped herself from saying, "not when it's the last night we'll have." She didn't want to ruin this with a confrontation. "Not when I want you so badly."

She watched his eyes open, saw his imminent surrender in those pale blue depths. He wasn't even going to try to deny her this time. He reached out to touch her, trailing his fingertips from her cheek, all the way down her neck and over her breast to her belly. She closed her eyes and sighed in longing.

And then he pulled her close and kissed her again, and it was so bittersweet that she had to battle tears. To love him this much, to know he was leaving her...she wanted to hate him, but she couldn't find it in her. He'd told her this was how it would be, after all. He'd warned her again and again, but she hadn't listened. She had no one to blame for her heartbreak but herself.

But she'd have this. One last night to cling to, to remember him by. She lowered her hands between them, and one by one opened the buttons of his shirt. Then she pushed the material away and pressed her palms to his chest. Warmth and firmness under her hands. His heart pounding, his breathing ragged.

His hands were at the hem of her shirt, and he pulled it off over her head. And then he pushed her back against the seat, and trailed his lips over her breasts, capturing one peak and suckling it as if he were feeding there. As if he needed this sustenance to survive.

Then he sat up slowly, eyes blazing. "I should put the top up," he whispered.

"I like it down."

"Someone could come along."

"I really don't care." She reached out and tugged

the button of his jeans loose, then carefully lowered the zipper.

"This time," he told her, "I brought protection."

"Hope you didn't buy them at Mr. Henry's."

"Why—"

"Shh..." she said, and she pushed his jeans down, skimming her hands over his hips. "It might not matter now, anyway," she whispered. "Make love to me, Lash." She pushed him down until he was sitting on the seat of the car. Then she knelt up and managed to kick free of her own jeans. She looked at him sitting there, aroused and waiting for her. And she slowly lowered her head into his lap, taking him into her mouth, working him with her lips until he was trembling and tangling his hands in her hair and making desperate, pleading noises deep in his throat.

She sat up again, and slowly, she straddled him, lowering herself over him, down into his lap, while she held his gaze with her own.

He closed his eyes and released a slow, long, shuddery sigh.

Her hands clasped his shoulders, nails digging slightly into his flesh, and she lifted herself up, lowered again, drew away, came back. Over and over she moved, her pace so slow it was agonizing. He clamped her waist, urging her faster. His head fell backward, and he grated his teeth, his lips parting in delicious anguish as she made him insane. She could see the cords in his neck standing out. She could feel his pulse skyrocketing.

His hands slid lower, cupping her buttocks and squeezing her. And then he brought his head up, caught her nipple in his teeth and suckled it as if trying to extract its nectar. She moved her hands to the back of his head to pull him closer, hold him to her breast, and she quickened her pace. He was moving, now, too. Arching himself up and into her, clinging to her, moaning her name. And then she didn't hear anything as the climax broke over her in waves, each one more powerful than the one preceding it. She whispered that this night would last her forever, and then she relaxed against him, sliding her arms around him and lowering her head onto his shoulder.

And he held her, just that way, stroking her hair, for a very long time. But she knew it couldn't last. And finally he said, "Jessi, I don't want to, honey, but I have to go."

"I know," she said. "I know." He'd told her all along, hadn't he? How could she not know?

She slowly got off him, reaching for her clothes.

"We're going to have that talk," he said. "But it's gonna have to wait, for now. If I wait too long—"

"It's all right, Lash. There's nothing you need to explain to me. I understand." She pulled her shirt on, climbed out of the car, where it was easier to stand, and yanked her jeans on. Lash was struggling into his inside the car. She smiled gently as she watched him. "Goodbye, Lash." She turned to start walking toward her pickup.

"Jessi?" He looked up as she left, still trying hard to right his clothes in the confines of the vehicle. His shirt hung open, his hat was on crooked, and his jeans were still undone when he jumped out to stand on the roadside.

A car buzzed by, and its occupants blew their horn at him and hollered something obscene out the window.

"Dammit, Jessi, wait. At least you have to know that when I said I wanted to marry you before, I—"

"I know," she whispered. "I already know." She blew him a kiss, climbed into her pickup, started the engine and drove away fast, heading for home instead of the highway. She had to get out of there before the tears started flowing. If he saw them, he'd go back to believing she was some innocent, naive little girl who couldn't handle reality.

Problem was, she was wishing she could be the naive girl he thought she was. But she couldn't. Not when reality was staring her squarely in the face. She loved him, and he was leaving. And there was still a slim chance she might be carrying his child.

Hell, reality was just no fun at all.

Jessi tried really hard to act perfectly normal at home, but she suspected her family saw right through her. And whenever anyone mentioned Lash's name, she had to avert her eyes so that she could have a minute to blink them dry.

"Speaking of Lash..." Wes said, after someone mentioned his name yet again, this time as they gathered for leftovers in the kitchen. No one could sleep, after the rustling, and now, at midnight, everyone was hungry. "Where the hell is he? I thought he'd be out here with you, Garrett, seeing as how we were the latest victims of the rustlers."

"No need of that," Garrett said. "We've pretty much figured it was that lowlife Zane who did it. Now all we have to do is track him down."

"Oh." Wes frowned and reached for another piece of fried chicken. "So why aren't we doing it?"

"I'm just waiting for some information to come in," Garrett said. "Don't worry, we'll get him."

Elliot tilted his head, observing and listening. "Not like you to be so vague, Garrett," he said.

"Not like you to be so curious," Garrett said quickly. "I'm goin' up to bed. Can't do any good to sit up all night."

"Me too," Jessi said softly, drawing all her brothers' eyes to her face, every set of them studying her worriedly.

"You getting sick again, Jessi?" Wes asked.

"You're so quiet," Ben added.

"You should talk, Ben," she replied, injecting a lightness she didn't feel into her tone. "My brother, the epitome of the 'strong, silent type.'" Ben smiled at her, and she smiled back, but it felt strained. Then she said good-night and headed up to her room, but she was far from ready to go to sleep.

She put on her nightgown, and actually crawled into bed. She lay there, wide awake and staring at the ceiling, for over an hour before she gave up the notion of getting any rest tonight. She couldn't even close her eyes.

Garrett must already know that Lash had moved on. After all, they'd solved the rustling. They knew now that Zane was the mastermind behind the whole thing, and since he'd no doubt left the state and maybe even the country, it was up to the FBI to bring him in. Lash's job was done. He'd only promised Garrett he'd stay until it was, and he'd probably turned in his badge tonight, when they went to his place in town.

But Garrett had his suspicions about Jessi and Lash, and he didn't have the heart to tell her the truth.

Poor Garrett. It would be easier on him if she told

him she knew, and that she was all right with it. But she wasn't quite sure she *was* all right with it yet. So she paced, and worried, and she figured she might as well just buck up and get used to the fact that she'd never see Lash Monroe again. It wasn't the end of the world…as much as it felt like it was.

Wes said over a hundred head of cattle had been taken. It was a terrible loss, but the ranch would probably survive. Still, she felt personally responsible for the loss. So as long as she was pacing anyway, she went ahead and worried about that, as well.

The pregnancy test was still in its wrapper in the bottom of her purse. So she paced still more, and she worried about that, above and beyond all else. She gnawed her lip and told herself she couldn't use it tonight. She stopped pacing, stared at her purse, took a step toward it, then shook her head hard and resumed moving along the path she was trying to wear in her carpet. She had enough on her mind tonight without knowing the results of that stupid pink pregnancy test kit. And what idiot decided to wrap them up in pink cellophane, anyway?

Ah, but if she knew the results were negative, it would be one *less* thing to worry about, right? And she had to do something. Anything productive.

"All right," she said, and nodded firmly. "What am I, a woman or a wimp?" She lifted her chin. "Woman. Pure Texas woman, toughest breed on the planet. Too tough to be so scared of a five-dollar package from the drugstore." She nodded hard. "So, let's do it."

She locked her bedroom door, took the kit from her purse, unwrapped it and read the instructions twice.

Then she went into the adjoining bathroom.

She came out a few minutes later and scuffed aimlessly until she found herself sinking onto the stool in front of her vanity. She focused her blurred vision and saw that her face was very pale and her eyes were huge as they stared back at her from the vanity mirror. In something like awe, she laid her palms very gently against her abdomen. "I can't believe it," she whispered, and a tear made of sheer emotion spilled from her eye and rolled silently down her cheek.

She'd expected to feel panic-stricken, devastated, frightened, when she looked down and saw the positive results so clearly showing in the test kit. But instead, she'd felt something entirely different. A wave of warm, soothing, overwhelming joy. A glowing feeling that seemed to fill her up from her head to her toes. She could almost believe it was shining from her eyes like the pale amber glow of light from an oil lamp on a stormy night.

She was going to have Lash Monroe's baby. She was carrying the child of the man she loved. And there was nothing frightening or devastating about it.

She looked into the mirror again, and this time she smiled.

Chapter 11

"So," Garrett said to Chelsea as they lay in bed, her snuggled so close to him that he could feel her heart beating. "This aunt Kate person told Lash that his other foster brother, Peter, had gone back to Mexico when his uncle died, leaving him—get this—lock-stock-and-barrel ownership of his meat-packing business."

"You're kidding me," she said. "Gosh, how many rotten bad-news foster brothers did that poor guy have to put up with, anyway?"

"Three," Garrett said. "He doesn't think the other one is involved, though. But it seems Zane and this Peter were always stirring up trouble together. So Lash figures Peter has to be Zane's connection. He got an address for the company, and he's going down there to check it out."

"All by himself?" Chelsea sat up a little, staring down at Garrett with a bit of censure in her eyes.

"Yeah, I didn't like that part of it, either. But Lash says he and Zane have a score to settle that goes back a long ways, and that it's their own private war, and he has to take care of this himself. I did make him promise to check in, though, and to let us know if he gets himself into trouble."

Chelsea nodded. "You know how many men Zane must have had working with him to pull off as many rustlings as he did yesterday?" she asked him.

Garrett grimaced, and closed his eyes. "I promised Lash I'd give him a chance to handle this on his own."

"He's going to get himself killed, going down there alone. He's walking into a snake pit."

"Sweetheart, he's not gonna try to take them down or anything. He's just gonna check the place out, see if any cattle are walking into the slaughterhouse with our brand on their hides, see if Zane is down there. Then he'll call in the cavalry."

"The cavalry being...?"

Garrett shook his head. "Wes, Elliot, Ben and me, of course."

"No Feds?"

Garrett shrugged. "Depends on Lash. If he wants me to bring them in, I will. But, hon, if he'd rather not, we'll handle it ourselves. Hell, Lash is like family."

"Maybe more like family than you think," she muttered.

He bunched up his brows and stared hard at her. "Now that sounds like maybe you know something I don't know. Chelsea...is there something going on between Lash and Jessi?"

She shrugged. "Wish I knew. It would be nice, though, wouldn't it?"

"Nice, hell!" He sat up in the bed. "He's too old, and he's a drifter, and—"

"And he's a hell of a good man, and you love him like a brother already. Calm down, you big lug. I swear, I never saw any man as resistant to Cupid's arrow as you! I had to damn near get myself killed before you figured out we belonged together, and now you're pretending to know what's best for your sister. You've got to learn to let love take its own course, honey. And even if you don't, it won't matter, because it's going to anyway."

He didn't like the sounds of this. Not one little bit.

"Chels, there's one more thing. Lash made me promise I wouldn't say a word to Jessi—or to the boys, either, for that matter—about where he went or why. He says he's seen the way she dives headfirst into trouble, and he's right. Remember when I was facing an ambush in that canyon and she insisted on coming along to help get me out of it? She could have been killed then—"

"I remember. I was there, too, you know. And the way I recall it, Jessi held her own and made a few of those criminals sorry she'd come along at all."

"She's just a kid, Chelsea."

"She's a grown woman with a career and a business of her own. You've got to get that through your head."

"Lash thought it best she not know what he was up to until it's over with. He doesn't want her rushing off half-cocked and getting hurt, and I agree with him."

"She'd realize how stupid and risky what he's doing is, same as I do," Chelsea said.

"She'd get herself hurt trying to go after him, especially if she's got some hare-brained notion that she's in love with him."

"Yeah. Hell of a hare-brained notion that would be."

"Don't tell her, Chelsea. Promise me?"

"What could I tell her? Mexico's a big country. And for that matter, how are you going to know where to go when Lash needs your help?"

"He's going to call tomorrow night at midnight. Sooner, if he gets into trouble. He'll tell me where he's at then. So do you promise to keep this from Jessi?"

"I promise," she said. "I won't tell her unless it becomes absolutely necessary."

Garrett frowned at her and tried to see just what mischief was working behind her eyes. But, as always, his Chelsea only revealed what she chose to reveal. Which most of the time was everything, at least to him. But once in a while it was not quite everything. He had a feeling this was one of those times.

Six times Lash caught himself driving way over the speed limit. He was in one hell of a hurry, and he told himself it was because he wanted to catch Zane red-handed with those cattle. But it was a lengthy drive, over deserted stretches of dark nighttime highway, and it gave a man time to think. Maybe a little too much time to think.

So he got to thinking, and he didn't like what it was he was thinking about. He blamed it on the heat, then the darkness and the lack of streetlights, and finally on the heartbreaking crooning of country music, which was all his radio could pick up for a while. Songs belted out by men who were hurting so bad their voices cracked, just as their hearts apparently had. Crying over that perfect woman they hadn't realized they loved un- til it was too late. Moaning about wishing for a second chance as they watched her walk down the aisle with somebody else. Sheesh, it was enough to drive a man nuts.

Of course, he didn't quite have enough willpower to lift his hand and turn that knob in search of a different station, though he couldn't figure out why. So he listened until he lost the signal a little while later. After that, all he got were Spanish-speaking stations, and the music they played ranged from sexy Tejano to hot Latin beats that only served to remind him of the look in Jessi's eyes just a little while ago, when she'd driven him out of his mind with sensations in the front seat of his car. And then there were the heartfelt, emotional ballads with Spanish guitar accompanying them, which reminded him of her eyes when she'd realized he was responsible for that mariachi band at her grand opening. And he remembered dancing with her later.

Hell, everything reminded him of Jessi Brand. And he was more convinced than ever that he had to do the right thing by her. He'd taken advantage of her, and he really ought to make up for that. And if she thought marrying her was some kind of punishment in his eyes, she was wrong. It wasn't punishment at all. It was compensation. And hell, it wouldn't be so bad to be Jessi Brand's husband.

Just who did he think he was kidding, anyway? It would be the closest thing to heaven.

"Jessica Lynn Brand Monroe," he muttered, and then he grinned. "Jessi Monroe." It had a nice ring to it. "Dr. Jessica Monroe, D.V.M."

Well, hell, there was no question about it. He had to at least try to convince her that this was the right thing to do. And what her brothers, with their old-fashioned sense of values, would expect them to do. What the

Reverend Mr. Stanton would have flat-out ordered him to do. Hell, it was what he expected himself to do. He'd been raised to do the right thing. And the good book said it was better for a man to marry than to be burning up with lust. And he certainly was that.

A little voice in his head whispered that it was more than any of those things he'd just listed in his mind. Marrying Jessi wasn't just what he *should* do. It was what he *wanted* to do. And maybe that was what she'd been needing to hear. Maybe if he told her that, she'd change her mind.

Maybe he should just tell her. He nodded his head. Yeah. He'd just tell her.

That decided, he started humming along to the tune of the music, and then he frowned. Considering what he was facing a few more miles to the south, he had to wonder just what in the hell he was feeling so good about.

"You have to tell me where he went," Jessi went on. "Chelsea, I wouldn't ask if it wasn't important."

"I promised Garrett I wouldn't say anything." Chelsea had every intention of saying something—Jessi could see it in her eyes.

"Look, this is silly. I know he left. I'm okay with that, but there's a reason I need to know where he is. I'm going to have to get in touch with him...when the time is right...and..." Jessi frowned then, and tilted her head. "Chelsea, why in the world wouldn't Garrett want me to know where Lash has gone?"

"Because they both think you'll go running after him."

Jessi's eyes widened. "Like I'm so desperate I need

to chase a man down and throw myself at him? God, Chelsea, you don't really believe that, do you?"

"No one believes that," she said. "No one thinks you'd go after him to throw yourself at him. It's…" She let her voice trail off.

Jessi frowned. She knew something more was going on than what she already knew. And if she couldn't find out what it was, her name wasn't Jessica Brand.

"If I wasn't chasing him to rope and brand him, Chelsea, why would I be going after him?"

Chelsea lowered her eyes.

"He's in trouble, isn't he?" Jessi whispered, and she searched her sister-in-law's face.

"No. Not yet," Chelsea said.

She wanted to say more, Jessi could see it plainly, but she also knew that it was up to her to ask the right questions. Chelsea couldn't just break her promise to Garrett. It was one of the things Jessi respected most about her. That deep-running sense of loyalty.

"But he's in danger, isn't he, Chelsea?" Chelsea didn't nod, but her eyes affirmed Jessi's guess. And then Jessi caught her breath. "He went after that sleazy Zane, didn't he? I'm right, aren't I?"

Chelsea met her eyes and said nothing.

"Where?" Jessi pressed.

"I can't tell you that, Jessi. I promised Garrett…"

"But…?"

"But if the phone should ring around midnight, and if you were to pick it up and be very quiet, you might find out exactly what's going on with Lash. I'm only saying so because I think you deserve to know and because…of this…"

She dipped a hand into her pocket, and Jessi heard the crinkle of cellophane. Then Chelsea pulled out the pink bit of wrapper and opened her palm to reveal the home pregnancy test's brand name across the front.

Jessi snatched it out of Chelsea's hand and jammed it into her jeans pocket, looking around them to be sure no one else had seen. "Where did you get that?"

"It was my turn for housework," Chelsea said. "I was taking out the trash, and it sort of fluttered out of a bag. Darn lucky it was me and not one of your brothers who picked it up."

Jessi closed her eyes and tried to slow her escalating heartbeat as she realized just how easily that might have happened. "It was those damned condoms that little freckle-faced monster poked full of holes," she confessed, her words emerging in a fast, harsh whisper. She rushed to get them out before she could change her mind.

"Oh, Jess," Chelsea muttered. She was watching Jessi's face, waiting, all but holding her breath. "Are you going to tell me?"

"Tell you…?"

"Jeez, Jessi, tell me the results! I'm dying here."

Jessi closed her eyes and lowered her chin to her chest.

"Positive," she whispered. "I'm pregnant, Chelsea."

Chelsea's arms came around her, pulled her close and held her hard. "Oh, baby, it's gonna be okay. I promise you that. This is between you and me for now, okay? No one's going to know until you're ready. And, honey, you know I'm gonna be here for you, no matter what you decide to do."

"Thanks," Jessi said, and then she let herself hug Chelsea back, and a few tears burned her eyes.

"Thanks. God, it's good to hear that. But I think I've already decided…I want to keep it, Chelsea."

Chelsea stroked her hair. "Then I'll help you. You're going to be all right." She stepped back just a little and looked down at Jessi's face, smiling. "Are you going to tell him?"

"No," she said. "No, I can't. Not yet. I want him to fall in love with me, Chels. If I tell him this, then he's going to say and do anything he thinks necessary to get me to marry him, and I want to know it's real. I won't marry a man who doesn't love me."

"But, honey, what about the baby?"

"What baby?" Garrett said from the doorway. Jessi stiffened and saw the look of shock in Chelsea's eyes. Then Chelsea painted her face with a great big smile and kept on talking as if she hadn't seen or heard her husband. "You going to watch that baby for me next weekend or not, Jessi? 'Cause if you can't, I need time to find someone else. I promised to fill in at the Women's Center."

"What? Oh…um, sure. I'd love to watch little Ethan for you. Anytime." Without turning around or even glancing her brother's way, Jessi hurried out of the house.

She closed her eyes in relief when she heard Lash's voice on the other end of the phone line at midnight that night. Her bag was already packed and waiting in the truck outside. She had a map. She'd filled the gas tank and checked the oil. She was ready.

She covered the mouthpiece with her hand so that neither Lash nor Garrett would hear her relieved sigh when Lash's voice—sounding perfectly normal—

reached her ears. She hadn't even realized she was holding her breath.

"It was Zane, all right," Lash told Garrett. "He's here, with about a dozen others I suspect are part of his rustling operation. Then there's Petey and his crew of cutthroats. All told, I'd say this is going to be a tough nut to crack."

"You'd better sit tight, then," Garrett said. "You got a room somewhere?"

"Yeah, fleabag hotel called Casa del Coronado. But I can't just sit here, Garrett. I have a feeling Zane and the boys are just gonna take the money and run. And we might never track them down if that happens."

"You stay where you are," Garrett said. "I'll call the Federales and get them started, and then the boys and I will be—"

"No, you guys stay out of this. I don't want to be responsible for Jessi losing one of her brothers. This is my fight."

"Hey, pal, those are my cattle about to become fajita filler, so how do you figure it's your fight?"

"It's a family thing, like I told you. I want you to stay out of it, Garrett."

Garrett muttered, but agreed. Jessi stood there gaping, not believing her brother would be such an idiot. Lash was going to end up dead!

"All right, pal, but wait for the Federales, okay?"

"Unless he makes like he's leaving town, I'll lay low."

"Good. Now give me the pertinent details, so I can get some help on the way."

Lash recited the address of the hotel where he was staying, and gave a phone number. Jessi grabbed for a pen and copied both down rapidly, then tore off the sheet of notepaper and jammed it into her pocket, where her pickup keys were digging into her thigh.

"Be careful," Garrett said.

"How's Jessi?" Lash asked. She was halfway to hanging up when she heard that, but she snapped the phone back to her ear.

"Still acting pretty darned strangely, Lash. And I can't figure her out. First she was depressed again, and then tonight, she seemed kind of...I dunno, wound up and tense or something. I was hoping she'd have snapped out of it by now, but—"

"You haven't told her where I am, have you, Garrett? You promised you—"

"Hell, no, I haven't told her."

"Oh." His voice sounded vaguely disappointed. "Then, she hasn't asked?"

"Asked? Hell, Lash, she demanded. You know Jessi. But I kept my word. I guess she figures you decided it was time to move on."

Lash was quiet for a long time.

"Lash? Did you hear me? I said, she figures—"

"I heard you. I didn't want her to go thinking that, either."

"Well, you know how she is. Jumps to conclusions quicker than a prairie dog diving for his hole."

"Do me a favor, Garrett?"

Jessi gripped the receiver a little tighter as she listened.

"You tell her I'm coming back. Just so she knows I didn't pull up and move on without even saying so long. Okay?"

"You know, Lash, I've been trying to wait on this, because you asked me to, and because I agreed in good faith, but I think it's about time you tell me about it."

"About what?"

"About Jessi. And you. I mean, it seems to me that you and she have—"

"Sorry, Garrett, you're gonna have to be patient just a little bit longer on that one. I told you we'd talk it out, and we will. But I think it's only fair I talk this through with Jessi first." There was some noise in the background, and then Lash came back on the line. "Just know I don't want to see Jessi hurt any more than you do, okay? Now I gotta go. There's a big Mexican here shaking his fist at me and shouting about *el teléfono*," Lash said. "Goodbye, Garrett." And then the line went dead.

Jessi restrained herself from slamming the living-room extension down and hurrying on her way. Instead, she waited for Garrett to hang up first. Then she put the phone down quietly and walked to the pickup truck parked out front. She got inside, and pulled the door closed quietly.

She was not chasing after Lash Monroe. Her pride wouldn't allow it. And she wouldn't agree to marry him until she was sure he loved her, respected her and truly wanted her to be his wife. Not even if he got down on his knees and begged until his ears bled. No way. But maybe…maybe he was getting a little closer to loving her for real. Maybe he even did already, and just hadn't realized it yet. Maybe there was still a chance.

She bit her lip and told herself not to get her hopes up. She didn't need him. She wasn't worthy of the Brand name if she couldn't have her baby and raise it perfectly well on her own without any help from any man.

But, God, she wanted him. She wanted him so much

it hurt all the time, like a toothache that wouldn't go away. She even ached for him in her sleep.

But there was a whole other issue here. He was the father of the child she was carrying. And there was no way in hell she could sit safe and sound at home while her baby's father was out there getting himself killed. She had to do something. Lash wasn't going to rob her child of the chance to know its father.

Besides, she loved the damned fool.

Jessi coasted the pickup truck as far as it would go, and then she turned the key.

Garrett sat up in bed at the loud protests coming from the holes in Jessi's muffler. "Where the hell do you suppose she's off to at this time of the night?"

"Veterinary emergency?" Chelsea suggested.

"The phone didn't ring."

Chelsea was quiet for a very long moment, and Garrett reached out to flick on the lamp so that he could study her face. Damn. She had something to say. Something she was dying to get out. "Chelsea, hon?"

"The phone *did* ring, Garrett. And when the phone rings in the middle of the night, and you're a veterinarian, you probably tend to dive for it in case it's a veterinary emergency, wouldn't you think?"

Garrett just looked at her. Just sat in the bed and stared at her. She was telling him something. "If Jessi did pick up the phone, she would have said something."

"I don't know," Chelsea said. "I mean, if she picks it up and starts hearing the answers to questions she's been wondering about for a day or two, she might not say a word."

"She went down there after Lash, didn't she?"

"My goodness, I hope not!" Chelsea sat up in the bed. "I mean, it sounded to me like Lash was in trouble right up to his neck down there." Then she frowned. "Oh, but that can't be right. You didn't think it was necessary for you and your brothers to go help him out, so it must be perfectly safe for your baby sister, as well, right?"

Garrett closed his eyes, feeling the barb of guilt his wife had no doubt inflicted on purpose. He flung back the covers and pulled on his jeans, opened the bedroom door and hollered. "Ben, Elliot, Wes! Get up, and get dressed. Time for a road trip."

Jessi's old pickup truck wouldn't go above forty-five unless it was out of gear and going down a steep hill. Going uphill, she didn't think it would hit fifteen, but, thankfully, these roads were pretty much flat. There was another route that would have been a bit shorter, but there were one or two inclines on it that would have been too much for the old engine, so she chose the flat way, knowing it would be faster in the long run.

She'd breezed through customs without incident, though one young officer had advised her not to drive too far from home in *that truck.* Hell, the truck ran fine, just a little slowly, was all. Once she got past the border, she pulled off the road, turned on her dome light and consulted the map she'd purchased earlier. She was nothing if not prepared. She found the little town of Pueblo Bonito and mentally plotted out her route.

But then a pair of bounding high beams cut through the windshield, glaring into her eyes, and she couldn't see a thing. Panic seeped into her brain when the lights stopped, facing her, the vehicle having pulled off onto the shoulder, right in front of hers. Instinctively she reached out to lock both doors, and then she turned her key to crank the motor. She'd just back up, fast. All the way back to the border guys, if necessary. These lowlifes were going to be sorely disappointed if they thought they'd found some lost American female who'd make easy prey for their night's amusement. The dirty—

The headlights went out, and Jessi blinked in the sudden darkness. Was that—?

Four tall shapes emerged from the shiny new over-size pickup truck and sauntered toward her. Shapes she wished she didn't recognize. She thought about shifting into reverse and making a run for it anyway, but she knew she didn't stand a chance of outrunning Garrett in his brand-new umpteen-horsepower machine. Maybe they'd believe she was just out for a little evenin' drive.

She unlocked her door and rolled down her window. Garrett leaned his crossed forearms on the door, then smiled at her. "Honey, you gotta come home now."

"The hell I do," she said, instantly on the defensive, no matter how sweet his smile.

His smile turned to a frown. "What good do you think you can do down here? Hmm? You'd just get yourself hurt, and then Lash would have more to worry about than he already does."

Jessi wrenched on her door handle, shoved it open, pushing her oversize brother out of the way as she got out, and then slammed it again, standing toe-to-toe and nose-to-chest with him. "Seems to me I did *you* quite a bit of good when *you* were in trouble, Garrett Brand. Seems to me when one member of this family needs help, there are usually Brands coming out of the wood-

work to see he gets it. And you and I both know that
Lash is in trouble down here.''

Wes, standing off to one side, tilted his head and
eyed Garrett. ''That true, brother?''

''He'll be fine so long as he keeps his head down.''

Elliot piped up. ''Well, sure, Garrett. But supposing
he *don't* keep his head down?''

''You know, Garrett, he did get his face all busted
up defending our sister's honor. Don't we kind of owe
him one?'' Ben asked.

Garrett sighed heavily and turned to face them all.
''Look, guys, this isn't my decision. Lash made me
promise to stay out of this. It's a family thing. A long-
overdue showdown between him and his foster brother,
and he wants to handle it alone. I gave him my word.''

''Yup,'' Wes said, voice deep and slow. ''Just like
you made all of us give you our word not to get involved when you were walking into an ambush in that
box canyon. But remember, Garrett, if we'd kept our
word back then, you'd be dead right now. Maybe Chelsea would, too.''

''Exactly,'' Jessi said. ''Lash needs our help, and
I'm going to give it to him. Whether he wants it or not
is completely beside the point.''

Garrett shook his head. ''Look, I get the feeling this
thing with him and Zane is private. It would be different if Lash were family, but he's not, and—''

''You're wrong about that,'' Jessi said, and then she
bit her lip, because her brothers were all staring at her,
waiting for—and probably fully expecting—her to
have the last word. Only…they were gonna flip when
they heard what that last word was. She closed her eyes
and drew a breath. ''Technically, Lash *is* family.''

''How's that?'' Elliot asked innocently. She opened

her eyes just to slits, and saw Wes and Garrett's tempers sizzling to life. Ben stood calmly, no emotion showing on his face.

She scrunched her face up tight, clenched her hands into trembling fists at her sides and blurted out, "I'm carrying his baby."

Silence. Dead, stony silence. She opened her eyes just enough to peek out at them. Their faces were shocked, but turning mean. Reddening. Jaws tight. Teeth grinding. And yet they didn't speak. It was so quiet she could hear the ghostly moan of a distant wind in the desert, and the crunching, skittering sound of a tumbleweed rolling around somewhere out there. It all felt like a scene in an old western film—the one just before the big showdown. That moment when all the townsfolk hustle their women and children off the streets, and the black-clothed gunslingers step out on opposite ends to face each other. Death seemed to hang on the air. It might be after midnight, but there was a definite "high noon" feeling to all of this.

Then, finally, someone spoke. It was Wes. He said, "I'll *kill* him! I'll kill that double-dealing snake in the grass. I'll—"

"Can't kill him," Garrett said, and it tore at Jessi that his voice was a little choked with emotion. "We can make him wish to God we'd kill him, but we can't kill him. 'Cause there has to be enough of him left to marry her."

"Oh, no—"

"Man," Elliot said, "I sure hope Zane has Lash in a coma or something before we get there. He'd be better off."

Ben touched her shoulders. "Are you okay, Jessi?"

"I'm gonna take my bullwhip to that yellow-bellied

liar and strip every inch of hide off his sidewindin'
body!" Wes threw his precious Stetson on the dusty
road and stomped on it. "I'm gonna pull my bowie
outta my boot and—"

Jessi put her fingers to her lips and cut loose with a
piercing whistle that should have broken their ear-
drums—probably would have, too, if they hadn't all
been so thickheaded.

"No! You boys are gonna listen to what I have to
say if I have to hold you at gunpoint to make you do
it! Now get this straight. I am in love with Lash Monroe. Have been ever since the day he first set foot on
the Texas Brand. I wanted him, and I set about the
business of getting him. If you doubt that, boys, just
think about it for a minute. I always get what I want,
don't I?" She glared at each of them in turn, but only
paused a second, because if they started in again she'd
never shut them up. "I seduced Lash, not the other way
around. And I'm not one bit ashamed of it, either. He
told me right from the start not to fall for him, but I
did it anyway. He doesn't know about this baby, and
I don't want him to know until I'm damned good and
ready to tell him. You understand me? You keep your
big fat mouths *shut!*"

Then she turned to Ben. "And yes, I'm okay. I'm
just fine."

Ben nodded, big and gentle and accepting. "I'm
glad, honey. But I'm gonna have to kick your boy-
friend's ass for this."

Jessi rolled her eyes as her brothers all started talking
at once, voices raised as they described what they were
going to do to Lash in the most colorful terms possible.
They swore and ranted and hollered. She sidled away
from them, all the way up to that pretty new shiny red

pickup truck, and peeked in to see the keys dangling from the switch. Glancing over her shoulder, she saw her brothers standing in a huddle the Dallas Cowboys would have been proud of, each one trying to top the other's threats. She opened the door and climbed behind the wheel. She closed the windows, secured the locks, released the emergency brake, slipped the shift into first, then depressed the clutch. All systems go.

She twisted the key. As soon as the motor came to life, her brothers turned like one collective testosterone-enhanced male entity. She waved and popped the clutch as they all surged forward. But it was too late. She pulled it into second gear, then glanced in the rearview mirror and smiled at the distance the big lugs chased her before giving up. She faced front again, flicking on the headlights and shifting up another gear.

She could have taken the keys to her old pickup, leaving them stranded. It would have been intensely satisfying to think of them having to hoof it back to the border and use a phone to call Chelsea. Imagine them trying to explain that their little sister had stolen their big manly truck and left them high and dry. Ah, it was almost too good. But she'd denied herself the pleasure of that. She'd left them the keys. Because she had a feeling Lash was going to need a little bit more help than she could give him. So it was necessary for the boys to follow her on her journey south.

She turned on the radio and hoped this little town was far enough away to give her brothers plenty of time to cool down. One thing was for sure, she was going to have plenty of time to kill, waiting for them to catch up to her in that slowpoke of a truck. Which

was good, in a way, because she was starved. Nice that
she finally had her appetite back. Must be all this excitement.

Chapter 12

Lash had been holed up in the sleazy hotel for just
about as long as he could stand, and no Federales had
shown up yet. Zane was in a little cantina a few yards
down the dirt track that passed for a road in this hole-
in-the-wall town. Pueblo Bonito, indeed. If ever there
had been a misnomer...

A good portion of Garrett's herd of prime beef
stock—and those of many of his neighbors—were a bit
farther down, penned up in open-air corrals and waiting
for the morning shift to show up to slaughter them.
Seven a.m. was when the workers would arrive to begin their gruesome task, or so Lash had been told when
he asked around in stammering, very bad Spanish. That
gave him barely four hours, and it wasn't going to be
enough time.

He had to do something. He couldn't just keep on
waiting for help to arrive. He'd scoped out the slaughterhouse yard, and seen men sorely in need of bathtubs

and razor blades standing around the cattle pens holding rifles. He figured if he even got close, they'd use
them.

The town was obviously poverty-stricken. Buildings
were in tumbledown condition; brown water flowed
from the faucets, when they chose to spew any at all.
More interesting was the rat poison strategically placed
underneath the sink. The few vehicles in town looked
as if they were held together with coat hangers and
baling twine. Broken windows were patched with large
pieces of cardboard. The place reeked of despair.

But, hell, he couldn't sit around here much longer.
He couldn't stand to. All he could think about was
getting back to Texas. To the ranch. To Jessi.

And it had just started to occur to him that maybe
he'd been wrong when he told her he wasn't a settling-
down kind of guy. At first, he'd only thought he should
marry her because it was the right thing to do, but then
she'd gone and turned him down, and it had made him
think. Long and hard. Hell, he'd been *disappointed*
when she refused him. And when he pondered that
feeling, he'd realized that if he'd only been proposing
out of guilt or a sense of duty, then he'd have been
relieved. But he hadn't been relieved at all. In fact, he'd
been pretty crushed. He'd told himself he wasn't, but
that had been bull. All he'd been doing since then was
trying to think of how to talk her into changing her
mind. Into saying yes. Into being his wife.

Being his wife. God, the phrase whispering through
his brain made him feel warm and soft inside.

So the question remained—why? If it wasn't guilt
or remorse—if suddenly the idea of jumping into his
old car and heading for a new town and a new adven-

ture seemed like a nightmare instead of a thrill—then why?

Damn. Could he actually be...*in love?*

Seemed beyond his wildest imaginings.

He settled down in a rickety chair behind the filthy window in his hotel room, watching the cantina's entrance through the hole where the glass was broken, because it was the only part he could see through. There was little activity in the streets, but the cantina was busy. Men staggered in and out. Rough-sounding Spanish and deep laughter spilled into the street. He watched it all, and pondered his feelings about Jessi Brand for a long while.

And then he leaped out of the chair so fast that it clattered to the floor behind him. He stared, aghast, out the window, rubbed his eyes and stared again. Because the girl he'd been thinking about had materialized right before his eyes. She was sauntering down that dusty road in a pair of straight-legged jeans that hugged her where they shouldn't, and tall slender boots that reached almost to her knees. She wore one of those sexy ribbed tank tops, glaring white, the ones that were made for a man, but did incredible things on a woman. Over it was a plaid flannel shirt, lightweight, unbuttoned and gaping, sleeves rolled to the elbows. She wore a hat, a Stetson like his, only hers was a soft brown felt that made the red in her hair look even prettier.

She was eating a fajita about a foot long as she walked, and she was looking around—probably for him, he figured.

He heard the wolf whistle, saw her stop and turn her head toward the cantina's swinging doors. She turned so fast that her short auburn hair kept swinging even after her head had come to a stop. He could see it brushing her shoulders in the shadow of her hat.

Lash pulled his handgun and, without taking his eyes off the street below, checked to see that it was fully loaded.

The swinging doors of the cantina flung outward and his nemesis, Zane, staggered out, said something obnoxious to Jessi and gripped her forearm. Jessi smashed what was left of her fajita into his leering face, and he laughed as he swiped it off.

The bastard. He pulled her inside. Lash whirled and ran, as fast as he could out of his room and down the hall. His booted feet landed so hard that chunks of plaster jarred loose from the walls as he passed. He slammed down the stairs, skipping the lowest one—the one with the missing board—so as not to break a leg, and headed out of the hotel. He could hear the cantina's radio blasting from here. A cloud of dust followed him across the road, and he burst into the noisy Mexican bar, pistol drawn and ready, to see Zane on a stool, with Jessi on his lap. She had a big, heavy beer glass in her hand, and Zane was telling her to be sociable and drink with him.

"Get your filthy hands off her, Zane."

Someone stopped the music. The laughter and talk in the place died a beat later.

Zane blinked a little drunkenly, finally located Lash's eyes, squinted at the gun and laughed. He waved a hand around the bar to the patrons there. *"Mi hermano,"* he sang out. Then to Lash he said, "Little brother, these are my friends. They love me, because I bring jobs to their impoverished little town. I could run for mayor here and win. So I suggest you put that gun down before you upset them."

Lash glanced around at the men. They were all wearing ponchos and beards. The stench of body odor and stale beer and cigarette smoke surrounded him. And the glare of hatred flashed from their eyes. Then he looked at Jessi, and her eyes were so beautiful and big and sparkling. And not scared. Not at all scared. She looked…excited. There was a twinkle in those brown eyes of hers. Mischief. Devilment. The hellion was planning something.

He sent her a message with his eyes, silently telling her to stay still, and not draw any undue attention to herself. He didn't want her getting hurt. She smiled very slightly at him, as if to say, "Yeah, right."

Swallowing hard, Lash faced his worst enemy again. "If they like you so much, Zane," he said, "they'll sit still and keep out of this. Otherwise, they'll see you with a big hole in your head."

"I don't think so, *amigo*."

Jessi yelled, "Behind you, Lash!"

It was too late, though. The blow to the head took him by surprise, and as he staggered sideways, the gun was yanked out of his hand and tossed out into the street. The man who'd hit him loomed over him, and Lash pretended to cower, then hooked one leg behind the guy's feet and swept them right out from under him. Someone else jumped in front of him even as he got to his feet, but Lash came up swinging.

From the corner of his eye, he saw Jessi bring her giant beer mug down on top of Zane's head. Glass shattered, beer splashed and spilled, and Zane was bleeding. Zane gaped at her in disbelief, but only until she jabbed her elbow into his belly, hopped out of his lap, picked up a bar stool and swung it at him like a baseball bat.

The bartender ducked as a chair sailed over his head
to smash the mirror that hung on the wall behind him.
Then about eight guys jumped on Lash at once. But
for some reason, they didn't stay long. He'd been holding his own, but, if truth be told, he had been getting
pretty winded, ducking all those blows and taking a
punch or two every now and then. He closed his hand
around the neck of a bottle and broke it over one head.
While that attacker sank to the floor, he turned with
the broken bottle to face another. But before he could
blink, a big hand closed on the guy's shoulder, spun
him around and plowed a fist into his face with a teeth-
shattering crunch.

Lash frowned and looked up at the owner of that
beefy fist. Garrett looked back at him. Only he wasn't
smiling. In fact, he looked as if he were planning to
knock Lash's teeth out next.

What the hell—?

Another guy leaped on Lash from behind then, so
he had to turn around and tend to business. But damn,
Garrett had looked meaner than a bear with a toothache
just now. What the hell was wrong with him?

Lash ducked as a small round table sailed past. It hit
the guy he was fighting right in the chin. He crouched
low and made his way back toward the bar, where he'd
last seen Jessi, worrying about her being in the middle
of the riot that had broken out. He had to stay low to
avoid flying bottles, glasses, furniture and the occasional body sailing past. One guy got hurled right
through the front window, landing on his back in the
street. Damn fool got up and dived right back in again,
swearing a blue streak in his native tongue and uttering
some kind of battle cry.

He stepped on something soft that grunted in response. "Excuse me, pal," he muttered, and stepped over the body on the floor. Someone blocked his path, and a fist came toward his face. Lash grabbed the first thing he could close his hand on, and brought it up like a shield. Turned out to be somebody's dinner plate, and it smashed to bits. The owner of the fist howled and clutched his bleeding knuckles. Lash punched him in the nose and kept on going.

And then he saw her.

Jessi Brand was using an upturned table for cover, ducking behind it. Every time one of Zane's guys walked close enough to her, she popped up like some demonic jack-in-the-box and rapped him over the head with a full bottle of liquor. Seemed she had a cache of them back there. Lash made his way toward her, and when he got within reach she popped up again, bottle in hand, ready to add him to that pile of bodies lying in an unconscious, liquor-soaked heap all around her little battle station. Fortunately, he'd expected it, and he caught her wrist before the bottle could connect with his skull. "It's me, Jess."

"You big jerk, I oughtta clobber you anyway!"

He frowned, confused, but she twisted her hand around to grip his arm and yanked him behind the table with her, pulling him down low, so that they were both kneeling in the dubious safety provided by the toppled table.

She glared at him for a full minute, and then her face softened. "Damn, I'm glad to see you," she muttered, and she snapped her arms around his neck and kissed him full on the mouth.

Lash's arms slipped right around her waist, and he held her close, tasted those lips, and loved every second of it. The noise of the brawl faded, and a buzz of longing filled his head instead. He didn't want to stop kissing her. Not ever.

But he did, after a long moment. And he lifted his head in time to see a glass pitcher flying toward her. He pulled her out of its path and watched it crash to the floor. Then he shook his head. "Jessi, what the hell are you doing here?"

"What the hell am *I* doing here? Hell, Lash, you care to tell me how you were planning to get out of this mess on your own?"

"I wasn't planning to get *into* this mess on my own, you little hellion! You really think I'd have walked into a bar full of drunken men who see Zane as their hero if I hadn't seen the bastard yank you in here first?"

She blinked. "You saw that?"

"Sure I saw that."

"And you only came charging in here because of that?"

"Well, hell, Jessi, I couldn't just leave you here."

"And you knew all hell was going to break loose and that you'd be facing twenty-to-one odds?"

"I kinda figured."

She smiled. Then she slid her arms around his neck and she pressed her lips to his all over again. Man, she was going to kill him with kisses if she kept it up. She kissed him thoroughly, so thoroughly that it made his head swim and his gut clench and a sheen of sweat broke out on his forehead. And he thought he must have been a damn fool not to have been working his tail off to sweep this lady off her feet from day one.

A body sailed over the table and hit him on the way to the floor, jarring him away from Jessi's lips. And he looked into her eyes, and opened his mouth to say the words he'd been afraid to utter to any woman, ever. "Jessi, I—"

A whistle pierced the noise of the battle, and a pair of gunshots caused the combatants to cease and desist. Lash looked up to see what looked like a small army of Mexican police, shouting in Spanish and heavily accented English and hauling men to their feet and out the door.

Damn. They were arresting Jessi's brothers right along with everyone else. He had to do something.

But as he got up, one of the officers gripped his shoulder, and slapped a pair of handcuffs around his wrists.

Jessi couldn't believe her eyes. One by one, her brothers were hauled out the door by Mexican police, and so was Lash. While she was totally ignored.

She stepped outside, walked right up to the nearest uniformed man, a handsome, olive-skinned Don Juan with a cute mustache. She tapped his shoulder. "Hey. Why aren't you arresting me?"

He smiled charmingly down at her. "You are too pretty to be in jail, *chica*. Go home now."

"Now wait just a corn-shuckin' minute, here. I was fighting just the same as they were! Hell, *I'm* the one who started it. You have to arrest me! You can't *not* arrest me just because I'm a woman."

He shook his head, grinning indulgently. "You Americans! You make me to laugh." And he did laugh, and she thought that in about a minute he was going to ruffle her hair.

Then she peeked through the windows of the van where the guys had been installed and saw her brothers, all of them, looking at Lash as if he were a steak and they were a pack of hungry pit bulls. She tapped Don Juan again. "You can't put them all in the same cell, okay? See that one, the one they're all glaring at? He ought to be in a cell by himself."

"Why, pretty one? Is he a prince? A king?"

"No, but if they're alone with him, he's gonna be a dead man."

The officer frowned, then shrugged. "Women worry too much. Our space, it is small. You stop worrying now, and go home." And he turned and climbed behind the wheel. Then he blew her a kiss, sent her a wink and drove away.

Jessi stomped her foot and shouted after him. "Chauvinist pig!"

Lash didn't claim his handgun when the officer showed it to him and asked if it was his. He figured he'd get in less trouble that way. Then he allowed himself to be led to a cell in the back of the crumbling structure that passed for a jail in this town. He was shoved inside an adobe room with a barred door, where Garrett, Ben, Wes and Elliot Brand all sat on benches. None of them said a word. None of them grinned. All of them looked suddenly meaner than a pack of junkyard dogs on the hottest day in July, and for one brief moment, he thought longingly of his childhood with the preacher and his houseful of bullies.

"Hey, guys," he said.

They said nothing.

"I really owe you for coming down here like this. I'd have been dog meat in that cantina if you hadn't showed up when you did."

Garrett got up, nice and slow. Elliot reached up to

grab his arm, but Garrett shook him off and stepped forward.

"So I guess we got Zane by the short hairs, huh?" Lash said, and he took a step backward, only to meet up with the cold steel bars behind him. "I explained everything to that officer out there," he said, speaking quickly. "Just as soon as they confirm it all—and he's not gonna let 'em slaughter any cattle until they do—we can just send some rigs down here to fetch 'em back home and..."

Garrett gripped the front of Lash's shirt in both hands and picked him up off the floor, backing him against the bars.

"Gee, Garrett, is it just me, or have I done something to tick you off?"

Garrett said nothing. It was Wes who spoke up. "Jessi's pregnant, Lash. She says you got her that way."

"Jessi?" Lash blinked, his gaze swinging to Wes's, then back to Garrett. "Pregnant? She's pregnant?" He blinked slowly, some kind of warm yellow light filling him up inside from his head to his toes. "My God, she's carrying...my...my baby?"

"What the hell are you grinning about?" Garrett demanded. "Don't you feel the cold breath of the reaper on the back of your neck, son?"

"Jessi's gonna have my baby," he repeated. And he smiled even more. He couldn't seem to help himself. It was like a miracle. It *was* a miracle. And he loved her. *He loved her,* and had for quite a while now. It was going to be okay. Everything was going to be...just fabulous!

He dragged his gaze back to Garrett again. Well, it

was going to be fabulous, assuming he lived long enough to marry her.

"You're gonna do right by my sister, Lash Monroe. Make no mistake about this. You're gonna marry her, and not just because she's pregnant. You're gonna treat her like she's made of twenty-four-karat gold, pal."

"You're damn right I am," he said.

Garrett's eyes narrowed.

"I love her, Garrett," Lash said. "I love her so much I'd take on every one of you, if that's what it took to be with her. And maybe you'd break me up into little pieces before we were finished, or maybe you wouldn't. I've had some experience with bullies on the rampage, you know. But it wouldn't matter. I'm so high right now that I probably wouldn't feel it if you broke every bone in my body. So you gonna put me down, or you wanna take me on, here and now?"

Garrett's eyes widened. Then widened still further when his little sister's voice came to them, loud and low and mean as she shouted, "Open that cell door right now, mister, or prepare to meet your maker!"

He dropped Lash, and they all turned to stare through the bars at a guard with shaking hands held high above his head, and a pretty desperado with a neckerchief tied around her face, pointing his own gun at him. She backed the guard all the way to the cell and waggled the gun barrel at him. The guard put the key into the cell door, turned it and opened it.

"Good," she said. "Now, just so we're clear on this, those guys in that other cell are the criminals. These guys aren't guilty of anything. And I'd wait for you to figure that out for yourself, but I have pressing business to tend to, and it can't wait. You got it?"

The guard just nodded as the Brands and Lash

crowded out of the cell. "Truck's waiting out back. You boys pile in. In the back, dammit, or I'll leave you sitting here. Lash, you wait right here. You, *amigo*—" she dipped the gun toward the guard "—into the cell."

He moved into the cell and she locked it, then tossed the keys back down the hall. Then she popped the cylinder of the guard's gun open, and gave it a spin. "Just so you know, pal, it wasn't loaded. I'd never point a loaded gun at a peace officer. Even a chauvinist one." She dropped the gun on the floor. The boys were already piling into Garrett's pickup. She told Lash to get in the front, and then she got behind the wheel, yanked the neckerchief down to let it hang around her neck and pointed the vehicle toward the border. "I only hope we get past the checkpoint before they report us missing," she said. As she drove, she dug Lash's wallet out of her pocket and tossed it onto the seat. "Found this on that officer's desk. Didn't look like he'd been through it yet."

Lash couldn't take his eyes off her. Her cheeks were flushed with color, and her eyes just sparkled. And his gaze dipped down to her flat tummy and he thought about the tiny bit of life she was cradling inside her. And then he thought he was gonna just about burst with the love he felt for her. It was unbelievable to him that he hadn't ever recognized this feeling for what it was.

He *adored* this woman.

"Jessi," he said, and he slid closer, reached out and touched her hair.

She smiled at him. "We could get in big trouble for this," she said. "Garrett's a sheriff. I hope he had the good sense to give a false name. But I figure we can gift the town with some cattle. Breeding stock or something, to make up for their loss. Maybe with a show of goodwill like that, they'll let this little incident slide."

"Jessi," he said again, and he knew he was smiling stupidly.

"I found a prostitute outside the bar and gave her twenty bucks to drive my truck back to our side of the border. We can pick it up there tomorrow."

"I love you," he said.

She blinked, turned her head fast, and stared up at him.

"I want to marry you. Not as penance or out of guilt or anything else. I just want to marry you."

She smiled, and tears sprang to the surface of her brown eyes. "Lash..." But her voice trailed off, and that bright smile faded very quickly. The moisture in her eyes, though, remained. She looked away. "So my bigmouth brothers told you, did they?"

He didn't know what to say. So he decided to tell the truth. "Yes. I know about the baby."

He should have lied. He could see the tears that glittered in the glow of the dashboard lights. "That was so good, Lash, you know? For a minute there, I almost believed you."

"You have to believe me, Jessi. It's the truth."

"Hell, Lash, you were willing to marry me to pay for my virginity. Naturally you see it as even more necessary now. Your preacher sure as hell raised you right, I'll give you that much. But I'm sorry. It's not gonna work."

"You're wrong. Whatever you're thinking, you're dead wrong."

She braked so hard and fast that the Brands in the back were jostled against the cab. Lash could hear the tears in her voice, see her distress. "Promise me...not one more word about this. We'll talk later, okay? I can't...discuss this right now. It's making me physically ill, to tell you the truth. I could just about..." She put a hand to her stomach and shook her head. "Just...just sit there and shut up, or I'll make you ride in the back with those idiots."

"Don't be mad at them, Jess. This isn't their—"

"The hell it isn't! Dammit, Lash, I was just beginning to think there might be some chance for us. And they ruined it! You'd say anything to get me to marry you now, and how the hell could I ever know if it was true?"

"Jessi, I—"

"No. No more. The last time we talked, you told me you didn't want to marry, to settle down, to have a family. You said you just weren't that kind, Lash. Now you say you've changed your mind. I'd be a fool to believe you. It's because of the baby. That's the only thing that's changed, the only thing you know now that you didn't know before. No. That's the end of it. Don't say any more."

He closed his eyes, and he knew that from where she was sitting, what she'd just said made perfect sense. And how the hell was he ever going to convince her now?

"Jessi, the thing I know now that I didn't know before is that I love you. I have all along. I've done nothing but think about you since I left, and it hit me like a—"

She clamped a hand over his mouth, reached past him and opened the door. "Get out."

Lash got out. Jessi did, too. She stepped up to the pickup's bed and said, "Garrett, drive. Wes, you come up front with me. Lash, climb in with Ben and Elliot.

Ben, if you lay a finger on him, I swear to God I'll leave you stranded in the desert. I've never asked you for a damn thing, but I'm asking now, and if you can't do this for me, then—''

"All right, all right. I got the message. I'll behave."

"Elliot, if he does anything, toss his oversize bulk right over the side."

Elliot gave her a two-fingered salute. "On your side, sis. Just like I always am."

She got back in the truck, Garrett and Wes doing just exactly what she'd asked them to.

Lash felt defeated. He'd hurt her, all over again. And maybe caused her to lose any trust she ever could have had in him. How in the world was he ever going to convince her that he really did love her? How?

He racked his brain all the way back to Texas, but didn't have any flashes of inspiration. He stared miserably at the back of Jessi's head through the glass that separated them. When she leaned tiredly back against it, he pressed his fingers to the glass, as if he could touch her hair.

"You said you loved her," Ben said softly. "Did you mean it?"

Lash lifted his head and met those perpetually sad blue eyes. "I meant it."

"Then don't give up," Ben said. "Life's too short, Lash."

Lash held his head in his hands, and wished to God he could win. But it looked to him as if the game were over, and he'd lost. He felt just like one of those damned country songs.

Chapter 13

Jessi had a pounding headache, and her stomach was churning. Maybe because she'd pretty much figured out how she was going to handle all of this. She needed to tell Lash exactly how it was going to be, and then she'd tell her brothers. But Lash first. It was only fair.

When Garrett pulled into the familiar driveway of the ranch, she started to cry. She just couldn't keep it in any longer. Wes looked as guilty as Garrett did, and he slid an arm around her shoulders and hugged her. "Aw, honey, it's gonna be all right."

"I wish my mother were here," she sobbed, and she lowered her head, dropping her face into the haven of her warm palms.

"I know you do, Jessi," Wes went on. "Look, we were hotheads down there. You know we're gonna stand by you. You know we'll treat Lash like family once he marries you."

"Ah, hell, Wes, you just don't understand anything,

do you?'' She lifted her face to stare at him, and saw his wide-eyed confusion. "I can't marry him now. Don't you see that?''

Wes frowned at her. "Damn straight I don't see it. Hell, Jessi, you have to marry him now more than ever. You're carrying—''

"Lord, Jessi," Garrett said, touching her shoulder. "Honey, tell me you haven't decided to... I mean, I know, it's your decision. I know that. It's the nineties. But...honey...''

His stricken expression touched her, and she lowered her palms to her belly—damn, but it hurt. "I'm keeping my baby, Garrett. I love that idiot. How could I not want his baby?''

Garrett sighed in relief. Wes, on the other side of her, swore softly. "Dammit, Jessi, you aren't making any sense. If you love him, then why the hell can't you marry him?''

She met his eyes, wondering how he could be so dense. Then she just shook her head and got out. The guys piled out of the truck, and Chelsea stepped out of the house, onto the front porch, to greet them. Jessi was exhausted. Handling all these men was just too much. All she wanted to do was tell Lash her decision and collapse into her bed.

Chelsea met her eyes, and read them with that uncanny intuition of hers that sometimes gave Jessi the shivers. Chelsea nodded once and said, "Okay, boys, it's nearing dawn and you all have a big day coming up. Get your butts in here and get some rest. Give your kid sister a break for once, okay?''

Garrett walked up onto the steps and met his wife's eyes. "You knew about this, didn't you?" he said.

She drew a breath and nodded. "I gave your sister

my word I'd let her tell you when she was ready. And I love you too much—love *her* too much—to break a promise like that."

He closed his eyes slowly, nodding in understanding.

"It's gonna be okay, honey," Chelsea told him. "I promise you, it will." She hugged Garrett hard.

The others muttered in protest, but they went inside, and Chelsea kept one arm around Garrett, leading him in last of all.

Lash stayed outside with Jessi. She sat down on the topmost step of the porch, and he came over to sit beside her. "We really have to talk about this," he said.

"Yes, I guess we do, Lash. Because I've come to some important decisions, and you have a right to know what they are."

"But not to have any say in them?"

She met his eyes. He went silent. "Here's what I've decided," she said. "I've decided to keep the baby. I've got my own home, my own business, and I can support a child just fine all by myself. But if you want to chip in, I won't refuse you. And I'll give you all the visitation rights you could possibly want."

"Aw, honey, I don't want any damn visitation. I want us to be a family. Dammit, Jessi, you have to believe me."

She lifted her chin and looked him right in the eye. "I'm one hell of a woman, Lash Monroe. And there is no way in hell I'm gonna settle for a man who doesn't love me with every bone in his body. I shouldn't have to. You shouldn't ask me to."

"I'm not."

"Guess I'll never know for sure, will I?"

He let his chin fall to his chest. "I had my chance

and I let you get away," he said. "I suppose I deserve this."

She shrugged.

"Jessi, I'm not giving up. My drifting days are over, and I'm gonna convince you that I meant what I said. I'll follow you around like a lonely pup. I'll camp out on your front porch. I'll serenade you in the moonlight, and buy you flowers and write you poetry. All the things I should've been doing in the first place. Damn, I never thought I was a fool, but it's pretty obvious now. I love you, Jessi. Sooner or later, I'm gonna convince you."

She smiled very slightly, feeling a little dizzy on top of everything else. "I hope so," she said. "But I don't see how you can." She got to her feet, staggered a bit, and gripped the railing for support.

"Jessi?"

"I'm going to bed. I just can't take any more tonight." She turned and went up the steps, but had to pause in the doorway to catch her breath and battle the dizziness. The sudden, violent urge to get into her own warm bed overcame her, and she managed to propel herself through the doorway, stumbled through the house to the stairway, and gripped the bannister.

Lash was right behind her, his hands coming to rest on her shoulders as she trembled. "Jessi, what's wrong?"

"I don't know... I feel—"

"Garrett," Lash called. "Chelsea! Get down here! Something's—"

The first cramp hit her, and she felt as if she'd been kicked in the belly by a mule. She doubled over, clutching her middle, and she cried out in pain.

That cry more than Lash's, she knew, brought her brothers and Chelsea running.

"God in heaven, don't let her lose the baby," Lash muttered. He bent over her, and scooped her up into his arms. "I'm taking her to the hospital," he told the others. "Hold on, Jessi. Hold on."

Lash carried her gently through the automatic double doors of the emergency room, whispering to her that it was going to be all right. That he loved her. That he wouldn't let anything happen to her. Once inside, he shouted, "Get me a doctor. She's pregnant, and—"

Jessi cried out again, clutching her middle, tears pouring down her cheeks. And Lash felt a warm wetness on his own face. Several nurses rushed forward, one dragging a gurney with her and instructing him to lower her down onto it. Then these strangers wheeled her away from him.

He lunged forward, but one of the nurses caught his arm and shook her head. "Please, sir. We can take better care of her if you wait out here. I know it's hard, but it's best for her, really."

Lash stood there staring until they'd wheeled her out of sight, through another set of doors. Then he pressed both hands to his head and turned in a circle. Damn! If he lost her now... God, this was probably his fault. If he hadn't gone to Mexico...if she hadn't come after him... Maybe she'd been hurt in that damned brawl in the cantina. Maybe the drive over those rutted roads had instigated this. Maybe it was the stress, or the hurt brought on by not being sure of his feelings.

The doors swung open again, and Lash looked up to see the entire Brand family surging through. The boys stopped where they were, staring him down. Chelsea handed a sleepy-looking Ethan to Garrett and hurried forward, wrapping Lash in a warm hug. "She's gonna be all right, Lash. You'll see. She's tough."

"Toughest woman I've ever met," he said. "Stubbornest, too. Damn, Chelsea, I can't lose her."

"You won't." Chelsea stood back a bit. "You look like hell, Lash."

He closed his eyes and let her guide him to a chair. He took the coffee she brought him moments later.

He drank it, and watched those doors. Time ticked by, every second dragging out into a hundred of them. He got up and paced, stared at those doors some more, sat for a while, questioned a couple of nurses who knew nothing at all. And all the while, he felt the hostile eyes of Jessi's brothers on him. They blamed him for this. Hell, they ought to. He blamed himself.

Two hours later, he was on his third cup of stale, machine-generated coffee, and getting more nervous by the minute, when Garrett finally got around to saying what was on his mind. "So you guys talked, before she got sick?"

"Yeah," Lash told him.

"And you convinced her to marry you?"

"Nope." Lash crumpled his paper cup in his fist and tossed it.

"Well, then, we will," Garrett said. "She's gonna marry you, and that's final. We can't have her trying to raise a kid on her own."

Lash got to his feet, very slowly. "No," he said. He stared at each of the brothers, one by one. "No, it's time you guys figured something out. Your sister is tough, smart, beautiful, and perfectly capable of taking care of herself. She doesn't think I love her. And she isn't going to marry a man unless she knows beyond any doubt that he loves her the way she deserves to be loved. So no, I'm not going to marry her. I'm not going to let you pressure her into accepting me. The only way I'm going to marry Jessi Brand is by working my tail off to convince her that I really do love her. And it might take a while, but I'm gonna do it. I'm gonna do it whether she..." He closed his eyes, swallowing hard. "Whether she loses this baby or not. I adore that woman, and she doesn't deserve not to be sure."

He glanced back toward the doors, blinked his eyes dry, and faced the boys again, nodding firmly. "That's the way it's gonna be. So if you don't like it, we all might as well step out into the parking lot right now, because I love her too much to let her marry me before she understands just how I feel. I want her to be sure. I want her to know that I'd walk barefoot over hot coals for her, baby or no baby. I want her to know that."

The angry frown vanished from Garrett's face, and even Wes had the good sense to stop glaring. In fact, their expressions turned, one by one, into looks of grudging admiration.

Chelsea smiled outright. "You'll convince her, Lash. Damn, I'm so glad she's got herself a man who loves her the way you do."

Then the boys all shifted their gazes to look past Lash, and Lash turned to see what they were focused on, and spotted a nurse who seemed to be very upset as she spoke to a doctor, who looked puzzled. The woman raised her voice a notch then, and they could all hear her.

"I don't know how, Doctor! We only left her alone for a second, and....well, we just lost her!"

Lash's heart froze in that moment. The rest of his

body dissolved and he sank to his knees. "No," he whispered. "God, no, not Jessi..."

Elliot, Garrett and Wes stampeded past him, crowding the startled pair in white and demanding answers. Behind him, he could hear Chelsea crying.

And then Ben, that big, quiet, saddest of all Brands, was kneeling beside him, and dropping a big hand on his shoulder, squeezing gently. And when Lash looked up, he saw Ben's face, wet with tears. And he knew Ben had lost his own young wife, and the pain he was feeling was reflected in this man's eyes.

"Not again," Ben said softly. "God, not again."

"This can't be happening," Lash whispered.

Ben's arms enfolded him, and the two knelt there together, sobbing like a couple of kids. Lash didn't think he'd ever be able to stand on his feet again.

A shrill, piercing whistle cut through the grief in that waiting room like a fire alarm, and Lash managed to look up, toward the sound.

Jessi stood at the far end of the waiting room, clad in a hospital gown, hands on her hips. "What in the Sam Hill is everybody bawling about?" she demanded.

Lash's strength surged back into his body. He sprang to his feet and ran the length of the room, scooping her into his arms and hugging her hard, clinging to her as if he'd never let go.

He vaguely heard the nurse apologizing for her poor choice of words, and explaining that her patient was missing, not dead. By then, though, no one was really listening. Jessi's brothers were crowding around her, hugging her and Lash all at once, and Lash kind of figured they'd pretty much gotten over the idea of beating him senseless in the parking lot. For tonight, at least.

Lash set her on her feet, anxiously searching her face to be sure she was really all right.

"You really need to spend the night, Miss Brand," the doctor was saying. "You shouldn't even be on your feet right now."

And some of that joyous relief faded from Lash's heart when he heard the concern in the doc's voice. "Jessi?" Lash scooped her up again. If the doc said she shouldn't be on her feet, she damned well wasn't going to be. He held her gently. "Sweetheart, what's wrong? Is it the baby? Is there—"

"The baby's fine," she told him, and he almost sank to his knees all over again in relief. Then she nodded to the doctor. "Tell him, Doc."

The man smiled. "Food poisoning. A mild case, fortunately, though I'm sure it didn't feel that way."

"It was that damned fajita," she muttered, and she let her head rest on Lash's shoulder. "But I'm glad it happened."

Garrett shook his head. "How can you be glad? Do you know what you just did to us?"

"You scared the hell out of us," Wes said.

"When that nurse said she'd lost you..." Garrett began.

"I died inside, Jessi," Lash finished. "I swear to God, I felt myself die inside."

She met his gaze, held it, and he saw new moisture in her eyes. Chelsea cleared her throat, and Jessi pulled her gaze away from Lash's. "They wanted to keep me overnight. I wanted out of here, so as soon as they weren't looking, I sneaked out to see if I could convince my big brothers to spring me." Her gaze came back to Lash's, something like wonder in her brown eyes as she reached up and ran one hand through his hair. "And I'm glad I did, because I got a front-row seat for that little speech of yours."

Lash blinked. "You did?"

She sniffed, and nodded. "Yeah, I did. You convinced me, Lash. It's really not just the baby, is it?"

"No, Jessi. It's got nothing to do with the baby. I love you, and I'd figured that out before your brothers ever told me about the baby. I was down there in Mexico, missing you with everything in me and trying to figure out how the hell to convince you to marry me. God, Jessi, I never knew I could feel this way. But I do. I swear to God, I do love you."

"Then I guess I'm gonna hafta marry myself a drifter," she said. "Because I've loved you all along. You know that, don't you, Lash?"

He shook his head in wonder. "I know it. I can't quite understand why, but I know it." Then his face split in a grin. "You're gonna marry me?"

She nodded.

He leaned forward and kissed her, gently but thoroughly.

Garrett nudged Wes with his elbow. "Looks like we just got ourselves another brother."

"Well, hell," Wes said. "I've been saying all along that he was the only man around good enough for our baby sister, haven't I?"

"No, actually, you haven't."

The two grinned foolishly. "Somebody better call Adam in New York," Elliot chirped. "He's gotta be here for this wedding."

In the corner, Ben remained silent, and reached up to wipe a single tear from his eye.

Epilogue

Jessi gripped the doctor by the front of his shirt and growled deep in her throat. "I told you, I don't like pain. Now give me something or die!"

Lash pried her hands away from the poor guy's white coat, brought them to his lips and kissed them. "Sweetheart, the doc says it's better for you to do this without drugs if you can. You can do it, can't you? Come on, now—"

"*Where's my gun?*"

"Oh, boy."

The doc patted him on the back. "Jessi Lynn Brand Monroe, you settle down. Drugs are no good for the baby, and I know perfectly well you don't want to hurt the baby, do you?"

She glared at him. Lash figured she probably thought the doc was lying, just to keep the drugs from her and make her suffer. Since she'd been in the third stage of labor, she seemed to have formed the opinion that every male in the place was getting some perverse pleasure from her pain.

Ben and Garrett and Elliot were all smiling at her and speaking soft, comforting words. Adam, who'd come in from New York on the first flight out when they called to tell him she was in labor, was pacing like a caged lion. In fact, there were so many Brands surrounding the bed that the doctor said they were in the way. None of them wanted to leave though, and they wouldn't, Lash thought, unless they were bodily removed.

Except Wes. He was toughing it out largely to save face, Lash thought. But he was looking decidedly queasy.

Chelsea was on her way. She'd had to drop Ethan off with a sitter before she could get here.

The pain seemed to ease, and Jessi's face relaxed. She clutched her husband's hand in hers. "We should have sold tickets to this event," she said, panting to catch her breath. "Coulda paid for college."

"It's sure standing room only."

She nodded. "Good thing you don't have lots of family here, too, isn't it?"

"My so-called family? Heck, they wouldn't let Petey and Zane out of prison just to attend a birthing, would they? Besides, they'd contaminate the place. I don't want them anywhere near you...or our baby."

"Doesn't matter," she said. "You've got all kinds of family now. In fact, you have that big crowd of relatives you never wanted."

"And I love every last one of 'em," he told her, and he leaned over and kissed her mouth. Felt it go tight against his, felt her breaths coming faster on his lips.

"I...I can feel it... I have to push!"

"Go ahead and push, then," the doctor said. Lash straightened, and felt his heart flip-flop. This was it. He turned to smile crookedly at Garrett, and then Elliot, and Ben, and... Hey, where was Wes?

Oh, there he was, out in the hall, back to the wall, shoulders slumped, Adam seemingly holding him up. He was white as a sheet. What was that nurse waving under his nose?

Jessi clutched Lash's hand hard enough to break the bones and grated her teeth, and Lash felt helpless and scared as he watched her battle the pain, drawing on that endless reserve of strength deep inside her to push their child into the world.

"Damn, sweetheart, I'd do it for you if I could," he told her, bathing her face with a cool cloth.

"No man could go through this and live," she said through gritted teeth.

It seemed forever...and then it seemed it had been no time at all, because the doc was lowering a pink, squirming, tiny human being into Lash's waiting arms. And Lash was looking down into the face of an angel. "A girl," he whispered, and he bent close to Jessi. "Our little girl."

Garrett, Elliot and Ben crowded close, cooing and making the most ridiculous faces and basically sounding like a bunch of lunatics.

Then the door opened, Adam coming in first, to join them at the bedside, looking alien in his suit and tie. And then Wes came in, real slow, his black eyes wide and wet. The others parted to give him a chance to meet his new niece. And he knelt beside the bed, reaching out, letting the little one grasp his forefinger.

He reached into a pocket with his free hand, and pulled out a tiny suede pouch fastened to a thong.

"What's this?" Lash asked.

"A gift from Turtle, the shaman over at the reservation," he said. He'd been learning a whole lot about his heritage, and he seemed to be gaining a peace he hadn't had before. "It's a medicine bag. Hang it in her room until she's old enough to wear it. It'll keep her safe, and happy and strong."

"That's so sweet, Wes."

He shrugged as if it were no big deal, then ran one hand down Jessi's cheek. "You did good, little sister."

"I did, didn't I?"

He nodded, then straightened, averting his face to swipe at his eyes. "Maybe we should clear out now, leave you two and your little girl alone to get acquainted."

"Thanks, Wes."

The boys each leaned down to kiss their sister, and then they left the room. Lash lowered the baby into Jessi's arms, and bent to kiss them both.

"What will we name her?" he whispered softly, stroking the soft, downy head of reddish hair.

"Maria," Jessi whispered. "After my mother."

"Maria," he said. "That's nice. And what about a middle name?"

Jessi shrugged, her big brown eyes just drinking in the sight of the baby in her arms. "You pick one."

"All right. Michele. After Chelsea's sister."

"Chelsea will like that."

Lash touched Jessi's chin, tipping her face up so that he could stare into those eyes. "I never thought I could be this happy," he told her. "But I am. Don't you ever doubt it, Jessi. I adore you."

She smiled, real slow, eyes sparkling. "Hell, drifter, I knew it before you did." And she leaned up and kissed him.

* * * * *

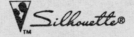

MILLION DOLLAR SWEEPSTAKES
OFFICIAL RULES
NO PURCHASE NECESSARY TO ENTER

1. To enter, follow the directions published. Method of entry may vary. For eligibility, entries must be received no later than March 31, 1998. No liability is assumed for printing errors, lost, late, non-delivered or misdirected entries.

   To determine winners, the sweepstakes numbers assigned to submitted entries will be compared against a list of randomly, preselected prize winning numbers. In the event all prizes are not claimed via the return of prize winning numbers, random drawings will be held from among all other entries received to award unclaimed prizes.

2. Prize winners will be determined no later than June 30, 1998. Selection of winning numbers and random drawings are under the supervision of D. L. Blair, Inc., an independent judging organization whose decisions are final. Limit: one prize to a family or organization. No substitution will be made for any prize, except as offered. Taxes and duties on all prizes are the sole responsibility of winners. Winners will be notified by mail. Odds of winning are determined by the number of eligible entries distributed and received.

3. Sweepstakes open to residents of the U.S. (except Puerto Rico), Canada and Europe who are 18 years of age or older, except employees and immediate family members of Torstar Corp., D. L. Blair, Inc., their affiliates, subsidiaries, and all other agencies, entities, and persons connected with the use, marketing or conduct of this sweepstakes. All applicable laws and regulations apply. Sweepstakes offer void wherever prohibited by law. Any litigation within the province of Quebec respecting the conduct and awarding of a prize in this sweepstakes must be submitted to the Régie des alcools, des courses et des jeux. In order to win a prize, residents of Canada will be required to correctly answer a time-limited arithmetical skill-testing question to be administered by mail.

4. Winners of major prizes (Grand through Fourth) will be obligated to sign and return an Affidavit of Eligibility and Release of Liability within 30 days of notification. In the event of non-compliance within this time period or if a prize is returned as undeliverable, D. L. Blair, Inc. may at its sole discretion, award that prize to an alternate winner. By acceptance of their prize, winners consent to use of their names, photographs or other likeness for purposes of advertising, trade and promotion on behalf of Torstar Corp., its affiliates and subsidiaries, without further compensation unless prohibited by law. Torstar Corp. and D. L. Blair, Inc., their affiliates and subsidiaries are not responsible for errors in printing of sweepstakes and prize winning numbers. In the event a duplication of a prize winning number occurs, a random drawing will be held from among all entries received with that prize winning number to award that prize.

5. This sweepstakes is presented by Torstar Corp., its subsidiaries and affiliates in conjunction with book, merchandise and/or product offerings. The number of prizes to be awarded and their value are as follows: Grand Prize — $1,000,000 (payable at $33,333.33 a year for 30 years); First Prize — $50,000; Second Prize — $10,000; Third Prize — $5,000; 3 Fourth Prizes — $1,000 each; 10 Fifth Prizes — $250 each; 1,000 Sixth Prizes — $10 each. Values of all prizes are in U.S. currency. Prizes in each level will be presented in different creative executions, including various currencies, vehicles, merchandise and travel. Any presentation of a prize level in a currency other than U.S. currency represents an approximate equivalent to the U.S. currency prize for that level, at that time. Prize winners will have the opportunity of selecting any prize offered for that level; however, the actual non U.S. currency equivalent prize if offered and selected, shall be awarded at the exchange rate existing at 3:00 P.M. New York time on March 31, 1998. A travel prize option, if offered and selected by winner, must be completed within 12 months of selection and is subject to: traveling companion(s) completing and returning of a Release of Liability prior to travel; and hotel and flight accommodations availability. For a current list of all prize options offered within prize levels, send a self-addressed, stamped envelope (WA residents need not affix postage) to: MILLION DOLLAR SWEEPSTAKES Prize Options, P.O. Box 4456, Blair, NE 68009-4456, USA.

6. For a list of prize winners (available after July 31, 1998) send a separate, stamped, self-addressed envelope to: MILLION DOLLAR SWEEPSTAKES Winners, P.O. Box 4459, Blair, NE 68009-4459, USA.

TAYLOR SMITH

Who would you trust with your life?
Think again.

A tranquil New England town is rocked to its core when a young coed is linked to a devastating crime—then goes missing.

One woman, who believes in the girl's innocence, is determined to find her before she's silenced—forever. Her only ally is a man who no longer believes in anyone's innocence. But *is* he an ally?

At a time when all loyalties are suspect, and old friends may be foes, she has to decide—quickly—who can be trusted. The wrong choice could be fatal.

THE BEST OF ENEMIES

Available at your favorite retail outlet
in June 1997.

 MIRA The brightest star in women's fiction

MTSTBE-R

And the Winner Is...
You!

...when you pick up these great titles
from our new promotion at your
favorite retail outlet this June!

Diana Palmer
The Case of the Mesmerizing Boss

Betty Neels
The Convenient Wife

Annette Broadrick
Irresistible

Emma Darcy
A Wedding to Remember

Rachel Lee
Lost Warriors

Marie Ferrarella
Father Goose

From the bestselling author of
Iron Lace and *Rising Tides*

EMILIE RICHARDS

JANET DAILEY AWARD WINNER

When had the love and promises they'd shared turned into conversations they couldn't face, feelings they couldn't accept?

Samantha doesn't know how to fight the demons that have come between her and her husband, Joe. But she does know how to fight for something she wants: a child.

But the trouble is Joe. Can he accept that he'll never be the man he's expected to be—and can he seize this one chance at happiness that may never come again?

THE TROUBLE WITH JOE

"A great read and a winner in every sense of the word!"
—Janet Dailey

Available in June 1997
at your favorite retail outlet.

MIRA The brightest star in women's fiction

MER1

New York Times Bestselling Authors

JENNIFER BLAKE
JANET DAILEY
ELIZABETH GAGE

Three *New York Times* bestselling authors bring you three
very sensuous, contemporary love stories—all centered
around one magical night!

It is a warm, spring night and masquerading as legendary
lovers, the elite of New Orleans society have come to
celebrate the twenty-fifth anniversary of the Duchaise
masquerade ball. But amidst the beauty, music and revelry,
some of the world's most legendary lovers are in trouble....

Come midnight at this year's Duchaise ball, passion and
scandal will be...

Unmasked

Revealed at your favorite retail outlet in July 1997.

COMING NEXT MONTH

#793 AN UNEXPECTED ADDITION—Terese Ramin

Intimate Moments Extra

When single mom Kate Anden and widowed dad Hank Mathison got together to talk about parenthood, things somehow led to the bed...and now *another* little bundle of joy was on the way! These veteran singles were making room for baby...but would the unexpected addition to their families bring them together—or tear them apart?

#794 MOMMY BY SURPRISE—Paula Detmer Riggs

Maternity Row

Prudy Randolph should have known better than to think that one night of passion with her ex-husband could change the past...and his paternal instincts. But it did affect their future, and now she had precious little time to heal his aching heart...and prove that little *miracles* really do exist!

#795 A MARRIAGE TO REMEMBER—Cathryn Clare

Their marriage was over—or so Jayne believed. But when an attempt on Nick's life robbed him of his memory, they went on the run together... and fell in love all over again. But could Jayne trust this changed man with her heart, or would the old workaholic husband reclaim the man she had come to love?

#796 RECKLESS—Ruth Wind

The Last Roundup

Soldier Jake Forrest was recklessly running from his past, seeking shelter from the memories that plagued his mind. Small-town doctor Ramona Hardy offered him more than just sanity and hope in her protective embrace. She gave him love...and vowed to prove to him that it really could conquer all.

#797 THE TWELVE-MONTH MARRIAGE—Kathryn Jensen

Newlyweds David and Carrie have just solved all their problems. Wedded bliss? Not exactly. David got the wife he needs to keep custody of his children, and Carrie got the children she's always wanted. Now there's only one thing threatening their twelve-month arrangement...*love!*

#798 STRANGER IN HER BED—Bonnie Gardner

T. J. Swift thought he had found the perfect apartment...until the supposedly dead—and very attractive—former tenant showed up to resume residence! Sparks flew, but if Robin Digby and T.J. didn't get to the bottom of this whole mystery—and fast—they just might end up getting burned!